PRAISE FOR *KINGS OF COWEETSEE*

"In *Kings of Coweetsee*, Dale Neal artfully loops his mountain tale in and out of the lives of innocents and villains, the lovelorn and the depraved, money-hungry newcomers and old-timers alike, in a present-day county ruled by men who buy votes and conspire in ruination for their own gain. Oh, the crushing weight of sin and shadow in such a kingdom, and oh, the possibility that a ruined girl could rise again sweet as a mountain flower in an old mountain song. As in Carson McCullers' *Ballad of the Sad Café*, the genius of this novel is that it sings like a ballad: dire, sweet, and fierce, each character's fate twisted and true."

— Marjorie Hudson, author of *Indigo Field*, *Accidental Birds of the Carolinas*, and *Searching for Virginia Dare*

"Dale Neal's *Kings of Coweetsee* has at its center a reconstruction of a community's history, and it's no ordinary history, containing, among other crimes, fixed elections and various forms of mayhem. This novel has a wonderful cast of colorful characters, good- and evil-doers, who show us the underside of local and national American life. Their voices will stay with you long after you close the book."

— Charles Baxter, author of *The Sun Collective* and *Wonderlands*

"'We don't consider ourselves a backwards people,' Dale Neal writes, 'but as the keepers of a lost kingdom.' Neal's ear for the Southern idioms and storytelling vernacular is uncanny and immersive. He also understands and vividly illustrates the underbelly of the still entrenched patriarchal political and social systems that corruptly govern the lives of the Coweetsee citizens. Enter this world and you will find familiar characters, but Neal's empathetic rendering of the travails of Birdie, Roy Boy, Maurice Posey, Aunt Zip, and Charlie Clyde, among many others, make this his best and most potent book. His respect for the trenchant backwoods wisdom of his characters is always present, as is the dirt-poor heartbreak of unrequited love and the high plaintive lonesome hiccups of the traditional ballads that stab into the listener's broken places and settle there. *Kings of Coweetsee* will shift the ground beneath your feet."

– Keith Flynn, editor of Asheville Poetry Review, co-author of *Prosperity Gospel: Portraits of the Great Recession*

"*Kings of Coweetsee* is a tale of power and intrigue with an ache at its heart as old as love itself. Dale Neal writes with the penetrating vision of an archaeologist unearthing the dark ironies of a thorny past. He's a born story-teller — his prose is graceful and his eye is keen."

– Kathryn Schwille, author of *What Luck, This Life*

"Simply one of the most natural storytellers writing novels today."

– Kevin McIlvoy, author of *At the Gate of All Wonder* and *One Kind Favor*

"Dale Neal, with a reporter's keen eye for detail, has brought to life a fictional mountain township, that, on further reflection, might not be totally fictional. Certainly the details ring true. This book is both an evocation of a disappearing culture and a picture of electioneering chillingly relevant to our times. A good read!"

– Wayne Caldwell, author of *Cataloochee, Requiem by Fire*, and *Woodsmoke*

KINGS OF COWEETSEE

Dale Neal

Regal House Publishing

Published by
Regal House Publishing, LLC
Raleigh, NC 27605
All rights reserved

ISBN -13 (paperback): 9781646034543
ISBN -13 (epub): 9781646034550
Library of Congress Control Number: 2023943432

All efforts were made to determine the copyright holders and obtain their permissions in any circumstance where copyrighted material was used. The publisher apologizes if any errors were made during this process, or if any omissions occurred. If noted, please contact the publisher and all efforts will be made to incorporate permissions in future editions.

Cover images and design by © C. B. Royal

Regal House Publishing, LLC
https://regalhousepublishing.com

Printed in the United States of America

In Memory of Mc

PART I

THE BOX

1

If you found us, you're most likely lost, we like to tease strangers. Coweetsee County lies at the tail end of the state, wedged deep in the Blue Ridge, as if a divine crowbar had prized open the high mountains for human habitation. Here, you find us, a few remaining families hanging white-knuckled onto steeply sloping, hardscrabble farms. Living back of beyond, we don't consider ourselves a backward people, but as the keepers of a lost kingdom. Yet no kingdom worth its salt, even in the sweetest of fairy tales, comes without its curse.

Once you had to take the slow-bending River Road east and west of town, the only way in and out of Coweetsee. Then the kingdom cracked open when the Feds moved the mountains and poured six lanes of concrete so a family of four in a minivan from Cincinnati could blow through here at 75 mph on their way to Disney World. Only the more adventuresome ilk might exit the beaten path to gape at our fall leaves or our many barns—even fewer stop by the Coweetsee County Historical Society.

Housed in the former jail, our museum holds captive memories, the imprisoned past, from Indian arrowheads to crazy quilts. Handmade banjos fashioned from cigar boxes and catgut strings hang from the plaster walls. Black-and-white photos show women in long dresses, the grannies who knew heartbreaking ballads from the hills of Scotland where young lovers died in each other's arms, or pricked faithless hearts with silver daggers, songs that Birdie Barker Price liked to hum to herself.

Birdie was on duty at the society when the antique sleigh bells sounded on the front door.

"Law, if you found us, you must be lost." Birdie alighted from her lonely chair, launching into her best tour-guide speech for the couple coming through the door, her first visitors in weeks. "Come on in. Look 'round. See the iron bars on the windows? Used to be a jail, but don't worry, I won't fingerprint you and you're free to go (after a sizable donation in that box. Ha, ha. Hint, hint.) Me? I'm the only inmate these days. Here was once the lair of lawmen—our own Sheriff Maurice Posey before he got busted for vote buying. Maurice served as the high sheriff of Coweetsee for so long, they say he once ticketed Jesus for jaywalking over the river."

"Honey, you can cut out the cornpone act with me," the woman said.

Birdie wasn't used to being so rudely interrupted and her mouth must have hung open for a spell.

The woman had a ferocious smile. "No need to convert us. We're regular folk like you, and believe me, we know the rock and the hard place you're up against."

Birdie had misjudged them as flatlanders from Florida, her in a floral silky swirl of a dress, sandals tied up around her varicose veins, him in a knit yellow polo, white slacks, skin leathery as the loafers he wore with no socks. The man walked briskly through, not taking time to read the little placards Birdie had typed and taped by each display.

"What you seeing, Bert?" The woman raised her voice.

"Churns, plow bits, the usual. Fair condition," her companion hollered.

The woman paged through the guestbook. "Not much traffic these days. What's your name, dear?"

"Birdie Barker Price. I'm the docent and director here at the Coweetsee Historical Society."

"Birdie, what a pretty name. I can tell you wear all the hats."

"Bunch of medals, helmets, army surplus stuff," Bert hollered again. He'd hit the war displays, highlighting Coweetsee's contributions to the Revolutionary, 1812, Civil War, Spanish-American, World Wars I and II, Korea, Vietnam, Grenada, and Panama (remember those little larks), onto the quick Gulf, and then the longer onslaughts of Iraq and Afghanistan. Photos of the grinning boys who didn't make it home. A sad room if you linger and look too hard.

"Holy moly, Margo. They got a bearskin back here, big one with claws."

"Add it to the list. Birdie and me are just getting started." Their lack of any historical reverence ruffled Birdie. "Who are you people? What do you want?"

The woman dug in her yellow leather purse and handed over a business card. Margo and Bert Lounsberry, Historic Inventory Solutions, with an Atlanta address.

"We are the saviors of small-town museums and collections, which unfortunately, no one values much these days. I guess you're a nonprofit, with little to no support from local officials, am I right?"

"We keep the lights on, and, yes, admissions are down," Birdie admitted, feeling somehow to blame. "But I can't sell off our exhibits, now can I?"

"Actually, you can." Margo's insistent smile never faltered. "Check with your peers. Cantor County just shed its collection. And we're consolidating the Franklin County exhibit in Georgia next week. Rural communities need the revenue. When it comes to closing your school library or keeping your small-town museum, necessity beats nostalgia."

Birdie felt her stomach drop, felt somehow she was to blame, that she had failed her own history, listening to this woman explain the market for the pastoral, the rural, what folks like to think of as more wholesome times. Margo's main buyers were the interstate restaurant chains that featured high-cholesterol menus and wood-planked walls hung with Americana artifacts.

"Which could very well include your bearskin in the back," Margo insisted. "Think about it. You have my card. Call us when you're ready."

Still smiling their greedy wet smiles, they left.

Long after the bells had stopped vibrating on the closed

door, Birdie stood in her empty museum. She held the business card in her sweaty palm, its sharp corners pressing her flesh like a shard of broken glass.

Coweetsee, a pretty place to be poor in, remains rich in stories, songs, and sayings. Birdie couldn't live with the betrayal of surrendering all that past, even for a solvent future. But what if the Atlanta lady was right? Even she wondered if the exhibits didn't look more flea market than museum. All Birdie could offer the public, those passing through, was a sanitized, bucolic vision of Coweetsee. If not her, who would share our true stories, the real dirt, the lives that were buried everywhere on the land?

Coweetsee's curse was that it never changed.

Birdie Barker Price locked up for the day and stepped out to the empty street.

Downtown was largely deserted, a ghost town, lacking the bustle of folks Birdie remembered as a girl coming to town with Aunt Zip for their Saturday shopping. What used to be mercantile, hardware, and dress shops left only empty storefronts, dusty glass arenas where rats perform their rodent ballets. Tattoo parlors and video stores took their turn in recent years. Then the vape shop opened, hawking flavored oils and electronic cigarettes, instead of honest tobacco once grown in these parts, contributing to the cancer of the world.

A gaggle of girls loitered out front, blowing bubblegum-scented clouds into the chill March air. They had dyed their hair pink and purple. They wore too much mascara and rouge on their faces and work boots on their big feet, both prissy and manly, trying to look mean and cool and dope, whatever the password is in their circles these days. They posed for selfies with their sequined smartphones, holding the screens overhead, putting their heads together and pouting their lips. Then they broke apart giggling, admiring their social savvy.

"Aren't you young ladies in school, haven't you someplace

better to be?" The schoolteacher in Birdie wanted to know.

"No'm," they said in resigned unison.

And Birdie began to put names to their painted faces, calling the roll from an old homeroom: Tammy Lunsford, Sara Snook, Melinda Mabe, and one older, meaner looking, familiar, but whom she couldn't quite place.

"You could go on home and help your mamas out, you know."

"Yes'm." Their mascara-matted eyes rolled. They blew their bubblegum-scented vapors in clouds.

Birdie walked on.

"Bitch."

Birdie heard the catty word scratching at her back, the sort of sass she would never abide at the blackboard when she ruled the classroom. Oh Lord, Rhonda Harmon Jr.—Birdie's worst student. That scowling face, arms always crossed, slouched in her desk, forever chewing her insolent gum, muttering under her breath. How often had Birdie whirled around? "What did you say, young lady?"

"Nothing." The girl would sink lower, her chin about desk high.

"Better be nothing," Birdie said to no avail.

How could she forget? Birdie kept walking.

With only a few parking spaces assigned for the rare visitors in front of the society, she usually parked across the bridge. The river below runs quick and cold through Coweetsee, and more than a few bodies have been pulled from its deeper waters. Her face still burning, Birdie was rattled by the curse leveled at her back by young Rhonda Jr.

That troublesome girl had taken after her mother, the original Rhonda Harmon, who ran hard and loose with all the boys. She had been found naked in the water, bloated beyond recognition of the pretty young thing she had been.

And remembering Rhonda, while walking over that terrible current, Birdie found herself mouthing an old song.

We went to take an evening walk about a mile from town.
I picked a stick up off the ground and knocked that fair girl down.

It was a ballad she'd learned as a girl from her aunt Zip, sitting on the front porch knee to knee, helping to shuck corn and snap beans in the summer. The old woman sang in cracked a cappella.

She fell down on her bended knees, for mercy she did cry
Oh, Billy dear, don't kill me here, I'm unprepared to die.

Zip always sounded hoarse, like she'd spent her life hollering at wayward dogs, errant children, and drunken men. It wasn't a pretty sound she made, more of a keening than any crooning heard on the radio, but it sounded like Death come to set you straight.

She never spoke another word, I only beat her more
Until the ground around me with her blood did flow.

Love songs, Aunt Zip called them, though the lyrics concerned hateful things that happen to women. "Men," the old woman more than once warned Birdie, "don't you trust a one of them. Many are bluster and some are harmless, but they ain't like women. And a girl your age is likely to be boy crazy, moonstruck and man stuck."

But Birdie, like those girls loitering on the sidewalk, didn't listen. Same as me thirty years ago, Birdie thought, hoping to get noticed, wary of anyone looking too hard at them, waiting for some approval, a prince to sweep them away from this tired place.

I took her by her golden curls and I drug her round and around.
Threw her into the river that flows through Coweetsee town.

Now no spry young thing herself, but forty-eight years old, Birdie found herself afraid, crossing this concrete span with its low railing, secretly wondering if she might someday decide to jump. Maybe that's what had happened to poor Rhonda Harmon.

Go down, go down, Coweetsee gal with your dark, alluring eyes.

Go down, go down, Coweetsee gal, you can never be my bride.

That overcast day, huddled in her Pendleton coat, Birdie could see a man walking along the opposite side, hunkered in a black hoodie. He looked familiar, someone Birdie should have known. She raised her hand, waving at him by instinct or the good manners that Coweetsee prides itself for, but he kept heading into town.

A slight hitch slowed the man's gait only a little, and she swore she heard taps on his shoes.

She crossed the bridge to the bank where the old grade school had been turned into artist studios. Shawanda Tomes pieced and sold her quilts there.

In the former classroom, quilts hung over the chalk boards where schoolchildren had once studied how to diagram the King's English, pruning sentences from their trunks into branches and twigs. Birdie had taught most of Shawanda's babies and they had continued their teacher-parent conferences in quiet years afterward.

Birdie slumped into one of Shawanda's cane-bottom chairs.

"Lord, what a day."

"Tell me about it."

"A couple from Atlanta stopped in, wanted to buy out the items in the historical society."

"Didn't know history was for sale."

"That's what I told them, and they left in a tizzy."

"Good riddance." Shawanda bit off the thread with her white teeth and inspected her handwork.

"What's that you're working on?"

"Pattern's called Drunkard's Path. Woman from Florida wanted it on commission."

Shawanda spread the panel and Birdie could barely see her stitches, faint as a spider's web in the sun. She loved the names of all Shawanda could do, hung about the room, Lover's Knot, Shoo Fly, Sister's Choice, Dutchman's Crossing, Old Maid's

Fancy. Looking at a warm colorful coverlet could summon a whole story.

Shawanda was the best quilter in the county and her work was worthy of the Smithsonian, but she was often overlooked because of the blackness of her skin, and how that doesn't jibe with the official white-bread version of hillbilly Appalachia.

"Girl, you okay? You're looking kind of peaked." Shawanda peered over her sewing specs.

Birdie finally let out the breath that she had been holding hard under her sternum. "Strangest thing just happened. I was walking over the bridge, thinking about poor Rhonda Harmon. Remember how she drowned?"

"Now there was a wild white girl."

"No sooner did I think of poor Rhonda, and who did I see but Charlie Clyde?"

"Naw. That devil's still in Craggy Prison last I heard."

"Remember how he wore taps on the soles of his shoes? You could hear him coming and going."

"You didn't want him sneaking up on you, that's for sure."

"That's how I knew it was him on the bridge," Birdie said.

She was still shaken by the coincidence. Like merely thinking of the drowned woman had summoned the woman's criminal brother.

But it was Shawanda's turn to look troubled. "It just ain't right. Nobody told us they were turning the likes of him loose."

If Birdie had a history with Charlie Clyde, it was nothing as bad as the blood between him and Shawanda Tomes and her family. Charlie Clyde's checkered record of public drunkenness, barn break-ins, and grand theft auto had culminated in the arson of the Nebuchadnezzar Missionary Baptist Church, better known as Old Neb. Tragically, Shawanda's uncle, LeRoy Hubbs, had been sleeping off one of his drunks in the last pew when the church went up in flames one August night in 1996. The fatal fire drew FBI attention as a potential federal hate crime since burning Black churches was all the rage that summer. But then the Atlanta office pulled back on the investigation since everybody in power knew that African Americans were mythic creatures in Appalachia. "We're in the mountains, not goddamn Mississippi," Maurice insisted.

And no one was sad to see Charlie Clyde finally convicted and sent away for good.

"Maybe you should mention it to Roy Boy," Shawanda said.

"Why?"

"Since your ex is running for sheriff."

The election was still eight months away, but the face of Roy Barker was already plastered in the window of the hardware store. Birdie's high school sweetheart and first husband, the familiar features larger than life, the rolls of fat around his neck, the bristle-cut of his military crew cut, the earnest jowls and his little boy eyes. "ROY BARKER, 2014—He's a True Native!" the sign shouted.

"Lord, another election," Birdie sighed. "Folks get so riled up."

"You going to vote this time? I mean it is your ex or the Yankee."

Francis "Frank" Cancro, a retired cop who had relocated from New Jersey, had been appointed by the state attorney general to fill out the term after the Feds arrested Maurice Posey. Roy had served as Maurice's chief deputy and driver for years. His campaign was a promise of a return to older, better ways.

On principle, Birdie Price refused to participate in local elections, not wanting to be part of the corruption Coweetsee could never shake. "I'm free as an American not to have to choose the lesser of two evils. This isn't the Soviet Union where everybody voted for the top man every time." That's what she had told herself, friends, and family for years.

Shawanda was watching Birdie with her warm eyes.

"Listen, girl. I don't think you crossed the river to tell me about Charlie Clyde or Roy Boy or history. Maybe you come to get a little something-something."

And she unfolded a corner of her ever-growing web of quilting and slid a plastic baggie across the table. Birdie pulled the hundred from her leather wallet and tucked the folded bill beneath the corner of the quilt. Their eyes did not meet in the practiced transition.

While church ladies brought casseroles and cards of concern during that long last year Talmadge spent with the cancer grinding him under heel, the life and fight draining slowly from his gray eyes, Shawanda proved the most Christian among them all. She brought baggies of Coweetsee's highest-grade, homegrown cannabis. What was good for his cancer was good for her grief. Birdie rolled and smoked a doobie each evening on her front porch, drifting off to her happier days with Talmadge.

Birdie stuffed the baggie into the bottom of her cloth tote without a word. She'd gotten what she had secretly come for, Shawanda's secret something to sooth her frayed nerves. But today, she still felt anxious, still hearing those sharp taps echoing over the bridge and the rushing river.

"Charlie Clyde back in town. I would never have believed it." She gave it some thought. "You only hope he's changed after all this time."

"Girl, you grew up here same as me," Shawanda snorted. "You know nothing changes in Coweetsee."

Heading home, she had been down this road so many times, Birdie could about drive it blindfolded. When she was teaching, she would leave school and arrive on her front porch with her key in the lock, not knowing exactly how she had traveled the dozen miles in between. At least, the door would be bolted shut, not like that lie of the good old days when folks in Coweetsee never had locked their doors. If they didn't, it was because they never left the house.

Birdie passed by barns, local landmarks that she'd grown up with and never noticed until Talmadge (an outlander) pointed them out. Coweetsee boasts more barns than people, the largest number anywhere in the state. Talmadge was a true Barn Believer, making it his mission to document and photograph all the forgotten shelters for cattle, burley, and hay before their shingle roofs rotted and leaning frames collapsed. "There, the Anderson barn." Tal never failed to point out the stately tobacco barn across the creek, as pretty a postcard as you could imagine.

Too much reverie and rubbernecking nearly brought her into a front-on collision when a beige beater swerved over the yellow line in a blind curve. Birdie saw Deana Harmon mouthing curses as she whipped by. Birdie was off the road, nearly into the ditch before she wrestled Tal's old VW onto the road again and came to a shuddering stop. The adrenaline surging through her arms as she gripped the wheel. "What the hell? Harmon whore," she cussed aloud, unconsciously what she had heard muttered by Aunt Zip, and by most other women in Coweetsee.

Seemed more than a terrible coincidence to be thinking of poor Rhonda Harmon drowned in the river, only to be passed by her devilish brother on the bridge, and then nearly get run over by the eldest Harmon sister on the way home. What made her really shiver? The close call was on the same road where Charlie Clyde had taken his wrong turn years ago.

She was a girl when she heard all about the Harmons from Aunt Zip, sitting knee to knee on the old woman's porch, learning the love songs, a warning to what men were capable of and how women suffered for their crimes. Zip allowed that Charlie Clyde was a little liquored up, but inebriation alone didn't explain his actions that night.

The youngster had been driving home when his headlight caught a glimpse of a body in the roadway. He pulled off to the side and let the engine idle before he turned the key. He stepped out, the insects flying in the cone of his one bright headlamp, the other busted out when he'd kicked his own car out of a fit of pique and never bothered to have it replaced. He walked over, stopped, studied the situation. As a test, he put his boot toe in the ribs of the body, which snored and snuffled.

He squatted on his heels and studied the sleeper. Drew Adcock who had made it halfway home from the country store where he'd sat most of the evening with a jar of homemade spirits. Drew was an accomplished drunkard and sometime house painter, a ghost in his latex-splotched whites. Most of the time, he wandered into a ditch to sleep it off, but this night he was stretched across the yellow line.

"Well, looky what we got here." Charlie Clyde studied the soft face of the dreaming drunk, who snuffled and licked his lips and scratched himself like a troubled dog.

Useless to talk to a passed-out drunk, just as useless to ask a psychopath like Charlie Clyde what he had in mind.

He walked to his car, lit a cigarette, sat thinking in the dark. He shifted the gears and rolled forward until there was a slight rise of the car and a sickening crunch underneath. He looked in the rearview mirror but saw only the red glare of his taillights. He pushed the clutch and shifted the stick into reverse and still looking into the mirror, edged backward until he could feel that sweet, sick lift once more and the muffled crunch underneath.

When he tired of the sport, Charlie Clyde spun his wheels in a thick smear on the now wet asphalt and raced into the night, leaving a real roadkill in his wake.

He had just turned sixteen, gotten his driver's license.

But the worst of the tale was yet to come. He drove to his parents' house and slept like an innocent. The whole week, he'd bragged about his deed at Clark's Mercantile where the never-do-wells and the loiterers hung out. He laughed again at the squishy sound a two-ton car makes traveling over the speed bump of a two-hundred-pound man.

When the sheriff got wind of the boy's bragging and drove out to arrest him, Charlie Clyde freely admitted what he'd done. He was driven like a prince in the backseat of the patrol car and ushered into his waiting jail cell. The lad stretched out on the hard springs of the cot with his lithe arms laced behind his dark-haired head, whistling bright tunes through the iron bars.

The Harmons, too poor to have a pot to piss in, and no real land to sell, somehow found a way to hire fancy lawyers for their son. They married off Charlie Clyde's fine young sisters, turning those old men's heads to look the other way. Lady Justice stood, a blindfolded bystander atop the domed county courthouse, which echoed with the judge's heavy gavel and pronouncement.

Charlie Clyde got off with manslaughter and was sent to the juvenile detention outside Morganton, like a prep school for future perpetrators. By the time Birdie and her friends hit high school, he was back in town. He had always been a handsome devil, who hammered those silver taps into the heels of his oxfords. He could kick up his heels and flatfoot on the plywood floors laid down at Friday night shindigs. He favored tight jeans and white T-shirts with sleeves rolled. Of course, he carried a comb to tend to his shiny pompadour. He smiled, he looked you over, nearly made you swoon. A bad boy all right. A regular recidivist, he would do different stretches in the state penal system, but he always kept coming back to Coweetsee, up to his old tricks.

It was during one of his later stays, courtesy of the state corrections department, that his youngest sister, Rhonda, had accidentally drowned or been pushed into the river by a drunken lover, depending on who was telling the story. Hurt always followed that family. Years later, a man in a black hoodie was seen standing over Rhonda's grave in the slanted cemetery on the hillside above Meadow Fork, paying his respects. When he walked away, the grass muffled the taps on his shoes.

From the main road, Birdie chugged up the gravel grade to her private knob, pulling into the worn spot beneath the shag-bark hickory shading the side of the cabin. She was still surprised when the lights weren't on, the warm lamps glowing in the windows. Talmadge will be there. He isn't there. I can't bear to think of it as just mine yet, it will always be ours.

The hurt hit her all over again, that yawning hole within. A widow's homecoming.

But UPS or FedEx had made it here before her. A delivery awaited her on the front porch by the sliding door. Birdie couldn't recall what she may have ordered.

Then she saw it was no flimsy cardboard, but a square wooden box. Not the slim slats of an apple crate, but hardwood fit for a king's casket, hand-hewn and jointed, stained with age, charred by fire, coated with mud. The number thirteen scored and burned into its side. Raw wood shaped like a tongue where the latch had fit but had been pried away ages ago. The ring that would have held the missing lock was all that remained of its security.

The lid was cut with a thin slot where a folded paper had been partially stuffed. Probably a donation to the society. Folks often left their cast-off antiques, mostly junk at the doorstep of the historical society for potential displays. Birdie had to drive most donations to the county landfill.

She unfolded the note, looking for an explanation.

HISTORY MUST BE HERD

Printed crudely in No. 2 pencil on blue-lined notebook paper torn from a wire-bound composition book. Like a note passed so often in her class in school. Misspelled of course. Anonymous, almost with the air of a ransom note. Where was the treasure, the pay-off but inside?

The label "13" might have put off a more superstitious soul, but just like Pandora, Birdie couldn't resist.

The rusted hinges creaked as she lifted the lid. The smell of the past, stale, stifled, dusty, nearly made her sneeze. At the bottom was a dried corn cob, mouse droppings, and dozens of yellowed, shriveled scraps of paper. She raised a brittle page to the light, which promptly fell apart at an ancient crease. She was more careful and lay the next scrap on the porch floor. She bent closer. Much of the wording had been erased evidently by the elements and time itself, but she knew from the very feel in her hand that here was history.

In large, faded type, the top of the paper still faintly read Coweetsee County Ballot.

Below, a whole smaller paragraph of type hard to make out,

and then again at the bottom left, two squares arranged atop each other beside a pair of names.

Maurice Posey

Shad Smathers

Could it be? Birdie began to tremble, as if she had opened an ancient tomb, with mummified remains of the long dead. Maurice Posey had been the longest-serving elected sheriff in Coweetsee and indeed the whole state. But he was an upstart in the election of 1982 when he squeaked by the incumbent Shad Smathers, the son and grandson of high sheriffs. Everyone knew the tangled history. Some said the boxes had been stuffed, others hinted those votes had gone missing. Maurice always contended he'd won it fair and square.

The box was history all right, and she was the unofficial county historian. If she was right in her suspicions, this could prove a godsend. With the upcoming election, she could envision a special exhibit for the historical society. Clear away some of the churns, roll up the bearskin. What if she put on a show about Coweetsee's checkered history of politics and local elections? That could be a real crowd-pleaser.

But lifting the lid raised other disquieting questions. Who put it on her front porch? Why now? With Coweetsee facing its first contested election since Maurice had been convicted for vote-buying, which nobody considered a crime in Coweetsee, the anonymous note seemed somehow more of a dare, even a threat. She didn't like the looks of those muddy boot prints left by a man of grim intention, not bothering to wipe his feet or cover his tracks.

If you found us, you're not lost. You must be local.

She carefully lowered the lid, too late for the hopes and fears that had slipped free.

Birdie pressed her teeth into her first knuckle, a habit from girlhood whenever she was beset with strange news, a decision to make. A little pain on the bone did the brain good.

She fished out her phone and texted her ex.

2

Roy Barker felt the buzzing on his thigh again, like a bee had flown into his pants when he wasn't looking. He patted his right front pocket. No phone. But that phantom tingling was telling him something. A premonition. He found his cell phone where he'd left it on the dash of the jeep. When he swiped his finger on the screen, he saw the message: WE SHOULD TALK. COME ON OVER. No smiley face emoji. This couldn't be good.

A more sensible man might not have jumped so high at his ex-wife's beck and call, but Birdie sounded like she was in trouble, which Roy could never resist.

Roy found himself in his Jeep Wagoneer, roaring up the gravel grade to her place, that high cabin that she had built with her second husband with the big money vistas, a far cry from the shotgun bungalow Birdie and Roy had rented as newlyweds.

She sat in the chained swing. Roy caught a whiff of what she was smoking.

"That stuff's still illegal here, you know. This ain't Colorado."

"No, it's always Coweetsee." She took a deep inhale and let out a cloud that would fog any man's mind. "You gonna tattle on me? Like what you did to Talmadge?"

She couldn't let it go, that time Roy arrested her hippie husband on a simple possession charge. Roy was going to write up his VW Bug for a broken taillight when he happened to see the baggie sticking out of the ashtray. Seek and ye shall find when the dumbshit was sporting a cannabis leaf bumper sticker. Talmadge didn't have to spend any time in the jailhouse, but he was sentenced to the trash pile of community service. Roy had smiled, passing him in an orange vest on the shoulder of the bypass, collecting litter on weekends that whole long fall. Of course, Birdie wasn't so amused.

"You know I was just doing my job."

"You didn't have to take such a pleasure in it," Birdie said. Don't get angry. Roy had been a wrestler in high school. He'd learned that sometimes you let your opponent tire themselves out if they have you by the neck. He'd learned to outlast her tirades.

"You call me all the way over here to dig up ancient history?" he asked.

"No, something I wanted you to see. I found that when I got home tonight."

The strongbox stood by the sliding door, and muddy boot prints trailed across her porch. Roy bent and studied the wooden chest. The number 13 had been branded into its front panel. One end of the box looked charred, like it had been set too close to a fire, or maybe survived some blaze. The other side was coated in riverbed, like maybe it had floated downstream in a flood.

"Looks old."

"Best look inside."

He lifted the lid. Roy could smell tobacco leaf and animal droppings, an ancient aroma. The papers at the bottom were brittle to the touch, which made his own skin crawl with impropriety, like he had pried open a casket and was rooting around for the corpse that had turned to dust.

"Those papers show Shad Smathers and Maurice's names. I believe that's a ballot box from the '82 election," Birdie calmly explained. "The one they say Maurice stole from Shad Smathers."

"That was an awful long time ago." Roy took a deep breath, then slammed the lid shut. He didn't like where all this was headed, what Birdie was putting into his head.

"I was thinking it would be a good display for the historical society, but I don't know who put that box on my porch. They left a note but no name. That worries me."

He could see her point. Those boot prints belonged to a good-sized man, bigger than Birdie.

"Something else."

Birdie alighted from her swing, the chains jangling, and walked to the edge of her porch. She crossed her arms, the way that Roy would always remember, the bony points of her elbows always jutting out, echoing her sharp hip bones.

Roy groaned inwardly. There was no hurrying her, never had been.

"Now this just may be a coincidence. I saw Charlie Clyde crossing the bridge today."

"Charlie Clyde?" Roy Boy couldn't help himself but let out a short sharp whistle. "Lord, last thing we need around here. Reckon he finally got paroled."

"Isn't somebody supposed to say something when a convict like Charlie Clyde is turned loose on his hometown?"

"Why you asking me?"

"You're the one running for damn sheriff, aren't you?"

"Folks asked me. Maybe I can get Coweetsee back to its old self."

"So you're going to be the next Maurice Posey?"

"I'm my own man. I don't aim to repeat Maurice's mistakes."

"Like stealing elections? Good Lord, Roy Boy. I hope that's not your stump speech."

She was the only one who called him by his boyhood name, at least to his face. Yes, he was a junior, but his daddy had been dead for thirty years. Roy had trained most everyone else to call him by his grown-up name. Don't get angry. Don't get angry.

He should have kept his mouth shut. They were finished ages ago. She went and married that hippie and was by all accounts a happy and satisfied woman until Talmadge Pierce got cancer and died on her. Kept his distance all these years, gave her that space she said she needed, like being next to his bulk in bed made her claustrophobic. Twenty years, yet they couldn't help but hunker into the trenches of their marital wars, aiming at old targets.

Tired and frustrated, she kicked the porch post, then sat on her swing, her feet crossed at her still-thin ankles. Roy Boy's backside strained against the vinyl webbing in the metal lawn chair. The mystery box closed between them.

He noted the lawn needed cutting on the slope down to the woods where a small redbud glowed its early bloom as the sky pinked over the far ridges.

Roy swallowed hard and tried harder. "Sure is pretty up here."

"Pretty lonesome, sometimes," Birdie allowed.

Then, as if on cue, an owl hooted once, twice from an already dark holler.

"You keep a gun in the house?"

"I've got Aunt Zip's old revolver somewhere, after we put her in the home."

"Are you okay here, all by yourself tonight?"

"No, I'm not okay, but I can take care of myself. I didn't know who to call, since Talmadge…" And she suddenly melted, a twitch at the side of her mouth, her eyes welling.

Roy sprang to his feet, a man able to move faster than you would think for his bulk. But she raised her hand, warning Roy not to come a step closer.

"Don't you dare," she said. "Don't you be pitying me."

She held her arm out, her hand pressed flat as if against a wall of invisible bricks, a barrier to keep everyone out of her space, her thoughts. He watched her face fighting against the wash of grief, the blackness surging over her. Roy could see the girl he'd loved and married so long ago when they were young and knew no better. He looked away from her grief, to give her some privacy.

"I'm okay. I'm fine." She wiped her eyes hard with the heels of her hand.

"Probably, the weed. You ought to stop that."

"Bad habit, I know." She pinched out the joint in her ashtray. "Talmadge used it for the pain. I suppose I do too."

"Sorry." Roy took a chance. "Truly. For your loss, for your pain. Everything." He waved his hands, like that might help his feeble words take wing.

What should you say to your ex as the dusk crept up the mountain, and the sun set over the ridge? That damn owl gave its hoot somewhere in the trees, then came that silence that blankets the world in the shift from day to dark.

He stooped and hoisted the ballot box on his shoulder.

"Where do you think you're going with that?"

"If this is what you say it is, this box might be valuable to someone. Let me run this over to Junk Jackson's. See if he thinks it's legit, and what is worth."

"That dirty old scavenger wouldn't know historical significance from a dried turd," Birdie said. "Put that down. That's history and that's my box now."

Reluctantly, he lowered it back to the porch and rubbed his shoulder.

"Take you some pictures," Birdie suggested. "You can show Junk those."

"I don't have a camera." Roy Boy looked befuddled.

"You've got your phone. It takes pictures, you know."

Technology was not his friend. He handed over his device to Birdie's outstretched hand, and she snapped some shots of the box from different angles, then closeups of the ballots. She handed the phone to him.

"I still might use it for the historical society. Let me know what you find out."

After Roy left, the dust settled on the gravel road, and the dusk lingered. Birdie sat on her swing, smoking the last of her joint. She was still rattled by the ballot box, and the muddy footprints of whoever had left it there as a message, maybe a warning.

She wasn't so much afraid of the woods and the dark, as she was going inside to that empty and cold bed. Perhaps it was only Shawanda's weed whispering in her ear as she watched the smoke curl from her mouth.

She was glad she had called Roy Boy even though the man still infuriated her after all these years.

You always were the angriest woman I know. You were always the slowest man I know. All that time together and many more years apart, they still knew each other. They didn't even have to say the worst out loud when they fought. Perhaps a part of her still missed her beau from their high school days. Roy Boy was a big-boned lad turned into a sad man with a drum belly after he'd spent the better part of his life in law enforcement, gallivanting about these hills and hollers with the high sheriff himself, burning moonshine stills and marijuana patches, then raiding meth labs.

Who had put the notion in his thick head that Roy should run for sheriff, Birdie didn't know, but she had her suspicions. All those hangers-on, loiterers, and layabouts who used to be Maurice's unofficial deputies at the jail. It was a wonder any crime ever got solved in Coweetsee since all those men did was park their butts on broken cane-bottom chairs, drink bad coffee, and then the harder stuff after hours. Now instead of the jail, they hung out at the McDonald's on the bypass.

All talk. Men are all talk.

They had talked Roy Boy into believing he could possibly win. After all these years, she didn't want to see her childhood sweetheart pinned, too proud to slap the mat in surrender.

In high school, Birdie had sat in the bleachers in the gym, hollering at the top of her lungs for Roy to pin his opponent. He circled slowly, looking for his opening, grappling the other guy's beefy arms, then suddenly, he was on top, or sometimes underneath with his adversary on his back. He made his move, the deceptive flab that proved to be solid muscle, and Roy would bend his foe to his will.

At his last match, she had heard him snap a boy's arm, a terrible sound like a rifle shot that cracked across the cavernous gym, followed by the boy screaming, Oh God, oh God, a high-pitched cry like a bird that had flown inside, desperate to flee.

Roy Boy quit wrestling after that, and didn't go out for football, even though his poundage was half the offensive line that poor Coweetsee High could muster against the other Single A division schools around the mountains.

Now she feared Roy Boy was up against something that outweighed him, could overwhelm him. Birdie didn't know what was sadder—not that he'd never win, but that he'd never give up. She couldn't blame Roy Boy when she was the one who gave up on their marriage. She had seen the bearded, beautiful boy shuffling his sandals down the sidewalks of Coweetsee on a summer day. An outlander if she'd ever seen one, but this one caught her fancy.

"Why you hanging out with that long hair?" Roy once asked her point-blank.

"Because he's a sight more interesting than you ever were," she fired back.

Talmadge Pierce was born and schooled in Washington DC, where his daddy served as a government attorney. He went to school at the university down in Chapel Hill, but came to Coweetsee during the heyday of the hippie homesteaders.

He was greeted by Coweetsee natives with a slow drawl. "You ain't from around here, are you now?"

"Nope," he said. "But I'm here now, thank God."

It took an outsider like Talmadge to make Birdie see what she'd grown up with.

"You could roam all over America and not find a place, a people more authentic than here in Coweetsee. This is a treasure trove, I mean, the tall tales, the ballads, the barns are beautiful. All this disappeared a century ago in the rest of America. You've got roots here, Birdie. Do you know how rare that is in our corporate consumer society?"

Coweetsee had beaucoups of barns, but just how many no one had really counted until Talmadge came along. He started driving the roads in his VW Beetle, doing a windshield survey. It quickly averaged out to five barns a mile in some sections of the county. He did the math. With a conservative estimate of 10,000 barns, Coweetsee boasted a barn for every two people living in the county.

"Somebody needs to write their history before they all fall down," Talmadge insisted. He wrote a grant from the state cultural office, and he began collecting oral histories of the owners, checking property records in the county courthouse, and taking photos with a Nikon. He wore tall rubber boots, to ward off the copperheads and rattlesnakes that were the main inhabitants of these abandoned barns.

"You and I made love in more than a few barns."

She blushed and punched his arm. "Talmadge!"

Where she had only seen utilitarian structures to shelter livestock or harvests, Talmadge Price summoned bucolic bowers of passion with maids and swains. Lolling in the hay after their trysts, he would recite Chaucer and old English. Tal was the only one she would trust enough to lay down in the vermin-infested, shit-smelling places. Looking into those blue eyes, Birdie would have laid with that man in the middle of the road, and it would have felt like a goose-down mattress, to be with that sweet man.

She divorced the deputy sheriff, weathered the titters of the church ladies, who frowned on adulteries and affairs, and kept her job as a fifth-grade schoolteacher. And for fifteen years, the couple made a life together in this cabin, her teaching children and him believing in barns until the cancer came along.

Tal had been feeling tired and he went in for a physical. The tests weren't good. It was in his blood, a leukemia. They fought hard, chased all the latest treatments, the experimental drugs. It was bad when all his beautiful hair began to fall out after the chemo. He surrendered to the inevitable before she did. He was only a year older than she, but he looked and moved like a suddenly senior citizen.

"I can't go on. You need to help me out."

"I can't believe you're giving up on us like this," she said one night, words that she would regret until the day she died.

It wasn't fair, of course, her railing against a skinny man with his shaved head, the strange bony knots of his skull, the vertebrae poking through the long nape of his neck.

Talmadge blinked in disbelief. "I'm dying here, babe. I can't do it anymore."

Tal had never owned a gun and had his reasons. His father had shot himself and Tal thought it might run in the family. Depression. You must break the cycle somehow. Having a gun at hand maybe wasn't a good idea when you hated yourself. No guns, no silver bullet.

Instead, Birdie asked Shawanda if she could get ahold of anything more potent than the primo weed.

"What you need that for, girl?"

"Don't ask."

She got a hold of morphine. Birdie didn't ask, though she suspected it might have come through Shawanda's daughter, Kezia, who had some access to medicines as a caretaker at Laurel Trace nursing home where they had moved Aunt Zip.

On the last night, the Prices sat on the porch and drank a bottle of fancy French wine, the best they could find in Asheville, a Bordeaux. "I wanted to take you to Paris, I wanted you to see that countryside."

They watched the moon rise to their right over the hills, the sun off to the west, reddening the rims. The first stars start to shine, the planet Mercury. Talmadge had been a Boy Scout, never made it past First Class. He wasn't the Eagle type like an astronaut or a general, still the Scout code had stuck with him, trustworthy and loyal. He could point his finger to the night and draw out the constellations for her. The names of Greek gods and heroes, the sad women like Cassandra. Birdie would blink and said of course, she saw. She was fibbing. Pinpricks of light, but it was nice to think someone could see a pattern, trace a story in the night skies, even if she couldn't follow it.

She had crushed the pills and stirred the deadly debris into the last glass as they finished off the bottle. He drained it to the dregs and went inside to lie down. She waited as long as she could bear, then Birdie went in and lay with him, wrapping her arms around him. "Don't go," was what he said.

She listened to the hard rasp of his breath, felt the terrible shuddering of his chest beneath her hand. She closed her eyes. His stayed half-lidded but the light had leached out of those blue irises.

When he was gone, Birdie went out on the porch and smoked. A cigarette this time, not the weed. She was weeping when the sun came up and the body of her husband was cooling in the bed. They had agreed. She had to wait before she called for help that Talmadge wouldn't be needing. No one was coming to save him or her now.

Sheriff Cancro—it was hard to get used to someone wearing Maurice Posey's badge—had stopped by the house after Talmadge had passed.

He stood on the porch and interrogated rather than consoled the new widow. Birdie sat dutifully in the middle of her swing, not to the side, weighing the chains equally after her soulmate, his weight had been removed from those terrible scales.

"He died quick, that was a mercy, I suppose. In his sleep," Cancro muttered.

"It was a mercy," Birdie agreed. She swayed slowly in the swing, her ankles hooked one behind the other, floating in this suddenly strange, empty space.

"Your husband," Cancro coughed. "Went awfully quickly."

"He had cancer and he died."

"Maybe he had some help."

"What are you saying, Sheriff?"

"People talk." The uniformed man shrugged.

That son of bitch was going to let his accusation hang in midair.

"People talk all kinds of shit in these parts," Birdie said.

That had been over a year ago. Birdie had kept her silence, her secret and not told a soul. If he led me away in chains and locked me in the cell of his new facility, no bars, but just a thick metal door with a small glass window to peer in on the prisoner in coveralls, it would be all that I deserved.

3

If anybody knew the value of a ballot box from a shady election, whether for hard cash or as a nostalgic collectible, Roy knew it'd be his old classmate, "Junk" Jackson. Coweetsee had a cast of those folks known as "characters," but Junk had staked out a particular niche, trading on his shiftlessness and cunning. His instincts as a packrat paid off handsomely in rusted implements and cast-off appliances, heaped in his front yard and piled on his porch. Even getting inside the house was hard, since you couldn't quite open the door but had to shoulder past teetering stacks of *Life* and *Playboy* magazines, columns of crockery, and piers of plastic buckets. He hoarded African masks, Cherokee masks, Mardi Gras masks, WWII Hun helmets and rusted bayonets, 78 rpm vinyl records, Elvis memorabilia, comic books, crock pots, busted toaster ovens, the loot of flea markets and swap meets across the Southeast. Long before recycling became routine, Junk was the king of refuse.

In grade school, he had been plain Walter Jackson with bad teeth and body odor from not having a shower in the house. His nickname came later, from his stint on a TV reality show on the History Channel, *American Trash*. The producers wanted to play up the Junk persona. Sporting long locks of dirty blond hair and a stained mustache that bristled with menace while a jangly banjo played the background music, Junk stared at the camera for the opening credits. It helped that Walter owned several pair of bleached overalls, which he strapped over his bare chest. He looked the part of an untrustworthy yokel who would know the lay of the land and steal any outsiders blind, the spitting image of our contemporary Snuffy Smith.

"Wasn't much of a paycheck in the end. TV ain't all it's cracked up to be, American Dream-wise," Junk allowed.

Roy pulled into his eyesore of a place. A trio of tractors sat in the front yard in various states of disassembly. A couple of early model sedans hunkered side by side, their hoods raised on treasure troves of engine parts. The car seat had been detached and dragged to the front porch where Junk had parked his lazy self. Roy climbed the steps and looked for a place to sit himself.

"How's business? You ever sell any of this shit?"

"Sometimes," Junk said. "But now it's mostly to set the scene."

Junk's latest scam came on the heels of his TV fame. Only a mile from the interstate exit, he saw plenty of traffic going past his place. How to make them stop? He had painted "Ask a Real Redneck" in red barn oil on a warped sheet of plywood leaning against his mailbox. Flying the Confederate battle flag from his front porch probably hurt his cause with younger folks, but he sat his station, shirtless, his belly hanging out like a Buddha, ready to dispense his salt-of-the-earth, homegrown opinions to any outlander who wanted to snap his photo. The gallon jar stuffed with greasy dollar bills served as a reminder that such wisdom was not free.

"You won't believe all the wackadoos I get and what they want to know. Hell, I have to make up shit," Junk complained.

Roy swatted at the Rebel flag that kept flapping into his face. "You're giving folks the wrong impression of us."

"Just giving the people what they want."

No worse than what the Cherokee did down on the reservation, Junk explained. Chiefing by the roadside, getting paid for pictures by tourists, never mind no Cherokee wore a warbonnet or slept in a teepee. People have their own ideas of what Indians and mountaineers look like.

"You'd be surprised how many followers I have on Instagram these days. I'm what they call a social influencer."

"You should get an honest job."

Junk smiled, revealing his yellow-stained teeth. "Look who's talking, Mr. Sheriff's candidate. How goes the campaign?"

"Not too bad. I reckon I can count on your vote come November."

"You put that money in my tip jar?"

"We don't operate like that, no more. Maurice got sent away for buying votes."

"That's a shame," Junk said. "I suppose you'll have to just win on personality."

Enough with the small talk, the polite busting of balls that was male etiquette in Coweetsee. Roy got down to business.

"Birdie found something on her front porch. Called me to come take a look."

"And you went running right over. She's still got you pussy whipped, I see."

Before he became Junk, Walter had been married once, like Roy, fresh out of high school, but Alma Jackson had left him, ran off one night with a drive-through trucker. It had been years now, but even between men who didn't particularly care for each other, there were places you didn't poke into, wounds that were still never quite healed. It wouldn't be fair.

"She's my ex. Let's watch the language."

"Or what? You gonna arrest me? You ain't won that gold star just yet."

"Or I could just kick your ass like I used to."

"Come on, fat boy. We can rumble."

Roy could still flinch at the clammy touch of Walter's sweating skin against his when they faced off on the mats in the musty gym of Coweetsee High, the light of another time pouring through those high windows. They circled each other, grappling, looking for the weakness, the take-down. He had Walter slapping the mat with a headlock, his head scissored between Roy's stout thighs when Walter bit him. There weren't any rules the way mountain boys wrassle.

"We'd look like fools, pair of old fellows like us. You'd take a swing and then me. We'd have to sit down to catch our breath."

"Speak for yourself." Junk flexed his flabby biceps and Roy had to laugh.

"So back to this box Birdie found. Sounds like it might be something historic, worth some money."

At the mention of money, Junk's eyes began to shine. He was a man who could almost weep when it came to currency, perhaps landing in his pocket.

"If you're asking a real redneck, my expert advice ain't for free." He nodded again at the gallon jar on the rail of his porch.

Roy raised a haunch to free his wallet, pinching a twenty for the tip jar. "Happy?"

"I try to be contented with my lot in this life." Junk flashed a grin of yellow teeth.

Roy fished out his phone. "Birdie took some pictures of that box. They're in here somewhere."

Junk held out his dirty hand. How come everyone knew about handling technology except for me, Roy thought. The old scavenger pursed his lips as he thumbed through the photos on the screen, squinting at the details.

"Birdie says that's a missing ballot box from the 1982 election, when Shad lost and Maurice took his star," Roy explained. "See that number thirteen on the side, that's the Meadow Fork precinct, Shad's old stronghold. He expected to get more votes out of Meadow Fork than people who lived there. They say he lost by only thirty-one votes."

"Ain't much into politics," Junk said. "One side's same as the other. Money keeps changing hands but always ends up in the back pocket of the big fellow."

"You do remember I am running," Roy said.

Junk handed over Roy's phone. "Bring me that box. I'll give you ten bucks."

"I just gave you a twenty."

"Don't know what to tell you then, good buddy," Junk said. "You could always ask W. D. Clark."

W. D. ran the Clark Mercantile, a two-story wooden general store in Meadow Fork. He had been a fixture in that part of the county forever and a fixer in every one of Maurice's campaigns after Shad got knocked off in that shady '82 vote.

"He's the only one I know who collects this stuff, or used to. I hear W. D. has moved on from politics. Now he's snatching up land along the interstate exits, looking to get ahead of the development. That man always knows which way the wind is blowing and how a few more greenbacks might line his pocket. He's the man you ought to ask if you ask me."

"I'd rather ask a rattlesnake for a favor than that cranky old cuss," Roy said.

"Some say he's the one who might have ratted Maurice out to the Feds."

"That's why I'm not asking him squat."

Junk stared off into space, his forehead furrowed as if scraping his brainpans for some helpful advice.

"I do recollect Rhonda Harmon once asked what a ballot box might be worth."

"Rhonda?" Roy hadn't thought of that drowned woman in forever.

"Years back, said she and her sister had come by one, thought it might be of some interest to some people in power. I told her what I told you, go ask W. D."

"Did she?"

"Never came up again between us." Junk drummed a beat on his bare belly. "This was when I was seeing her some on the sly. Until things got ugly between us."

You and me both, buddy, Roy thought but kept his mouth shut. He hoped the blush in his face wouldn't betray him. That drunken one-night fling after Birdie had abandoned him. No need sharing all his secrets with Junk, who was known to talk too much with anyone who showed up on his porch.

"Sad how that old girl drowned like that," Junk said.

Roy remembered that Deana Harmon had called the sheriff's office, said her sister had been missing for a few days. Everyone thought she was at a weekend party is all, and no one paid that much mind, until a fisherman found her body snagged in the branches of a felled tree under the riverbank. A shame, maybe suicide, maybe an accident when she fell drunk into the water.

But many said she'd been punched and pushed. Another story, another cautionary tale we tell ourselves in Coweetsee.

Sad, what else could a body say?

They fell silent. Roy stretched his legs. Junk raised his scrawny arms over his head and yawned. They were two aging men, not old, but they were sitting on the porch, surrounded by the manmade salvage of Junk's front yard and the God-given mountains rolling away to the horizon. The breeze was coming off the ridge and cooling their faces. They had known each other all their lives and had little to say to each other. No hurry came in Coweetsee with any conversation. If it wasn't a deep dark secret, a dirty deed, a body buried in the woods, folks generally would speak their minds.

"Speaking of Rhonda, you hear tell that Charlie Clyde is back in town?"

Junk whistled. "That's news to me."

"Birdie saw him downtown. I could tell she was scared."

"Women scare easy in Coweetsee. A bunch of nervous nellies if you ask me."

"Charlie Clyde is someone to be afraid of," Roy insisted. "Given what he's done in the past.

"Oh, I don't know if he's all that bad. I did some trade with him off and on."

"That old boy always gives you the willies the way he smiles."

"Lots of ladies seemed to like that smile," Junk observed.

"You still think he really burned down that church like they say?"

"Who else is wicked enough in Coweetsee?"

"Charlie Clyde swore on his mama's Bible that he was framed," Junk said. "As if his mama ever owned a Bible."

"He done the crime so he paid the time, like Maurice always said." Roy shook his head.

"I reckon he's paid his dues if they let him out."

"Maybe," Roy observed. "Funny how that old ballot box shows up the same time as that old devil."

"That's a fact."

A fact but the mystery remained.

About that time, a car pulled into Junk's gravel driveway and a couple in sunglasses, cargo shorts, tank tops and sandals got out of the SUV with big grins on their faces.

"Looks like you got business."

"Yep, back to work."

"I'll leave you to it."

The young outsiders bashfully approached the porch, passing Roy as he headed to his jeep.

"You ain't really going to 'Ask a Real Redneck,' are you? You know it's all just a joke."

The lad in his aviator sunglasses and cargo shorts snorted. "We get it. We just want a photo."

"Y'all are in luck. I ain't broke the camera on a smartphone yet." Junk wedged between the couple for a selfie as he brushed the girl's breast and elbowed the boy, squeezing into the frame of the phone the lad held at arm's length.

She was telling them what hashtag was best. The big old smirk that Junk Jackson usually wore fell off his face as he got into character as mournful mountaineer.

4

The historical society was open Wednesdays through Saturdays, so on Tuesdays, Birdie ran her errands, did her grocery shopping, then at mid-afternoon, drove to Laurel Trace Rest Home. Birdie always had to sit in the car for a second to catch her breath, collect her thoughts.

She hated that Zip was at Laurel Trace, away from her home. Her aunt fell off the porch a few years back and broke her hip. "Tough titties," she could hear Aunt Zip say. It was a terrible decision, but Birdie and Talmadge decided it was time for assisted living.

The first Tuesday she had come to visit, Birdie had locked her keys in the car and had to call Talmadge to rescue her. Now Tal was gone, and she was left with an aging aunt and a sad life.

From the parking lot, looking up, she could catch a glimpse of George's Gap where the two-lane road corkscrewed out of Coweetsee. The whitened trunks of dead hemlocks stood on the high ridge like the masts of shipwrecks, killed off by acid rain from the TVA's coal plants. The redbuds were already showing. Next the dogwoods would bloom. But a new cell tower loomed over all, blinking its baleful red eye over the county.

She'd rather be up there, than down here in the laurel hell that gave the old folks home its name. Birdie collected herself and put on her best smile. Life goes on and so should she. Zip always told her that, but that didn't make it any easier.

"How is she today?" Birdie asked the attendant on duty.

Kezia, still looking fresh in her pink smock, though it's likely been all day she's been cleaning up after old folks.

"Right as rain, Miz Price."

"Really? Shoot me straight."

"Sweet as she can be."

"Now, I know you're lying."

Kezia giggled. "She don't change. She'll give you a hard time, but she's a good soul."

"If she's feeling good, she's likely causing trouble."

Zip used a metal cane for her bad hip and traveled the long hall, calling on her friends, mostly lording it over the bedridden, counting her blessings. The old gal had gained weight after she settled into Laurel Trace. She would turn a hundred next year, and she didn't seem ready to go nowhere.

"Thanks for telling me the truth," Birdie said.

Kezia beamed like she used to, all cornrows and bright eyes in the front row of Birdie's fifth-grade class. She was one of Shawanda's babies. Smart like her mother. She had gone to community college, gotten an associate degree, and found steady work helping the elderly of Coweetsee in their last days.

"Tell your mama that you're righter than rain."

"I surely will, Miz Price."

Birdie hurried down the hall. Passing the small rooms of residents in their single beds and lounge chairs, she was reminded of all the artifacts she zealously guarded at the historical society. Old Mrs. Mabe with her mouth open to the ceiling, her braided gray hair splayed across her pillow. She looked for all the world like the antique butter churn in the back of the jail, its wooden plunger now stuck for all eternity, swollen in the drilled hole of the round wooden lid, mashing only the memory of ancient curds. Or the Widow Gunther with her wrinkles and rheumatism. She wore the same prim pout as her ancestors posed on porches by itinerant photographers back in the Depression, which had never really ended in some corners of the county.

Coweetsee, of course, was cursed to never change.

The fading souls carefully captive in their cells, serving out the sentence of their last days, gently snoring or loudly fussing, the same personalities as their six-year-old selves, underscored in their second childhoods.

Laurel Trace's clientele was mostly women, thin haired,

whiskery chins, many moaning or garbling. Out of twenty residents, a male was a rarity.

So the ladies were all atwitter with the former Sheriff Maurice Posey in their midst.

He still could get around on good days with his oxygen supply slung over a thin shoulder, making his way along the hall, knocking at doors. "I've come a courting," he'd sing out, making the wan cheeks of the widows glow again, their rheumy eyes sparkle. Hope always eternal, lust and love blushing even at the end of wrinkled days.

Birdie passed by Maurice's open door, and saw him sprawled in his bed, mouth wide open, snoring away innocently. The once fearsome lawman looked harmless enough when asleep. He'd received a compassionate release from his ten-year sentence in federal prison since his emphysema and cigar-choked lungs guaranteed a death sentence. Maurice's demise maybe wasn't as imminent as he'd convinced the federal officials. "I've seen 'em linger for years in his condition." Kezia shook her head. "Never can tell."

Aunt Zip was only one door down and across the hall. "Zipporah Sherrill" read the small interchangeable plaque by her threshold.

On her school rolls, Birdie had to call out more Tiffanys and Bethanys and Madisons and Skylars. No one inflicted biblical names on baby girls these days, no Zippora or Ava or Drusilla. Women like her aunt Zip were from a different time, cut from a coarser homespun cloth. "Lord, we had to make it all ourselves or make do without." She was a creature of a distant century. She'd seen everything from horse-drawn buggies to Apollo moonshots, but she was not impressed with the conveniences of our day, indoor plumbing and paved roads, electrification with stoves you plugged into a wall instead of feeding wood into to bake your biscuits, the idea of buying frozen biscuits. Microwaves, dishwashers, dryers, TV, AC, internet, all the things Birdie had tried to bring into her house by the end of her long life.

Zip had been a spinster, caring for her parents until they had passed. But Birdie believed her great-aunt had been a wild one in her youth, and knew what boys were all about. She just never saw the need to have one in the house forever underfoot.

Aunt Zip sat in her lounge chair by the window. Not that there was that much to see as far as a view, compared to the breathtaking vista from the parking lot. The twenty-bed Laurel Trace got started as a motorist inn back when folks came down the highway into town.

"How's Chip and Eve and the rest?"

"I think Eve is going to eat Chip one day." Zip had a view of a rock outcropping and vines and trees and growth only about ten feet on the other side of the big glass, but she had her own world there. She watched beetles and centipedes slide through their short lives on the rocks and leaves. She had a chipmunk she called Chip, and a long yellow snake she'd named Eve.

"I'm sorry. At least they keep you company."

"I get plenty of company. Tires a body out."

"Like who?" Birdie held her great-aunt's hand.

"Oh, the sheriff comes by for a chat. Says he might arrest me for being so attractive."

"That old flirt. I'll tell him to leave you be."

"Don't you dare." Zip jerked back her hand coquettishly.

"You remember he went to prison for vote-buying. He made Coweetsee the poster child for corruption."

"Maurice paid his dues. He's just waiting like the rest of us to die," Zip insisted. "In the meanwhile, we just talk about old times."

Damn if the whole town hadn't forgotten the terrible shame of his conviction and turned Maurice's return into a homecoming parade. Roy had proudly drove his former boss down Main Street in his jeep. Roy worshipped the old man, but Birdie had never been a fan of the Coweetsee kingpin.

Birdie didn't like the idea of a felon living next door to her great-aunt, but she wasn't going to pick a bone with the old girl today.

"What are we going to sing today?" Birdie asked.

"You remember all the verses to 'Henry Lee'?"

"Probably not, but you'll remind me." Birdie had to laugh. Talmadge had suggested that Birdie start singing the old ballads again with her great-aunt, a way to pass the time visiting, perhaps to relieve Birdie's guilt. Birdie had forgotten most of the verses and it gave Zip a little authority. "Sometimes, it helps for a teacher to be a student," Tal had said in his irritating wisdom.

Zip would start humming, as if fetching the words from deep memory. She raised a rheumatic bent finger skyward. "Pitch it higher," she said. If you started too low, the turns of the quatrains would spiral you down deep in your throat, like into the well where the bodies were always thrown.

With everything going wrong these days, Birdie counted on singing songs with this old woman to forget her troubles. Birdie sang loud, like her life was at stake, same as the poor souls in the lyrics. She could feel the cords of her neck straining around her larynx as she pitched it high.

They wound through the verses about a hapless boy named Henry Lee and the girl who was hot for him. The thick-headed lad turns the girl down and doesn't take to her bed.

She leaned herself against a fence, just for a kiss or two.
With a little pen knife held in her hand, she plugged him through and
*   through.*
Come all you ladies in the town, a secret for me to keep
With a diamond ring on my hand, I never will forsake.

Birdie began to giggle when Zip sang that verse. "That's wild. Kill a man because she can't get him to put a ring on her finger."

"Pay attention, girl. We're still singing," Zip admonished her.

Next verse, the murderous maiden enlists her friends, who take poor dead Henry Lee by his arms and by his feet and drop him down a hundred-foot well.

But then the ballad, as Zip's songs often did, took an even

stranger turn when a talking bird enters. The maiden tries to sweet-talk the little feathered messenger the same way that she'd tried and failed with her doomed lover.

Fly down, fly down, you little bird, and alight on my right knee.
Your cage will be made of gold, all I can give thee.
I can't fly down; I won't fly down and alight on your right knee.
A girl who'd murder her own true love would kill a little bird like me.

Remembering the bird in the tree, a sudden flash of wings seen from the porch where she sat in swing with Talmadge bundled close under a Pendleton blanket, Birdie felt this tightness in her ribcage, like every breath was measured before she could release it into this uneasy world.

"What's wrong, child? You seem off today." Zip could always see through her as a little girl, in a way she felt her own mama never took notice of.

"I guess my mind was elsewhere." Birdie hesitated, then blurted out her secret. "Guess who's back in town?"

"Charlie Clyde," Zip said as if clairvoyant.

"How did you know?"

Zip chuckled her toothless mouth. "Word gets 'round quick. Kezia told me."

Birdie should have known anything she whispered to Shawanda was likely shouted on the other side of the county by the end of the day. It's the way things worked here in Coweetsee.

"You best stay away from the likes of him," Zip said. "I recollect when you was but an empty-headed girl sweet on that bad boy."

Birdie had been hearing if not always heeding her great-aunt's warning since she was a girl. The summer she turned sixteen and got her license, Aunt Zip let Birdie drive to Coweetsee to get the old lady's hair done.

Birdie had already read the magazines in the beauty parlor and drifted out to the sidewalk to chew her gum in peace and perhaps people watch. She stared at the marque on the Coweetsee Strand—*A Star is Born*, with Barbra Streisand and Kris

Kristofferson. Streisand looked pretty, even with that big nose, but Kris was a dreamboat.

She didn't hear the tap of his shoes until Charlie Clyde cornered her against the car.

"Goodness, girl. How come I never noticed you before?" He reached and placed his warm palm against the sweat of her blouse, over her new bra and her perked breast. He pinched a pleasure out of her nipple. Decades later, the feeling could still swell inside her, a mixture of mortification, excitement, sweat, and heat. He was twenty-one or so, and she was sixteen. His mouth was on hers. He was pressing her body against the hot door of the Chrysler, her bare thigh burning below her culotte. She closed her eyes, swooning, falling deep inside herself.

"You back off that girl right now, before I put a bullet in your head."

Birdie opened her eyes to see the barrel of Aunt Zip's pistol tickling the ear she wanted to nibble on herself.

"You gonna shoot a man in broad daylight, lady?" Charlie Clyde asked innocently. "Here on the main street of Coweetsee?"

"Better believe I will if you don't move yourself away from my niece."

He held his hands up half-heartedly, like this wasn't the first time he'd been caught red-handed grappling with a girl, or maybe he was used to having people point firearms in his face.

"We were just having a little fun." He winked at Birdie.

"I said back off before I put a bullet through your thick head." Aunt Zip kept waving the gun like a magic wand.

Charlie Clyde stepped away with a sharp metallic tap of his shoe on the broken sidewalk.

"Keep on walking," Zip warned. "And you best stay away if you want to stay alive."

She was furious at Aunt Zip, driving home in the car. She couldn't say it was the first time she'd been kissed. Birdie had practiced pecking at boy's dry lips on the playground at school, but this was the first time that a man had put his mouth on her, and it was like he had drawn her very soul out with his sweet tongue.

"I think he really likes me," Birdie wailed.

"Charlie Clyde is sweet on any slut who's going to uncross her legs. Don't you trust that boy, not if you have any sense or wish to keep your dignity."

"They say he's a good dancer."

"Satan can do a jig as well, and they say he has a dick as cold as ice, if you want to know the truth of it."

That afternoon, Zip told Birdie the true story of what Charlie Clyde had done, running over poor drunk Drew Adcock, and how he was first sent away.

Besides the boy, the Harmons had themselves two fine daughters, Deana and Rhonda. In hopes of saving that son, they'd put a lien on their farm, and still that wouldn't be enough to pay for the defense of the indefensible. The Harmons mortgaged not only their property, but their progeny. The daughters were driven to a house by the river, where the town fathers of Coweetsee went for drink and cards and unsavory sport.

"His sisters had to pay for his meanness." Zip shook her head years later in her recliner at Laurel Trace. "My god, it sounds biblical, selling your daughters to whoredom in Babylon."

"Wait, I thought you said they were married?" Birdie said. Somehow her great-aunt had skipped over that part years ago.

"So they thought."

They were tricked, Zip explained. The Harmons believed they had found the right suitors for the sisters. Rich, well-fed, round-paunched lawyers and powerbrokers at the courthouse. Fourteen was the legal age for marriage with parental permission and Rhonda had just celebrated that fatal birthday. Deana was nearing spinsterhood at seventeen. But no marriage certificate was ever signed, stamped, and filed in public records at the courthouse.

The girls went on to party with their new beaus. Liquor flowed and fun was had. And when baby bumps started to show, well, the men knew a place to take care of that problem. The daughters came home, unmarried and un-pregnant as well, now worse for wear.

"No crying over spilt milk or lost maidenhoods," Zip snorted.

"They call that sex trafficking nowadays," Birdie protested.

"What happened to those men?"

Zip shrugged. "Nothing. They all died. Maybe a few are left, but they're old now."

"Didn't Posey investigate?"

"Pshaw, girl. That was even before Maurice's time, back when Shad Smathers wore the star. Everybody knew it was wrong, but it wasn't a crime," Zip snorted. "Women are like cattle, livestock, shipped off to slaughter after they are paraded at the fall fair and win their ribbons. Innocence, my ass."

"I don't recall you telling me any of this before."

"Your mother warned me not to scare you, give you nightmares. She was awfully protective of you."

Birdie believed she'd never heard a whole truthful story. Seemed there were always missing parts, the way that the women would lower their voices when she came into the room, how the murmur of murders came from the porch when she slammed the screen door, gone to fetch the iced tea. She'd always felt adults were keeping something from her.

"Lord, you were a skittish girl," the old woman said. "Staying away from Charlie Clyde was all you needed to know then. And now."

"I saw Rhonda Jr. the other day downtown. Was she the result of that fake marriage?"

"No, she came along later. Rhonda went wild after she came home," Zip said. "She would never say who the daddy was."

Not much of a mother, the original Rhonda liked the partying life, the comforts that gullible men might buy a willing girl. Until she drowned. Deana looked after the little girl, tried to keep a roof over her head and keep her fed. Generation after generation, the Harmons were bandied about among Coweetsee as a cautionary tale, a warning as to what lay in wait for un-suspecting, unguarded girls. How many times had Birdie been cautioned to watch herself, to not turn out like those poor girls? How many times had she said as much to her own students?

Kezia knocked softly at the threshold, then came in with her tray. "Time for medicine, Miz Zip. I waited until you came to the end of your song, though it took a while."

"You should join us," Birdie said. "Your mama always said you had such a sweet voice in church."

"Y'all sing such sad songs. All the time women getting killed or thrown in the river."

"You're probably into the hip-hop these days," Birdie said.

"No, ma'am, I like the good old gospel songs my mama sings at church. Lazarus rising up. Walking in glory. Something that raises the spirit." She smiled.

Kezia took after her mother. White women had it hard but Black women knew something more, Birdie reflected.

The young woman hesitated. "Miz Price, can I ask you something?"

Just the tone in her voice about broke Birdie's heart. Kezia was not a little kid in her class anymore, but a grown woman, single mother, abandoned by a man with a couple of babies herself. It still shocked Birdie how everyone kept getting older, worn down in Coweetsee. "Anything, Kezia. What is it?"

"My mama said you saw Charlie Clyde Harmon in town."

"I'm afraid so."

"Somebody saw him out on the road by our church. My mama's beside herself. You think we should be worried?"

"In all honesty? I don't know," Birdie said.

Charlie Clyde had been in the vicinity the night that Old Neb Baptist, Coweetsee's oldest and only congregation of Black folks, had gone up in flames that gutted the wooden structure and claimed the life of the deacon LeRoy Hubbs who had been sleeping one off in the back pew. Charlie Clyde had been hanging around the Gas 'n' Go where one of Shawanda's cousins had been working the counter that summer Saturday evening. It was from the pay phone there that the 911 call came into the sheriff's dispatch. "Nigger church on fire," the caller slurred, then hung up.

Maurice sent Roy Boy to bring in Charlie Clyde, who had protested his innocence throughout the trial, but a jury of his peers believed the circumstances warranted a guilty verdict. The sentence hadn't proved nearly long enough. He was back in town, causing who knew what kind of trouble.

"Anybody say something to the new sheriff?" Kezia asked.

"Not yet. I don't know. Maybe I will," Birdie said.

"It might be good." The orderly put her finger to her lips and nodded at her charge in the recliner.

Zip was tuckered out with her singing. She stretched her frail bones gingerly in her chair, soon her puckered mouth fell awry, gently snoring.

Kezia eased out of the room, waving bye-bye to her favorite teacher and patient.

Birdie studied her last surviving relative, asleep by the window. It was so peaceful, how the breath came and went, and then one day, it wouldn't. First, her mother. Gone in a matter of weeks with ovarian cancer while Birdie was in college, then her daddy a few years later, a heart attack in front of the television, then Talmadge helped along by her fatal cocktail. Zip was the last one left, and she would be gone soon. Birdie felt her absence already, a hole yawning inside. She would be all by her lonesome.

Her eye caught a movement out the window. The chipmunk was skittering around the rock and roots. Birdie finally spotted the snake, coiled above on a sunlit ledge. The littlest life went on, despite all the dangers.

Birdie bent to kiss her great-aunt's wrinkled forehead, fragrant with the scent of old lady and baby powder.

"Don't you go and die on me," she whispered. "You're all I got left."

5

Out making his campaign rounds, Roy found himself in Meadow Fork, Shad Smathers's stronghold, where the residents squinted their eyes, sizing you up before taking you down. He passed by the bent and broken sign for Harmon Lane, a gravel run angled up the hill from the main road.

He stopped and shifted into reverse, safe in the knowledge that in Coweetsee you could drive back-ass-wards as necessary. You could also idle in the middle of the road to converse with another driver or cheat on the yellow lines around the corkscrew curves. Common courtesies and conveniences. That was how things were done in the kingdom.

The lane up to the Harmons hadn't changed much since he'd last been here to arrest Charlie Clyde for the Old Neb church fire. Less gravel, more washboard ruts. At the top, the Harmon homestead came into view, half-covered with kudzu, the asbestos shingles flapping off the side, the front porch sagging. Cut into a red bank below, a newer aluminum mobile home squatted on stacked cinder block. Rubber tires held a blue tarp over the metal roof. You saw the same story driving all over Coweetsee. The old homestead traded for the manufactured modular shelter, easier to heat with electricity than woodstoves.

Roy parked next to a beige beater of a car, with its quarter panel eaten away to rust. Looked like someone was home.

He climbed the three steps to a small deck of unstained timber that was already starting to weather. He knocked at the screen door which rattled on its hinges. A girl appeared behind the warped mesh.

She looked at him with utter disregard. Her hair dyed a streak of magenta. Too much mascara on her close-set eyes, an angry blush on her fat cheeks. She wore a halter top and chains, like she was trying to audition for a biker chick.

"Rhonda?" he whispered, like he'd seen a ghost.

"Yeah, what do you want?"

She blew a pink bubble and popped it loudly. He'd seen that bubble on that face ages ago. Rhonda Harmon, whom he'd kissed and done much more with. Rhonda with her wild reputation, who drowned in the river. Yet here was her spitting image, alive and breathing.

"Rhonda?"

"Wait here." She stomped off in her boots into the dim parlor. Voices came from inside. Who is it? Some man. What does he want? How do I know?

An older woman appeared at the trailer's screen door. She wore a man's cardigan draped over her shoulders, a house dress, and men's work boots. Not an uncommon uniform for women living in this country, hardworking, chopping wood, or feeding livestock, though none of that was apparent on the Harmons' godforsaken hilltop.

"What do you want?"

"That girl. She said she was Rhonda."

"Yeah, that's her name. My niece. After my late sister."

Of course. His heart stopped thudding so hard in his ears. He swallowed. Roy had everyone sorted now. Rhonda's daughter had answered the door. The original Rhonda was still drowned. And this was the eldest sister, Deana. Once a looker, if always a little hard about the eyes, long legs, once long hair, now pinned back.

"It's me, Roy Barker. You remember? I used to be a deputy for Maurice Posey."

"You come around with the voting money?" she asked.

"No, no. We don't do that no more. That's illegal."

"Hard lesson to learn." She laughed bitterly. "Maurice Posey was all high and mighty until he got sent away."

"I am running for sheriff myself." Roy fumbled through his prepared pitch. "Hope you'll vote for me come November."

"You aim to be the next Maurice Posey?"

"Well, yes, uh, no. I'm not Maurice. I'm my own man." Roy dithered. "I'd just ask you to consider me as your next sheriff."

"Picking between the lesser of two evils? I got better things to do than vote when nothing ever changes." She glared at him, her hand fixing to slam the door in his face.

"Maybe you can still help me out." Roy hurried. "Seems an old ballot box from the '82 election showed up the other day on Birdie's Price's porch."

Deana paused. "Birdie Price? Don't she run the county historical society?"

"Why, yes."

"What's she planning to do with that box? She gonna put it in her museum or something?"

"Maybe," he said. "Anyway, Junk Jackson mentioned to me that your sister Rhonda once asked about a ballot box. You know why your sister might have asked that?"

"Junk Jackson is a flat-out liar. Just another example of the useless men who live in Coweetsee, if you ask me." The way she was glaring at him through the screen, Roy knew she was counting him among the useless men.

"Just one last thing. I heard Charlie Clyde was in town. Seen him around?"

"My brother"—her eyes flashed, and her voice was level and hard—"is the biggest bastard we know. Y'all sent him away to prison, but we had to grow up with him."

The woman was spitting through the screen, flecks of her saliva catching in the mesh. Roy could feel the heat of her bitterness, her wrath on his face.

"Now you can get the hell off our property before I call whoever is the law these days," Deana screeched.

And the door was slammed in Roy's face.

Roy sat in his jeep for a spell, his hands shaking, eyeing the abandoned house, the empty porch where he saw all the guilt, the ghosts. A pink-haired girl who looked the spitting image of a drowned woman Roy had once kissed. Deana, once a beauty, now a bitter crone. They had a sad history, these women who had been whispered about, shunned by more "proper" ladies their whole lives. All because of what their bad seed of a brother had done. He was afraid to look over his shoulder lest he see Charlie Clyde's leering face again. He had been here, years back.

Roy Sr. did not smoke cigars. So, Roy Boy was curious when his father came home with the King Edward's cigar box. When he opened it, he saw a snub-nosed revolver lying on top of a stack of grimy ten-dollar bills. His father quickly snatched the box away from the inquisitive boy.

"Mr. Smathers wants to help some families. Sort of like Santa Claus comes early."

The instructions were clear. Every four years, the Smathers machine fanned out across the county, into every cove and holler, down the riverbanks and up to the remotest ridge, anywhere with a mailbox and a likely voter. Make sure they register. Make sure they understand. No quid pro quo, of course. Just an early Christmas gift to a fine local family who knows what's good for the county, Shad Smathers explained. His index finger stroked the pencil-thin mustache over his fleshy lips.

What was good for Shad was good for Roy's family. The principal's paycheck, their house, the car they rode in, all depended on who wore the sheriff's starred badge on his lapel. Better for them if that sheriff was always named Shad Smathers.

The trees exploded in October color along the ridges and down into the hollers as father and son rode around the county that crisp Saturday. Halloween was a few days away, but they weren't going trick or treating when they rode up to the Harmons.

Roy's daddy had left the boy in the front seat of the station wagon while he went inside to deal with the man of the house.

The Harmon daughters were plump and full of themselves, in their private worlds on the porch. Rhonda sat splay legged on the floorboards, showing her panties and swatting the bejesus out of the behind of a naked girl doll with one flip-flopping blue eye. "Bad girl, bad girl," the little make-believe mother hissed. The eldest, Deana, particular about her preening, sat painting her toenails a garish red. She puffed her pink cheeks to blow on her foot.

They paid no mind to the boy, which was fine by Roy, all of eight and thinking girls were the strangest things. Then, slamming the screen door, came their brother Charlie Clyde. He kicked Rhonda's dolly and stole a swig from Deana's soda bottle. He spied the car in their yard and the little kid. Charlie Clyde jumped down the steps and ambled over to lean his head into the open car window.

"Nice hat, kid. You treed that coon yourself, I reckon."

A coonskin cap was a childish thing to be wearing, but Roy Boy was still a little kid, and who didn't like Davy Crockett, King of the Wild Frontier? He knew all the words to the song by heart. "Davy, Davy Crocket was raised in the woods, so he knew every tree and killed himself a bear when he was only three." Every kid his age had one of these hats.

"Hey, what you got in the box?" Charlie Clyde reached for the cigar box on the seat, at the same time as Roy Boy. He had his hand on the dirty bills, but Roy Boy had the gun pointed in his face.

"Careful there, quick draw."

Charlie Clyde blinked his cold blue eyes. He lowered the lid of the box, fat old King Edward looking up at the two boys. Charlie Clyde slowly withdrew his dirty hands, but he never stopped staring, daring Roy Boy.

"Feels good, don't it? Thinking about it, ain't you?"

Roy was all of eight, but he knew this was adult business. The revolver was heavy in his sweaty palm, more substantial than the cap gun he played with at the house. He shifted on the seat, not eager to get his backside tanned if he were to disobey his father, even if trying to defend the family's good name. The little boy said not a word, but in that autumn stillness with every leaf exploding on the trees all around them, the world stood still. You live any time at all on this earth, and you know moments come that you don't get back, cracks in the flow of your days, like time shudders to a halt and then lurches forward into the future. Moments that make you the man you will become.

"You going to shoot me, boy? Make up your mind, one way or another. I ain't got all day here."

"Charlie Clyde!"

He stood up straight. Roy Boy slipped the gun back in the box and the regular world resumed.

His daddy had emerged on the porch with Mr. Harmon, a skinny man in dirty overalls and a battered ball cap too small for his oddly large head.

"Charlie Clyde," Harmon called. "Come say hey to Principal Barker."

When Roy Sr. wasn't traveling the county as part of the Smathers political machine, his regular paycheck came courtesy of the Coweetsee County school board at whose pleasure he served as the principal of the high school. Charlie Clyde was his worst student, a bully who terrorized his teachers and goosed both girls and boys at the water fountain.

"You doing your homework these days for Miss Underhill?" Roy's father asked, already knowing the answer.

"Why yessir," Charlie Clyde said with the smarmy sass that would have gotten any other boy's rear end tore up in Coweetsee County.

"What were you doing at my car?"

"Me and your son were visiting. I was telling him how much I like his coonskin cap."

The father's face flushed with embarrassment. The boy knew it was his fault and his face went red with shame.

"Well, I best be getting along. More folks I need to see today." Roy Sr. took his leave.

"We appreciate you stopping by. We appreciate Sheriff Smathers." Mr. Harmon grinned.

His father plopped himself behind the wheel with a heavy

sigh, but Roy kept watching Charlie Clyde on the porch as they drove off. He pointed his finger at Roy, and mouthed the word *pow* in his thin lips, then blew the smoke from his imaginary gun.

Father and son had to stop at the bottom for a Nash Rambler trying to negotiate the ruts and upgrade. W. D. Clark, who had run the store in Meadow Fork forever, waited there with his arm hung out the open window. He waved at the Barkers.

"How do, Barker? I see you're about Shad's business."

The father gave a nervous laugh.

"How are them Harmons? Do we know which way they are leaning?"

"Who knows." Roy Sr. shrugged.

"Double-dippers. Ain't too many honest men left in Coweetsee." W. D. blew a cloud of cigar smoke into the air between the idling cars. "Glad election season only comes every four years. So much time and money. See you around."

And he gunned his car up the rough road, spinning a spray of gravel behind him.

The Barkers drove home, the lid of the King Edward's box jumping up and down on the money and the gun inside. Roy Boy tore that coonskin cap off his head and stuck his burning face out the window.

Roy felt as frustrated as that little boy when he got home that evening and fell into his father's worn wingback. He sat in the gloaming, the shadows creeping out of the corners of the room, his hands poised on the armrests where his father's once warm palms had oiled the cracked leather. As a school vice principal and baseball coach, Roy's father liked to lecture him on responsibility.

"Roy Boy, watch yourself. Some folks are in sad shape these days, but they don't make it any easier on themselves."

Yeah, but you didn't make it any easier for me, Roy thought.

Fair to ask what kind of responsible father leaves his eight-year-old boy in the front seat of the station wagon with a cigar box full of dirty twenties and a loaded revolver, the possibility of sudden murder seared in his memory.

He had outlived his father by decades now, but any day, the Barker heart might give out on him, and he would keel over to join his kin in the cemetery. Roy had inherited the thick bones and pot belly of his daddy's people, topping the scales at 290 these days. The muscle of his wrestling days had softened to fat in his middle age. Roy swore off athletics in high school, much to his father's consternation. "Son, it's your decision and I won't try to sway you, but—" He looked down at his big shoes and then back at his boy with big pleading eyes, but that was all his father would ever say on the matter.

Roy Sr. was waving the school buses out of the parking lot, end of the day, end of the causeway. Cracks in the concrete, grass sprouting. Likely needed to get some herbicide out there, make it look nice. He did all the planting himself around the school grounds, mowed the lawns himself on Saturdays. He bent over to pluck that pesky green growth when the pain snagged his left arm and pulled him into the sickening, swaying darkness. Oh, oh.

The last teachers leaving saw him lying in the parking lot. Mabel Honeycutt tried CPR and pounded on his chest, while Glenda Tucker ran inside to call 911.

Later, in that long-numbed time, Roy was surprised daily to not see his father or hear the echo of his heavy brogues along the tiled main hall of the rock school built in the Depression. The school board voted for a bronze plaque with his father's name to be put outside the glass panes of the principal's office.

That spring, Maurice Posey was waiting for Roy at the high school commencement ceremony. The sheriff stood at the bottom of the platform and shook each graduate's hand, complimenting each on their high achievement, and reassuring them of the community's pride in their achievement. He had special words for young Roy Barker. "Your father was a good man, an upright citizen, a contributor to the good of the county,"

Maurice said. "I always respected him, even on different sides of the election."

Maurice was looking for big strapping lads, young men of character who wanted to serve their community. Maurice had seen Roy in his wrestling glory, so the sheriff was certain about his strength. Did Roy know how to drive a stick shift? Shoot a gun if need be?

Charlie Clyde's face loomed like a target in his memory. He could have saved Coweetsee County much woe and trouble if he'd shot Charlie Clyde's smirk off his thin face, sent that bullet into that squinty eye. But he hadn't pulled the trigger, let the hammer fall, fired the fatal round, now had he? Coward, he forever called himself.

Maurice was getting impatient with his silence. "Son, you want the job or not?"

The Barkers had been Shad's constituents, his father a cog in the Smathers machine every four years, until the impossible had happened. His father was dead.

"Yes, sir," Roy said with all the good manners inherited from his father.

You could forget your family, swap allegiances, change sides. Even in Coweetsee.

6

One morning in April, Roy was driving the slow curves of the river road into town, through wisps of fog rising off the cold water, when he saw an apparition ahead. Not a trick of the eyes, not a ghost, but a man dressed in dark denim and a black hoodie walking on the broken shoulder. Roy swung the jeep wide, then stopped and watched the rearview mirror. Sure enough it was him.

Roy gunned the engine as if he might pull away. Guy didn't hurry, didn't hasten his gait, or even pull his hands from his deep pockets. He was his own man and not to be hurried even if you were doing him a favor. And as he came closer, the metal taps on the soles of his black shoes clicked louder on the asphalt.

"Why, speak of the devil. I heard you were back in town," Roy said when the man reached his window.

"Yes, and I thought I'd run into you sooner or later." Charlie Clyde grinned. "You headed to town?"

"Hop in."

Charlie Clyde settled into the seat and pulled the door shut as best he could.

"You need to get a better vehicle. A high and mighty man like yourself doesn't need to ride around in a rattrap."

The jeep had more than 150,000 miles on it, still chugging along, like Roy himself, a little worse for wear and tear.

"You want to ride or to walk?"

"Just making conversation, Roy Boy."

"I didn't know you were getting out. Came as kind of a shock to folks when you just showed up."

"No place like home, now is there? What do they say, home's where they have to take you in." Charlie Clyde's feet danced on the floormat like he couldn't keep still even in a moving car.

Roy couldn't help but poke a bit at him. "Gotta tell you, it's kind of strange you riding in the seat next to me, instead of in the back."

"Yeah, I always thought you had the softest hands when you were pushing my head down, putting me in the car." He was older, more wrinkles, the cheekbones more pronounced, skin loose now under his stubbled chin. But that smile was still the same, shiny and sharp.

"I see you're running to be the law again." Charlie Clyde nodded at the campaign yard sign that Moe Dinkins had out in front of his mailbox. "Driving around, handing out the money like the old days, huh?"

"Doesn't work that way anymore," Roy explained. "Coweetsee must get back to its values. Too many people moving here don't appreciate the old ways."

"Yeah, you sound like a politician, picking all that fried chicken out of your teeth," Charlie Clyde said. "I ain't met the new sheriff yet."

"Cancro. Yankee moved down from New Jersey. Retired military. Decent enough, if you like those folks."

"Nobody likes a Johnny-come-lately. You got my vote for free."

"Felons don't get to vote in this state. You lost that right when the gavel came down."

Only then did Charlie Clyde, his old nemesis, glare at him. Roy kept his eyes on the curving road ahead into Coweetsee, but he could feel that baleful look boring like a corkscrew into the side of his skull.

"Paid my debt even though I was wrongly accused. Kept my nose clean. Served my time. Model prisoner, model citizen. Maybe I've changed."

Like a skunk losing his white stripe. Roy didn't think so. He changed the subject.

"You got any plans? Working?"

"Things turn up. Paying propositions always present themselves to a man who's open."

"I went by the house the other day. Deana said they hadn't heard a word from you."

"My big sister can be such a bitch."

"So, where you staying?"

"Where I can. I still have friends, not in high places, like you, Roy Boy."

"Roy," he said, stone-faced, staring straight ahead. "Just Roy." Roy kept his eyes on the curving road, the tricky fog thick along the river bends. "You remember when I nearly blew your head off when I was little? That time you were trying to steal a cigar box of my daddy's money."

"No, not really. I've had a gun in my face more times than I can count," Charlie Clyde said.

That infuriated Roy, an incident that scared the child in him for life, perhaps directed him toward his calling in law enforcement, the terrible guilt and secret relief he hadn't taken a life, he wasn't sure he could live with himself—all that made no difference to Charlie Clyde. He just sat there with that faint sneer on his lips, his teeth always showing, but never a real smile you could trust.

"Funny story," Roy said. "An old box showed up on my ex's front porch. She seems to think it's a ballot box from the '82 election. The 13th precinct would be out Meadow Fork. Right where you used to live. They say Shad Smathers lost that precinct and the election to Maurice Posey."

"After Maurice found a way to steal the vote." Charlie Clyde sniggered again. "You know he framed me later for that fire."

Again, with that pitiful excuse. It didn't help that Charlie Clyde had called the dispatch office from the pay phone at the Gas 'n' Go out on Highway 9, just a half mile from Old Neb Baptist. It didn't help that Maurice had found an empty gas can in the trunk of Charlie Clyde's Rambler. No, it didn't help that the drunk deacon LeRoy Hubbs was sleeping it off in the last pew when the flames consumed the church in the summer night.

Roy fumed as he wheeled along the river. Like every lowlife he had encountered as a deputy. Never met a crook who was ever guilty in his own shifty eyes.

"Funny that you show up same time that box shows up on Birdie's porch."

"You accusing me of something?"

"No," Roy said. "Just pointing out the coincidence."

"I hear W. D.'s the man to ask about stolen elections. Hear he's got a whole stack of ballot boxes in his barn."

"And I hear folks saying things are going missing from their barns. You ain't walking off with stuff that don't belong to you, now?"

"Keeping my nose clean." Charlie Clyde flicked his finger across one nostril and grinned.

"You better stay away from Birdie."

"Your ex? What do you care? She still yanking your leash?" He smiled, the kind of smile your fist itches to smack off his face. "She used to be a fine-looking girl. I remember stealing a kiss and copping a feel from her downtown. And her aunt about blew my head off." He smacked his lips. "Fine, fine girl."

"Leave her be."

"Or what, Roy Boy. You gonna arrest me? You ain't sheriff yet."

"Not yet. But I will be, and then maybe you'll be sorry you've been giving me such grief."

"Hey, stop here," Charlie Clyde said.

"Thought you was going to town."

"Here's as good a place as any. I won't take any more of your time or gas."

Roy pulled to a stop by the side of the road.

"Better watch yourself. Everybody is keeping an eye on you," Roy warned.

"Who doesn't like the attention of pretty women and jealous men?"

❧

Charlie Clyde stepped onto the soft shoulder, making a sarcastic salute of two fingers to his arched eyebrow as he watched Roy roar away in a huff.

But as the jeep rounded the bend, out of sight, the easy smile slid from his face, the muscles tensing into a more authentic scowl. He saved his white shiny teeth for prison guards, authority figures, judges in black robes, unsuspecting women, everyone he was trying to win over or dazzle.

He did his time. The model inmate in his overalls, his hair pomaded, glistening. Sang with the prison choir. Steered clear of the drugs and the homemade hootch in the general population. Minded his business. No one bothered old Charlie Clyde.

Always a felon, but at last a free man again. One hundred dollars in five worn Jacksons again in his pocket's skinny wallet, its silver chain clipped to his belt loop. The same dirty bills were in the wallet ten years ago when he'd surrendered all his personal belongings. He'd traded his shoes and jeans and shirt to the Department of Corrections in exchange for prison overalls and ugly work boots.

Used most of the cash for a bus ticket. Riding across the Old North State and into the mountains, his eyes welling at the sight of the blue mountains heaved up in the afternoon. Rode into the night, stop after stop in podunk places until the Greyhound's last stop at midnight. Taps of his shoes echoed on the always empty sidewalks of Coweetsee. The river murmured beneath the concrete span as he walked over to the other side and slept on the riverbank.

At daybreak, he walked the roadside with his thumb out, hitch-hiking. Trucks would stop ahead, and he'd run up the tarmac with his taps sounding.

"Howdy. You remember me?"

The rides didn't last long, usually with the driver looking panicked, staring straight ahead, knuckles white on the wheel, just nodding along to whatever Charlie Clyde thought to say, or just letting the sinister silences fill the cab. He'd get out after a mile or so.

Riding with Roy had been his longest yet. They remembered him all right.

But then homecomings were hell, he reflected. Never any warm welcome in the cold bosom of his fucked family. Years ago, he'd taken a bus back from that first stint in juvenile detention, then hitched a ride out to their dirt drive and walked up to the property.

The old man was in the barn, pretending to be working, the lazy luckless farmer that he was, sucking up to politicians and powers that be for any loose change.

"What we had to do to keep you from hard time. Your sisters, my poor girls," the geezer blubbered, but these were no tears of joyous homecoming, just a nauseating self-pity.

Charlie Clyde felt his fist clench, a five-fingered mind of its own to punch his father's toothless face and keep punching it into a bloody pulp. "I can give you something to cry over, old man." The same rage welling inside him, from that night when he wanted to see if Drew Adcock's head could be smushed like a melon under the tires of his car.

When he got out this time, he'd tried to give fair warning. A week before his release, he'd placed a pay phone to Deana who he had not spoken to in years. "Guess who's coming home?"

She wasn't keen to offer him a place to rest his head. "Trailer's mighty small between me and Rhonda."

"Rhonda?" His baby sister had drowned early in his sentence. A felon wasn't allowed home for her funeral. Was she back from the dead, or had he been dreaming that in his cell?

"Rhonda Jr. You wouldn't remember her and how much she's grown."

Deana offered him a place to stay in the abandoned homestead, not that the electricity was on in the old house. "I reckon you could room there."

He'd been by, not bothering to knock on the screen door of the pathetic trailer but going straight to the empty farmhouse.

The front door unlocked, the rooms stored with ratty furniture and rat droppings. Floorboards creaking beneath his shoes. Ancient newspapers stuffed in the cracks of the walls. He couldn't believe Deana's hissy fit after he ripped out a few copper pipes and timbers to make a little money. His family. The old man and the old lady both dead now, Rhonda too. They shared blood between them, but nothing in the way of loving bonds. None of them had bothered to visit him during all that hard time, serving a sentence for a fire he hadn't even set.

Down the road, he left the asphalt. He slid down the embankment and nearly landed in the creek. Squatting on his heels, he palmed a mouthful of water and took a drink, even with the risk that an upstream outhouse or cow pasture had tainted the currents. He tried to dance his way over the river rock to the other side, but with slick soles, he slipped and splashed one foot into the stream, flailing his arms to keep from going ass over teakettle into the creek. He climbed the muddy side, grabbing at roots, until he reached a clearing. A barn stood across the fallow meadow, overgrown with belt-high brambles. He waded through broom sage and white-topped Queen's Anne lace, swatting at the flies that flew in his face, getting beggar lice on his black denims, his shoes squeaking with his wet socks, already wearing a blister on his pale feet.

He'd had luck before with barns, no telling what was left behind in the stalls and lofts. Sometimes tools, even lawn mowers he could wheel off and pawn to the good old boys like Junk Jackson who stood in the gravel lot at Clark's Mercantile, the tailgates of their pickups open and lined with all sorts of booty. Guns and knives, they kept hidden under blankets and tarps. They never asked where such and such an item might have come from but offered a cash price. They lowballed their offers, since they would charge double at a swap meet or flea market two counties over. But it was cash money that Charlie Clyde was needing.

He walked, blinking, from the bright sun into the shadow, inhaling the ancient aromas of dried dung and rich tobacco leaf from the last cash crop to hang from the rafters. Golden motes of dust and leaf still floating, suspended in the bars of light that fell through the slats. He kicked at dried hay, cowshit, a scuffed snakeskin. No plastic gas cans, or modern tools, or old TVs, or discarded appliances, the junk of a local household.

He stood in the slanted light in the empty barn. The stock sold off for a final slaughter, the cash crops abandoned. A useless hulk upright in the pitiless sun and the rain, heavy with age, kudzu creeping through the cracks. Worthless. Not a damn thing in there worth a dime.

He turned, his metal taps scuffing the soft dirt. He whirled faster, until his hands flew out. He kicked the slatted wall of the barn. The plank popped free of rusted nails. He kicked again harder, kung-fu kicks, soccer kicks, mule kicks. Goddamn it all, goddamn them all.

He bashed two or three boards loose. Hell, if he pushed hard at the post at the northern side, he could probably bring the whole thing down on his head.

Breathing hard, he squatted on his haunches, the creek still squishing in his shoes. He touched the wormy grain of the wood, the raised waves rough under his fingertips. He pried a board from the rusted nails, it gave way easily. What had taken weeks for a crew of men to raise a century past, he could likely dismantle in a matter of hours. Wood that was worth some coin, better than that strongbox he'd found last month. He'd brought the box to Deana as a peace offering for plundering the old house. At least, it got her off his back.

They all want to make him out as some sort of psycho, his family, a freak show.

Charlie Clyde smiled his straight white teeth in the shadow of the barn. He'd show them what monsters were made of.

7

At the appointed hour, Roy pulled into the parking lot of Mickey D's. No diner had been left downtown after Pete the Greek had boarded up the Rock Cafe by the courthouse, unable to make enough dough on bad coffee and fried pies when the lawyers came to town on court day. Nowadays, Coweetsee did business on the bypass, eating at fast-food places, hauling meals out in plastic bags that later blew along the road.

Regulars came for their morning coffee at the Golden Arches. The flat-screen TV showed the latest outrages in Washington, distant news while natives focused on local politics, the blood closer to home that ran hot. Roy had his own election to win, and Wednesdays was when he met with his advisers, his brain trust, the men who had put him up to running.

Roy shouldered the glass door open and was hit in the face with the smell of deep fry grease, warm cheese, thin black coffee.

"There's our next sheriff," cried Cutworm.

"Late as usual," Gene groused as usual.

They all had served with Roy as deputies on Maurice's last force before the Feds came busting in the jailhouse with their warrant. Carl "Cutworm" Mabe had a feed store now. Gene Hooper ran a well-drilling outfit in Yonah. Dwight Dewey ran a garage. Jimmy Lee Penland, he was a big old boy, played right tackle in high school.

They were waiting for him around the table bolted to the linoleum, swiveling in their plastic chairs. All had gained weight and wrinkles and seniority, knees were wearing out and hips were starting to be questionable. Jimmy Lee was worrying a molar in the back of his yapper. Gene was the runt of the pack, not hardly any bigger than when they were all in high school, but meaner now.

It was Gene who had first approached Roy about running. "You know you ought to do this. Somebody needs to step up." "Not me." Roy had tried to shrug him off. "You owe it to your dad. To Maurice. To everybody." That fall would mark Coweetsee's first election since Maurice had been stripped of office. Rich folks in Raleigh tapped a damned Yankee to keep the peace in the county. After a military career, Francis Cancro had patrolled some village on the Jersey shore, ticketing sunbathers and rousting drunks, before he balked at his tax bill and retired to the southern mountains.

"You're our best bet, hell maybe the last chance we got at keeping Coweetsee County for the folks born and reared here," Gene said. "Before the outsiders run us out of the kingdom."

Roy knew he operated more out of duty, obligation, and guilt than any ambition of his own for power and prestige. Birdie had often told him how his mind worked, and he knew better than to argue with a schoolteacher. Now it was all too real. He found himself running for sheriff.

So each week, his coffee buddies gathered to campaign strategize, looking to get a native in power again, to return the kingdom to its old ways.

But here was a new face Roy didn't recognize.

"Who's this?"

"You know Dylan Caldwell?" Gene said. "My sister's grandson, just graduated from the university."

"Glad to meet you, Mr. Barker," said a young man with a faint mustache and a shiny silver laptop open on the table. He halfway rose from his seat and extended his soft hand in greeting.

"Call me Roy."

"Soon we'll be calling you Sheriff Barker," Dylan said. "I had Mrs. Barker, your wife, as my teacher in fifth grade."

"Ex-wife," Gene hissed.

"She really encouraged me. Best teacher I ever had."

"I'm sure Birdie done a good job with you," Roy said.

Birdie used to talk all the time about her best students, though Roy tended to tune her out at the end of a long day patrolling the county or sitting in the jail awaiting a crime to occur. Dylan Caldwell, the name did ring a bell. After graduating from Cullowhee High, he went on to intern for a state representative in Raleigh, then onto Chapel Hill for a degree in political science. Wearing khakis and a polo shirt and loafers, he waa trying hard to look like a frat boy more used to lacrosse than dodging cow patties in a pasture.

"So what's new, boys?" Roy asked.

Jimmie Lee piped up. "Heard Charlie Clyde's back in circulation."

"I just gave him a ride into town." Roy took a sip of coffee, watched the swirl of creamer. "Told him he better keep his nose clean."

Dwight Dewey whistled. "Better lock up your barns and women is all I can say."

"Who's Charlie Clyde? Should I add him to our database?" Dylan asked innocently and the men burst out laughing.

"I didn't know that they made people as young as you," Cutworm chuckled.

"Dylan here can show an old fart like you some new tricks." Gene elbowed his nephew-youth. "Go ahead."

Dylan wheeled the laptop around on the table amid the coffee cups, and the old men brought their bald and graying heads together, squinting at the screen.

"I've been cross-tabbing the latest census data against proprietary zip code profiles. We can see that Coweetsee is at a tipping point, politically."

"What are you trying to say, Dylan?" Roy tried to be patient with the young man, who spoke a lingo he couldn't quite follow.

"Next time the census comes around, Coweetsee will definitely be different," Dylan said. "Take your birth rate, your death rate, in-migration and outflow, then match that against your registered voter rolls and add in what undocumented and off-the-grid folks there may be, and there it is."

"There what is?" Roy asked.

"The whole campaign is predicated on more natives more likely to know and like and vote for Mr. Barker than outsiders, who may be more aligned with your opponent. But what I'm trying to say is, that's not your trend line."

"Can you tell it to me in English?" Roy asked.

"Coweetsee ain't who you think it is," Gene interpreted.

The key to Coweetsee had always been precinct number thirteen—Meadow Fork. That had always been Shad Smathers's stronghold before Maurice cracked it. Now according to Dylan, Meadow Fork had morphed into Cancro country with all the rich retirees building the stone and timber mansions in Mountain Meadows. The upshot was, since Roy wasn't a member of the gated community, he wasn't going to be allowed to go knocking door to door for votes up there.

Cancro's campaign was making him out to be the professional lawman cleaning up corruption. Meanwhile, Coweetsee got stereotyped as the Carolina version of a banana republic, Dylan explained.

"Some people are so ignorant. Anyone knows we don't have the climate for bananas," Cutworm said.

"We do have pawpaws. Ain't that kind of a native?" Jerry Lee offered helpfully.

Gene nearly snorted his coffee out his thin nose. "Ain't the same."

"I am partial to a good pawpaw pie," Jerry Lee said.

He finally got his hand out of his mouth, and between wet, slick fingers he had the culprit, that bloody tooth, which he set on the white tabletop.

"Damn, son, don't you need a dentist?"

"I got it out, didn't I? That was about to bother me no end."

"Let's not get sidetracked," Gene said. "Go ahead and tell Roy the bad news, Dylan."

"You're looking at a $100,000 campaign, conservatively," Dylan said.

Roy laughed. "All we need is the people to come out and vote."

"This is how campaigns are professionally done these days, Mr. Barker." They would have to counter Cancro, who was going to hit hard with billboards and yard signs and robocalls to everyone in the county, fliers under the windshield wipers at all the dollar store parking lots, and commercials on the TV, and radio signals that crept in from the markets surrounding lonesome Coweetsee.

"But where do we get that kind of money?" Roy asked.

"I tell you who you need to talk to," Gene said. "You might need to ride out and ask W. D. straight out for his vote."

Roy nearly snorted his swallow of coffee out his nose. "That will be the day. Who do you think turned Maurice over to the Feds?"

It struck Roy that they had all been seated in the same way when fate had so brutally befallen their own sheriff. The Feds barged through the door of the old jail, the sleigh bell on the latch jangling to let the deputies know when they had visitors. They all sat, tilted in their cane-bottom chairs, not knowing what was about to hit them.

"Maurice Posey, we have a federal warrant for your arrest written by the U.S. Federal Court Judge in Charlotte," the federal agents said in their sharp suits and shiny shoes.

"Charlotte? You're in Coweetsee, in case you federal fuckers don't know shit." Deputy Dewey Hicks spit a great gob of tobacco chaw into his cup.

The point man in the FBI phalanx glared invisibly through his sunglasses. "Don't fuck with the Feds."

"This is the office of the high sheriff of Coweetsee County. Show some respect if you don't want to be locked up," Dewey said.

Maurice took the news like a gentleman. His knee cracked as he stood from his heavy oak chair and took the red bandanna from inside his pinstripe suit with its too wide collars, more fashionable in a previous decade. He wiped the sweat from his forehead and patted down the white wisps of hair floating like a halo over his crown.

"Boys, I believe it's over," the sheriff said over his shoulder as the marshals led him away in handcuffs to be arraigned.

No one knew it at the time, but Coweetsee was about to change.

Maurice struck a plea deal with the Feds and so he skipped out on what would have been the trial of the century for Coweetsee. What Roy and the rest of the deputies hadn't counted on was the loss of their own paychecks.

After Cancro was appointed to fill out the term, his first official memo concerned the summary dismissal of Maurice's men. For the last few years, the Yankee carpetbagger refused to hire anyone local, lest the corruption would creep back in the office. He recruited retired cops and troopers from distant jurisdictions, men with accents and crew cuts and brusque manners who were soon citing locals for speeding, jaywalking, parking in the road, all sorts of infractions no one had never thought were against state law.

There was plenty of incentive to rid Coweetsee of this cursed change for the worst and bring back better days. Roy could use a steady paycheck rather than having to hit the road again with his tractor rig, hauling trailers of Chinese-made crap cross-country.

And he'd promised Cutworm, Jimmy Lee, and the rest their old jobs on the force. First, they would have to win.

Despite all the brainstorming of the past hour, their sticky problem remained unsolved. Campaigning took cash, none of which the men of the table wanted to pony up. How would they win without more money?

"Too bad, you can't just ride over to Laurel Trace and ask the old man himself what to do," Jimmie Lee said.

"Why not?" Roy crossed his arms. "Wouldn't hurt to ask his advice."

"Fact is, Maurice is a convicted felon banned from election-eering ever again in Coweetsee. We're on our own now," Gene said.

They all bitched and blew on their lukewarm coffees, served in paper cups labeled with the warning *Hot coffee can cause burns,* another tribute to the obvious in the modern world these men found themselves living in, even though they desperately de-sired to turn back the clocks and calendars. They sat in silence, stewing over what could have been.

Roy decided to change the subject.

"Damnedest thing happened the other day," Roy said. "I was minding my own business when my ex texted me out of the blue, called me over to her house."

Jimmy Lee grinned, and Cutworm whistled.

"No, wasn't like that. Get your mind out of the gutter and listen."

"What was it then?" Jimmy Lee asked.

"She found this box on her front porch. Inside were all these paper ballots from the '82 election, the one Maurice just squeezed by. Number 13 it read, maybe the Meadow Fork ballot box."

"What the hell was it doing on Birdie Price's front porch?" asked Dwight.

"Historical donation for the museum, I reckon."

"Or a message. A warning. Sounds like someone's trying to fuck with your campaign," Gene said.

Roy thought Gene was overreacting, overly superstitious or spooked somehow. It was just an old box, filled with old paper. So what if Birdie put it on show, like some prize calf or jar of pickles at the county fair?

"What do you think I ought to do about it?"

"Get the hell rid of it. Dump it in the river, bury it in the barn. Throw it in a fire." Gene was whispering now, looking around the dining room of Mickey D's, afraid someone might have overheard.

People in these parts were born to talk and whisper, gossip

and conjecture, rationalize and lie, trading in rumors, stories, myths that make up history. Stories spread like kudzu in a small place like Coweetsee. You couldn't go a mile down the snaky road by the river or high on the ridge without running into a swarm of tales, myths, buried rumors, unburied ghosts. So many plots we couldn't get shed of them. Stories hung on us, weighed us down, kept us tied, even chained to a place like Coweetsee.

That fact never has changed in Coweetsee.

"But Birdie says that box is history."

"Cancro's already trying to paint us as a bunch of corrupt hillbillies buying and selling and stealing elections. You got to change that old story. You!" Gene leaned over and poked that cold well-digger's finger into Roy's chest.

"Do it, you win. You don't, we're all history."

8

With so few visitors to keep her company at the historical society, Birdie found herself watching dust motes drift in the golden light falling through the barred windows. The hours stretched by. She felt like a prisoner rather than a guard, confined by the junk left by past generations, treasures they couldn't take to heaven or the next life or whatever happens next.

To stave off boredom, she decided on the spur of the moment—why not inventory the society's collection? She squinted at the aging desktop computer, one finger on a handwritten list of artifacts as she typed with one finger into a spreadsheet. No one had ever asked just how many butter churns, apple dolls, petticoats, plowshares, harness rings and crosscut saws, mauls, adzes, medals, frying pans, flour sacks, tattered quilts, and arrowheads could one county jail contain. Birdie took it upon herself to tally an answer in case the question was ever asked.

She kept weighing what to do with the ballot box she had stashed in the closet. After her argument with Roy, she wondered if it would be too controversial to display before the election. She could see how it might reflect badly on a former deputy of that corrupt regime, looking to claim the brass star for himself.

Birdie still had the business card tucked in the guest register, the contact for the Atlanta collectors who would take history off her hands for a tidy price. Folklore Liquidators, History Erasers. They would hand over a tidy check, and a fresh start on a better future. It felt reassuring to have that number handy, like a fire ax under glass, to be broken only in an emergency.

Worst came to worst, she could always call.

❧

About noontime, Birdie powered off the computer and stretched her arms overhead, interlacing her fingers and flipping her palms skyward in a seated yoga pose. She needed fresh air, maybe take her cellophane-wrapped tuna sandwich over to Shawanda's studio for company at lunch. She locked up and stepped out on the deserted streets.

Coweetsee doubles as the name of the county and its seat, the only real town with 330 souls and a main street with a stoplight. Coweetsee comes from some likely garbled Cherokee word, which no one quite remembers its correct translation, something like "Place Where the Deer Drink" or "Where They All Got Killed." No Cherokee were left to ask in the county, chased off by smallpox and settlers, and the rest herded off on the Trail of Tears.

Legend was that the courthouse had been built atop an ancient mound, where a sacred fire had burned a thousand years, and likely the bones of chiefs and maidens lay buried, or so we liked to think. But change was always coming to Coweetsee. A drovers' road once followed the river. Flocks of geese and herds of pigs raised their dust and left their droppings for a hundred miles down to lowland markets. Money was made on the backs of these beasts headed to slaughter.

Then the railroad had punched through the kingdom, this godforsaken fastness of rushing rivers and thick laurel hells and no trails. Soon came the tourists and money men wanting to civilize it quick. The county courthouse dated to 1887. A statue of a blindfolded lady with a scale stood atop the white dome. If she weren't blindfolded, she could see down Depot Street past the railroad and the bridge over the fast-moving river.

Back at the museum, Birdie kept old-timey photos of the streets filled with midcentury cars, sidewalks packed with bib-overalled farmers and lawyers in seersucker suits and gloved and behatted women doing their shopping. Now all that history had been drained from the empty streets, the broken sidewalks. The street scene didn't so much change as collapse. At the corner of

Main and Depot was the rubble of bricks that was once Simms Hardware. The two-story, century-old structure standing more than a century suddenly decided to collapse in a plume of dust and ash, as the substandard mortar and suspect foundations gave up the ghost. Rats crushed beneath the plaster and lathe walls, the tin ceilings, the pine-board floors, the termite-infested timbers. It was a blight, and the town council was debating what to do, but the deed had passed onto the bank, which had sold it to some Atlanta equity investors. The upshot, no one was coming to clean up that mess anytime soon.

Birdie didn't recognize her at first, the girl walking aimlessly down Main Street. Wearing a green filmy gown, and good Lord, a tiara on her magenta locks. Maybe the statue of Lady Justice has snuck down from her perch on the empty courthouse, shucked her bronzed blindfold, and dropped her tilted scale with the bird's nest. Perhaps she wants to see for herself the world she was passing judgment on for the past hundred years.

"Vote for Cancro. He's got the cojones for the job," she shouted in the middle of the empty Coweetsee square.

Birdie couldn't avoid her on the sidewalk. She just wanted to get by. But then she recognized her.

"Vote for Cancro!" Rhonda Jr. hollered. "Man's got the cojones."

She sported the cheap green polyester gown she wore each spring for tax filing season, drumming up business for the tax return franchise out on the bypass. Not that that many folks owed much to the Feds in our piss-poor county, but you still had to get right with Uncle Sam and Raleigh if you were going to keep your disability or unemployment checks coming.

"Vote for Cancro. He's got the cojones," she shouted into Birdie's face. That was a hell of a better slogan than Roy Boy's.

"No thanks," Birdie demurred. She tried to step aside, but the Little Miss Liberty wasn't letting her go so easily.

"Who you voting for?"

"I'm sorry. I don't cast votes in local elections."

"Why not?" The girl kept pressing. "Ain't you American?"

About that time, a car come roaring down the street and squalled to a stop. Deana Harmon came screaming out at her niece. "What the hell do you think you're doing? Ain't you supposed to be up on the bypass, directing business into the tax office?"

"I'm moonlighting for the sheriff's campaign."

Deana pulled at the girl's filmy green sleeve, but Rhonda Jr. yanked her arm free.

"Leave me be, you bitch."

"Why you little bitch," Deana exploded. "You get in that car right now or—"

"Or what?"

Birdie marveled at the girl's backtalk, her pluck.

Deana tried to find adult reinforcements. "Ask Ms. Price here what everybody thinks of you."

"She knows damn well what Coweetsee thinks, and I don't give a fuck what these peckerwoods think they know about us."

"Hush your mouth," Deana hissed. "You'll have to forgive my niece. She takes too much after her mama."

"It's all right," Birdie mumbled. She just wanted to slip down the sidewalk to the safety of her jailhouse, lock herself away from this family psychodrama.

"She said in school we all had to vote," Rhonda Jr. said. "Now she's saying she don't vote. That's not right."

"That's her business. She don't have to say who she don't vote for," Deana said, then apologized to Birdie. "Sorry for her behavior. You were her best teacher. We appreciate that."

Not that Deana had shown any interest in her niece's education or shown up for any of the parent-teacher conferences as Birdie recalled.

Deana clutched at Birdie's coat sleeve and lowered her loud voice. "Glad I ran into you. Did you get that old ballot box?"

"How do you know about the box?"

"Why I left it for you on your porch, but you weren't home."

The misspelled note suddenly made sense. None of the

Harmons had done that well in school, judging from Rhonda Jr., or Deana. "Why didn't you sign your name?" Birdie suddenly wondered.

"I wanted to keep my name out of it."

Deana was no dummy. Birdie could tell she knew exactly what we all thought of that blighted family. Who would take a Harmon at their word?

"You're not afraid to tell the truth, the real history, are you, Ms. Price?" Deana said. "Not all the lies everybody believes around here."

"We try to separate myth and legend from the facts," Birdie mumbled.

"Oh, fuck the facts," Rhonda Jr. shouted.

"That's enough."

Deana got an armful of the girl's outfit and half ripped it from her arm, then she got the girl in a headlock, pulling her to the car.

"First Amendment. I can say whatever the hell I want," Rhonda Jr. yelped.

The Harmons' car roared up Main Street. Deana, as always, driving bat-shit crazed all over the road, and the Lady Liberty outfit of Rhonda Jr. flapping in the open window as aunt and niece screamed at each other.

Birdie kept trembling as she crossed the bridge, unnerved by the scene on the street. Her people had always been quiet, keeping to themselves, whether it be emotions or opinions. Rhonda Jr. was a Harmon at heart, loud in her makeup and her voice.

In Birdie's classroom, she had been the girl in the back row, twirling a curl of her hair around a crooked finger, staring slack jawed out the window, paying no heed to Birdie's blackboard, her blah-blah about algebra and social studies.

"Rhonda? Rhonda? You with us?" Birdie rapped a knucklebone on the desk to get her attention.

At recess, Rhonda Jr. would slap girls and slug boys. A terror among the monkey bars and swings, she liked to pin smaller boys beneath her knees, grinding her precocious girl parts into their prepubescent loins, sometimes leaning over to spit on their red faces, or even worse run her tongue over their crying eyes. "You want cooties? I'll show you cooties all right."

She carried that bad temper back into the classroom after eating a bologna sandwich, if she was lucky, for her lunch.

Social studies went no better, especially when Rhonda Jr. decided to participate.

"Who can name the state bird?"

"Cardinal," they called in unison.

"Does anyone know we have a state mammal?"

"In Coweetsee, it would be a dead possum." The girl giggled.

It was the hour for social studies, particularly state and local governments and how democracy should work, according to those periwigged founders in their white stockings, in Philadelphia, supposedly a city of Brotherly Love.

Birdie lobbed the class an easy question. "Is Coweetsee a democracy?"

Rhonda Jr. wasn't buying it, sitting with her arms crossed under her breasts, scowling at the very idea. "Only if you're dead."

Birdie stopped with her hand midway through the cursive of her chalk, spelling out the word *Democracy* on the board.

"Care to explain?"

"Votes get counted out in the graveyard. You're dead if you vote for the winner. That's what my aunt says." Rhonda Jr. sat, unsmiling, arms crossed, believing Deana Harmon to have the last word on everything.

No use arguing with a headstrong Harmon, Birdie moved past local politics to the safer ground of federal government in faraway Washington. She did write a note, requesting a parent/teacher conference with Deana Harmon. She folded the paper and gave it to Rhonda Jr., hoping it might be delivered.

Fortunately, Deana never showed for the conference.

❧

"Tough day, girl?" Shawanda asked when Birdie walked into her studio.

"Think I just dodged a bullet." Birdie settled into her usual cane-bottom chair.

"Do tell." Shawanda didn't drop a stitch but kept her silver needle moving slowly and surely through the fabric in her lap.

"Rhonda Jr. about tackled me out on the street. Wanted me to vote for Cancro. She was dressed like Lady Liberty, handing out fliers for his campaign. But the way she was badgering people, who would vote for him?"

"That poor Yankee don't know what he got himself into, hiring a Harmon." Shawanda shook her head, the beaded dreadlocks clicking about her shoulders.

"Then Deana comes along and yanks her up good. And I get dragged into the midst of their fight right in the middle of the street."

"What do you expect out of those folks?" Shawanda pulled her thread taut.

"Here's the strange part. We were talking and turns out it was Deana who put that old ballot box on my front porch. Wants me to put it on display at the historical society. She'd left me an anonymous note, misspelled, of course."

"No surprise there."

"It's like Deana almost dared me to tell the truth about that old election, like I wouldn't do the right thing. I said my job at the historical society is to separate the old rumors from the historical facts."

"So what you going to do?"

"My job, of course. Give the historical facts as best I can."

"Um-huh."

"I hate local politics. Folks get so hateful. People get hurt."

"You're too sensitive," Shawanda said.

"You know what Rhonda Jr. had the gall to say?" Birdie dropped her voice. "Fuck the facts."

Shawanda tittered. "That girl does take after her mom with that foul mouth."

It wasn't really the girl that Birdie resented, but her deceased mother. The original Rhonda Harmon had been thick of limb and neck. She sported the same clothes everyone had worn as teenagers in the more free-wheeling days. Denim skirts with white frayed fringe, more mini skirt than modest dress, always advertising herself beneath the buttoned fly. Her thick legs jammed into mid-calf pleather boots. Her hair too long for her age, and her mascara too thick. She looked the part everyone wanted her to play.

"She was awful loose with the boys," Shawanda said.

"And she paid the price for it." Birdie frowned.

No need to say the word that every woman thought of poor Rhonda. That word travels fast around Coweetsee, no sooner than a single female tosses her chin just so, fluffs her hair or bats a too-thickly painted eyelashes at a hopeless, helpless man.

Slut.

Birdie had felt herself the target of such talk, whispers across the county when she left Roy Boy, how she broke a good man's heart, her childhood sweetheart, took up with an outlander, a long hair, not a native, not one of us.

Birdie couldn't avoid the scuttlebutt about Roy Boy dancing at Cowboy's, the bar just over the county line. After she moved out, he become a regular for line dancing, back when it was popular to pull on your pointy-toed cowboy boots, shuffle your heels, clap your hands to the honky-tonk music on the juke box.

Maybe that summer night, Rhonda Harmon had looked different, her dark eyes somehow sexy or enticing or saying come-hither, and five long-necks too many, maybe Roy Boy was feeling lonely or lustful. They staggered out to Rhonda's Ford Pinto parked in the gravel lot. The two of them were too big to fit into that compact's rear seat, and so they went to town on the hood, were pawing and drooling all over each other. Roy Boy's jeans were down around his Tony Llamas and Rhonda's denim miniskirt hoisted up around her thick waist, with her boots bouncing on his shoulders. The headlights of the cars turning out of the lot spotlighted their rutting.

Birdie never asked for all those details, but Shawanda and the church ladies, and her hairdresser, and the other teachers at school in the faculty lounge, they made sure she got the picture. And wasn't she lucky to be shed of such a lug, a leech, a louse of a man? Wasn't long after that Rhonda was with child, and yet another baby girl was delivered to that cursed Harmon household. Rhonda would never say who the father was, but there wasn't a wife in all Coweetsee who didn't worry her husband might be milking other cows. Men dropped their eyes when they caught sight of Rhonda with her baby girl on the downtown streets.

Birdie had to seek some reassurance. "You don't think it was Roy Boy, the baby daddy?"

"Don't nobody know who's that girl's daddy, and I don't see many men getting in line for any DNA test like they got now." Shawanda bit off another bit of thread.

Birdie relented. "Maybe I should have been nicer to her and her mother. That poor girl must live with what happened to her poor mama."

It came as almost a relief or, at least, a fitting end to a tragic story when Rhonda got herself drowned. Her body washed up in the river, found by a fisherman who was out early, trying for a little crappie, something to feed his young'uns. Some said it may have been suicide or that the wild girl simply got too drunk and drowned by accident. But others whispered that the unnamed father, her secret lover, was the one who lost his temper and put Rhonda Harmon in her watery place. A paleness floating face down, hair streaming in the ceaseless current.

"My mama once warned me women always get the short end out here in the sticks. Coweetsee don't ever change." Shawanda made a face.

Fluffy white clouds crossed blue sky above the green ridges though the high windows of the former classroom. Coweetsee was still a pretty place to be poor in. They were surrounded by such beauty, such brutality.

"At least your girl turned out fine," Birdie allowed. "I can't tell you what a comfort Kezia has been to my aunt Zip over at Laurel Trace."

"Well, she was a handful herself growing up, but I did what I could."

"She was a good girl, good student, studied hard, made something of herself. You should be proud," Birdie said, trying to pay her friend a compliment. She always felt better after talking out her petty problems with Shawanda.

Shawanda put down her sewing, shaking out her tired fingers, cracking her knuckles. "Somedays I swear my fingers are going to fall off."

"That quilt's coming right along. So pretty."

"You just have to keep at it." Shawanda waved away any easy flattery. "Children or quilts, you just hope they turn out."

9

Back at the historical society, Birdie was motivated to dig through that ballot box. She handled each scrap of the yellowed, brittle papers with white cotton gloves, almost holding her breath, the artifacts were so fragile. Time and the elements had faded the pencil marks by either name, but the ballots were indeed from the 1982 election when upstart Maurice Posey upset the long-time incumbent Shadrack Smathers.

Her phone rang in her purse. She'd picked out a ringer sound replicating the doorbell she'd grown up with as a child at their brick rancher.

Roy's number showed on the screen. "You busy?" he said.

"Yeah," Birdie said. "Finally going through the ballots in that box I found. I'm counting thirty-one ballots in here, but I can't exactly tell which man got more."

"Yeah, I've been asking around about that box. Junk Jackson. Even Deana Harmon."

"Deana? I just saw her yanking Rhonda Jr. off the street. The girl was all dressed up like Lady Liberty and campaigning for Cancro."

"Maybe she'll scare folks off then," Roy said.

"How's your campaign going? You scaring people off?"

"Well, I was just talking with Gene and the guys over coffee, strategizing our next move, you know..."

She sensed his hesitation on the line. "What?" she asked.

"Do me a favor. Let's keep a lid on that box for now."

"Is that what Gene told you?"

She could hear him thinking, fumbling for the right way to say what she already suspected.

"You don't want to be putting the wrong ideas into voters' heads right now."

"I have an obligation as the unofficial county historian to tell the truth. And the truth is that Coweetsee politics have always been corrupt."

She could hear the deep intake of his breath on the line, then he let out his anger in a deep rush. "Are you calling me crooked because I'm running for sheriff?"

"No, I didn't say that."

"What are you saying?" He wouldn't let it go.

She swallowed hard. "I just wish you weren't running."

"I didn't know I needed your permission."

"It's not that. I don't want to see you lose."

"That's a real vote of confidence," he huffed. "Why can't you be more supportive?"

"I have to do what I think is right."

"That's always been the trouble with you, Birdie. You decide just what's right, everybody else be damned."

The silence between them was fraught, carried in the signals bouncing off the cell towers overlooking the kingdom of Coweetsee. What went unsaid but unforgiven between them, years of guilt, resentments, mutual betrayals. Free-spirited and strong-willed, she had run off with a pony-tailed hippie and left him, the crewcut good guy living with his widowed mother. How he had paid her back, when he couldn't hold his liquor or keep his pants up when Rhonda Harmon was dancing at the honky-tonk. All the sly whispers Birdie had endured as Coweetsee gossiped about their broken marriage.

"I'll do what's right," she said finally.

"Do what you will. You always do."

They hung up on each other. Her at her desk in the historical society that desperately needed more visitors, him sitting in his jeep on George's Gap, where he'd stopped to make his call.

Roy often drove up to the backdoor of Coweetsee, the winding two-lane to the state line. At the top, he could pull onto a wide shoulder beneath a shady buckeye tree, where he could look over the whole county, listen to the clatter of cicadas in the trees in summer, or the distant roar of a chainsaw in the fall, sometimes a faraway gunshot or two in hunting season. In the silence, he could daydream Birdie sitting beside him. They wouldn't say anything, they didn't have to. But they would be together. Maybe their hands would touch.

He savored the heartbreak in his chest, the Barker heart he'd inherited from his daddy, that bloody muscle doomed someday to skip a beat then shudder to a halt. Right now, he was still alive, still kicking. But still alone.

This used to be Maurice's favorite spot to oversee his kingdom. At the end of a patrol, Roy and the sheriff sat in the Chrysler with the windows rolled down. They could hear the ticking of the engine cooling under the hood. Maurice sat with his arm out the window, slowly waving the mountain air through his fingers, as if he were paddling along in an invisible river.

"Funny, ain't now?" the old man mused. "You shoot a man just a few feet down the road or run him over with your car, it's not my jurisdiction. Move that body just this side of the ridge and your ass is mine."

The sheriff liked to ponder the big questions. He could have been a preacher as much as he knew the Bible and could quote his verses forward and backward. "Which means nothing. Devil can quote scripture as well as anyone, and all I know from my years of law in Coweetsee County is that the devil goes to church every Sunday. Lord knows he might have even voted for me."

Roy didn't rightly know what to say to the older gentleman, whitehaired and wiser than he'd ever be. He could only repeat the conventional wisdom. "Nothing ever changes in Coweetsee."

But Maurice wagged his head. "Folks like to think so."

They sat until dusk fell over the kingdom. There were felons below, and crimes starting to creep out of the shadows, deeds to be punished within their power.

"Drive on. You can only waste so much time on top of the mountain," Maurice said.

❧

Down below, Roy could make out the flat roof of Laurel Trace, where he'd deposited Maurice Posey. He'd gone down to Fort Butner to fetch his sheriff home when the Feds finally decided to show the senior some mercy. Now beneath that distant roof, Maurice's failing body lay in his bed, breathing out his remaining days with the oxygen tubes in his hairy nose.

Last February, that buzzing on his thigh was bugging him again. Roy wondered if the cellphone in his pocket was going to give him prostate cancer or even of his balls.

When he answered, he heard a familiar voice.

"Been a while, Roy Boy. You still up to driving an old man around?"

"Sheriff? Is that you?" Roy felt his backbone stiffen. He almost came to a military attention, waiting for orders.

"Do me a favor. Come get me."

The Feds had aimed to make an example of him, but Maurice still had sway with lawmakers in DC. When he was diagnosed with the emphysema and the cancer that was going to cut short his life sentence, the powers that be decided to grant a compassionate release. It's a five-hour drive from Coweetsee down the state through the Research Triangle and its tangle of traffic to Fort Butner, but Roy made good time, missing the rush hour. He pulled into the parking lot. The gate was topped with coiled concertina wire that sliced the sunlight. The guards sounded the bell. The gate opened as a little gnome came walking out into the warm winter air.

Maurice had gone wizen and white as a mushroom or a stand of Indian pipe you see sometimes in the dark of the woods, color drained out of him by fluorescent lighting in the cells. He wore the same pinstriped suit as they had led him away in four years before. He had a walker and a shoulder-slung oxygen tank with plastic hoses feeding into his nose.

"You're a sight for sore eyes," Roy said.

"Thanks for coming." Maurice wheezed as Roy helped him into the jeep.

They had a lot of catching up to do on the long interstate drive.

"How was it? Inside, I mean. Did they treat you decent?" Roy asked.

"Played poker a few times with Bernie Madoff. We had a pretty good game going. There are Congressmen and celebrities, most everybody's trying to do their time, keep their heads down and not bashed in. Madoff got jumped in the lunchroom by some guy thought he'd lost some money. Broke a rib or two and punched out a tooth. Madoff's one tough sonabitch."

Roy laughed.

"Too much interstate. Not much to see other than gas signs," Maurice observed.

"We're in no rush, let's take the old road home."

They took the next exit and found the two-lane through the country, more farms and pastures and woods. But also dollar stores and convenience stores and auto parts stores.

Roy could feel the sheriff relaxing, rolling down the window, eating the wind that raised the wisps of white hair from his head. Maurice chuckled. "Feels like the old days, don't it? Just riding around. No rush in the world."

They stopped at a barbecue joint along the roadside, one of the real places that served the pork shoulder chopped with the tomato-vinegar sauce, the red vinegar slaw, and deep-fried crispy hushpuppies.

They were still far from the borders of Coweetsee, where anyone might recognize Roy's passenger, but folks kept eyeing them from the other picnic tables. Maurice looked the part, famous, with his white halo of hair and his fine cut suit. Roy fit the role of the muscle and the driver, a head taller than Maurice but always in his shadow it seemed.

Maurice snorted and shoveled his barbecue as if he hadn't eaten since he left Coweetsee.

"First meal as a free man. How does it taste?" Roy asked, his fingers red and greasy from the ribs.

"Not as good as what Shawanda Tomes' cousins can cook

in their smoker." Maurice kept chewing. "Lots of gristle in this Q."

"Maybe we can get you some real hog when we get home."

"Catch me up to what's going on in Coweetsee. How's the new man who took my badge?"

Roy made a face. "He goes about in this khaki uniform and a leather belt with a big gun."

Maurice had never believed in uniforms or showing off sidearms. He favored his pinstripe suits and let his deputies dress in their usual flannel shirts and dungarees. More of a civilian service than any paramilitary display.

"Heard he was from New Jersey of all places."

"Cancro does talk mighty fast and loud. Kind of rude if you ask me. He don't want to talk about the weather or how your folks are faring. Says he's just going by the book."

"You wonder who wrote his book."

After he fired Roy and the other deputies, Cancro had hired outsiders, professionals he said. Others might call them mercenaries, former beat cops, highway patrol troopers, military police. Men with hard voices and no ear for local conversation, and no small talk when they pulled folks over for infractions never even considered crimes before in Coweetsee.

"What you been doing in the meanwhile?" Maurice asked Roy.

"Driving long haul."

Roy had leased a Peterbilt rig and spent the past couple of years on the road, flying across the flat open country of the Midwest, hauling frozen chicken or cheaply made Chinese crap to the Big Box stores everywhere. Roy resented losing his career and a steady paycheck. He was ready to come home and work in Coweetsee.

"Sounds like this Cancro feller doesn't know what he's getting himself into. He might know about writing tickets and rousting drunks on a New Jersey boardwalk, but he don't know shit about the kingdom, now does he, Roy Boy?"

It was good to hear the old man's cackle, even if it was

strained with the extra oxygen piped into his nose. Maurice coughed slightly then again, deeper. And kept coughing, like a chopped bit of gristle had gotten caught in his craw. He waved away help as Roy stood, ready to hoist and bearhug the little man with a lifesaving Heimlich maneuver.

Maurice caught his breath and found his voice. "It's okay. I'm fine for a dying man."

Roy paid for their meal and helped Maurice negotiate the parking lot back into the jeep. They drove on into the afternoon, when they crested the hill on the highway and the first glimpse of mountains came on the horizon.

"Can't tell you how I've missed that view," Maurice said.

Soon the roads were getting crooked and climbing higher, and they were in the crest of the mountains, then took the winding corkscrew plunge down into Coweetsee proper.

"Slow down, Roy." Closer to town, Maurice suddenly rolled down his window.

"How do, Miss Mabel?" he hollered to Mabel Carter in her driveway, peering into her big black mailbox, checking her circulars and credit card offers.

The old lady turned at the call of her name.

"Sheriff?" she stammered.

"Been a while, Miss Mabel. How you been?" Maurice turned on his old easy charms, how he could butter up just about anybody and claim their vote.

"Lord, lord. It is you. I couldn't quite believe my eyes."

Word traveled fast as they drove into the town proper. Mabel with her cellphone for sure, and the Main Street was filling with people, more folks that Roy had seen downtown since he was a child.

Hey, Maurice. Hey, Sheriff. There were cheers and huzzahs and rebel yells and even a Cherokee war whoop that would raise the hackles on the nape of your neck.

Everyone was so happy to see the sheriff again, former sheriff, honorary or ex-temp. Folks were walking alongside Roy's jeep as he crept down Main to their cheers. It was for all purposes a parade, a hero's welcome, headed toward the court-house, underneath the cupola and the statue of Blind Justice on top with her scales. She couldn't see the crowd through her blindfold, but if her brass ears were unstopped, the commotion, the praise and profanities would have reached her perch.

"Stop here," Maurice ordered when they came to the court-house.

Roy helped Maurice out of the jeep with his walker and the oxygen tank. Roy kept a grip on Maurice's thin elbow, his spindly arm slender as a toothpick through the fine fabric of his suit's sleeve.

His old constituents—the men who frequented the park benches in front of the courthouse, spitting, smoking, gossiping over weather and petty crimes—came up, all smiles. "Maurice, how we missed you."

"Just glad to be home."

Maurice reached the top of the courthouse steps. He turned and the light caught his white hair and danced off his glasses like his eyes were on fire. He unhooked the plastic tubing from his nose. He began to speak in a surprisingly loud voice.

"Good afternoon, my friends. I can't tell how gratifying it is to a poor old public servant to be back among his people."

He licked his lips, and the breeze from the river caught the white wisps of his head. He coughed, bent double, and the crowd moaned. He waved away their concerns and began again:

"We have come through a hard time. They say justice has been done, but we have endured, and we will prevail. Our fathers fought over this land, this place, they died for what they believed, that no outlander from Raleigh or Washington has the right to just come riding into Coweetsee and tell her hardwork-ing, decent folks what they need to believe or who they need to vote for or how it should be done. There is the issue of local sovereignty, that we have a right to self-determination, that the kingdom of Coweetsee will continue."

Cheers and applause rose all around. Roy helped Maurice down the steps, through the crowd, their hands touching the sleeves of the sheriff's suit reverently, like he was the second coming of you know who.

"Where to, boss?" Roy asked when he got the old sheriff in the jeep again.

But Maurice was fighting for every breath. "Just drive me over to Laurel Trace, son. Like I said, I came home to die."

"But that speech just now? I don't believe I've heard better politicking."

"You give people what they want to hear."

All that time on the road, his hero returning home, Roy thought maybe Maurice would run and win his old job. And Roy could be his deputy, his driver once more. They would go patrolling the county, perhaps even park at the overlook at George's Gap, looking down across the kingdom of Coweetsee, returned to its proper self.

"You could still run again," Roy insisted. "And win."

"I'm a convicted felon," Maurice said softly. "I can't run. Can't even vote."

And Roy's heart just about broke.

"I'd just about forgotten how much chillier it is in the mountains than down at the camp." Maurice had rolled up the window against the February chill and rubbed his hands for warmth. All that fire and spirit he'd shown on the courthouse steps had fled.

"Drive on, son. Laurel Trace said they've got a warm room waiting for me."

10

MUSEUM ACQUIRES ARTIFACT OF CORRUPT ELECTION
By Birdie B. Price

With Election Day fast approaching, the citizenry of Coweetsee County have the opportunity to educate themselves on local political history, thanks to a new exhibit opening this week at the Coweetsee Historical Society.

The society has acquired, through the auspices of an anonymous donor, a wooden ballot box dating to 1982. Discovered inside were thirty-one ballots, mostly marked for Shad Smathers, the incumbent high sheriff in the 1982 election, running against Maurice Posey in his second bid for public office. The controversial election was close. Posey was declared the victor after two recounts by a margin of thirty-one votes out of 1,633 cast.

Smathers, who served a record nine terms as Coweetsee sheriff, died at his farm, after he was kicked by a mule.

Posey served seven terms until he was indicted and pled guilty to charges of vote buying and campaign finance fraud. Sentenced to ten years in federal prison, he was given a compassionate release due to failing health earlier this year. He is a resident at the Laurel Trace Rest Home.

The Coweetsee Historical Society is open afternoons to the public at the old jail.

&

Birdie's article appeared in the *Coweetsee Chronicle* where each week she had a column as an unpaid correspondent. She mainly wrote interesting histories about Civil War feuds and genealogy. But the mere mention of a ballot box that had suddenly surfaced or dropped out of the blue was like opening Pandora's box.

When she went to open the jail the next day, a crowd was waiting on the sidewalk, folks who had never before visited the historical society, men in blazers over their overalls and women in their Sunday best. The sleigh bells that had hung mute on the door began to ring a clamor as they filed in, crossing the threshold into the past. They didn't linger long over the military medals, nor the butter churns, they flew by the antique radio cabinets and the model kitchen from the 1920s, past ancient arrowheads and the shaggy bear hide.

They had come for what Birdie dubbed the Coweetsee Politics Past and Present exhibit. She'd cleaned out the inner cellblock, and let folks enter through the unlocked bars. They studied black-and-white photos of Shad Smathers cradling a double-barrel shotgun and of Maurice Posey in his natty pinstriped suit. Other photos captured feats of their law enforcement. Deputies in shirt sleeves and straw hats posed with a Ford pickup piled with confiscated cannabis on the county's largest drug raid, a ton of dope to be driven to the county sanitary landfill and lawfully incinerated. They say buzzards flew funny loops for days after in the heady air.

At the center of the cellblock stood a wooden table displaying the number thirteen Meadow Fork precinct ballot box with its lid open. A sample ballot was mounted under the protective plexiglass along with Birdie's carefully typed display card.

Nov. 3, 1982

COWEETSEE COUNTY BALLOT FOR COUNTY OFFICERS

Instructions

1. To vote for a candidate on the ballot, make a cross (X) mark in the square at the left of his name.
2. If you tear or deface or wrongly mark this ballot, return it to the registrar and get another.

SHERIFF
- Maurice Posey
- Shadrack Smathers

The folks came in quietly and read the captions, then departed quickly as if caught at the crime. They weren't smiling but shaking their heads.

Birdie might just as well have displayed Grandma's stained bloomers or tried to auction off a set of slave manacles, given the hate mail she would get.

They wouldn't say it to her face, but by their whispers, their dark heads like birds bobbing, she knew what they were saying: *Birdie Barker Price, we don't know what you're thinking, but what you're doing is killing this town's reputation. How dare you? Who do you think you are? Only an outlander would think this was interesting. You don't go airing all the dirty underwear with them bones stashed in the closet. What sins don't get called out, maybe don't count.*

The visitors filed in one by one, and if they saw someone already inside, they quickly ducked outside, despite Birdie's protestations and hand waves. "You found us, come on in. Plenty of room."

Mabel Carter came over and whispered, "I never did like Maurice Posey even after all those years. But there wasn't a choice, now was there?"

"Your secret is safe with me. I never voted for him either," Birdie confessed.

She also offered voter registration forms for the upcoming election. She urged people to sign up. "It's still a democracy. We can try again."

An hour before closing, her last guest slipped in—a bald man in dark trousers and scuffed brogues, a shirt once white now yellowed with washings. A shiny black coat hung on his thin frame, lapels too wide, the shoulders peaked. He looked for all the world like an off-duty undertaker.

"Why, W. D. Clark, what brings you to town?"

"I come to see that box of yourn."

"There in the back, Coweetsee Politics, Past and Present. It's a self-guided tour. Holler if you have any questions."

He drifted into the cell while Birdie sat at her desk, busily looking over the signatures in the guest ledger, twenty-five so far today. Some had even left a few crumpled bills and dirty coins in their donation box that sat at the corner of her desk. Maybe there was hope for history after all.

She must be doing something right if her museum could coax W. D. Clark away from his store to see her history exhibit.

The Clarks had always been at the heart of Coweetsee's corrupt power politics. His family had always chafed under the long run of the Smathers clan. A blood feud that likely dated to a disagreement during the Civil War. W. D.'s mother had been a Mabe, and he'd been fed from boyhood the bitter complaint, how Shad's great-granddaddy had shot a Mabe in downtown Coweetsee. Forget, hell. Forgive, never.

"W. D. Clark knows where all the bodies are buried, where all the dirt is in even the preacher's best dress shoe," Zip had told her.

The old man was standing at her desk again, slipped up on her while she wasn't looking. He moved like a wraith without a sound.

"Where did you get that box?" he asked point-blank.

"A donor who would like to remain anonymous. That donor thought that with the upcoming election this exhibit might be educational for the community."

"You been duped then." His Adam's apple worked up and down in his rooster-wrinkled neck as he worked himself into a righteous lather. That apple most certainly had a worm, Birdie thought.

"How so?" she asked.

"I bought this box from Junk Jackson at a flea market a few years ago. Had stored in my woodshed, I thought, until it was stolen. I'd like to know how it wound up in your museum?"

"Anonymous donation. I'm not at liberty to name names."

"It was that Harmon woman, wasn't it? She's been all around the county, talking trash about this box."

"I couldn't say."

"That box is a fake, I tell you."

"Those ballots look official to me. And number thirteen's the precinct out your way in Meadow Fork."

"Anybody ever think why a whole precinct in Shad's backyard would suddenly go for an outsider like Maurice?"

"All we're doing is showing the authentic artifacts from the election. We let our visitors make up their own minds how they feel about it." Birdie crossed her arms. "Maybe some folks just don't want to acknowledge the facts."

W. D. looked like he was set to explode.

"Fact is, democracy has always been about the almighty dollar. Politicians in Coweetsee are just more honest about how the game is played. No promises about a chicken in every pot once the man got into office and started lining his own pockets. In Coweetsee, voters got their dollars up front for voting for the right man."

She flinched as a droplet of his old man spittle flew from his lips and grazed her hand. "Maurice turned out to be the wrong man," Birdie argued. "He got sent away for a crime."

"That was never a crime before in Coweetsee."

"Maybe it's high time all that changed in Coweetsee. Maybe this election can be different, and not be all about the money, don't you think, Mr. Clark?"

He leaned over, planting his two tight fists on her desk, breathing his halitosis into her face as his voice dropped a register.

"You might be more careful, given your own history, dumping that deputy husband of yours and running off with that hippie boy. Probably up there the two of you smoking dope. I remember how your ex busted him for possession. It's a wonder they let you teach innocent school children after all that."

W. D. knew her business all right.

Birdie blanched. "That was just a misunderstanding."

"But then he got the cancer, didn't he? Went awfully quick at the end. Some folks might say way too quick."

What was he saying to her? How would that old man know anything about Tal's last night? Were there any secrets that could be kept in a place like Coweetsee? Birdie sat open-mouthed, unable to answer for herself, too afraid to fight back.

He straightened himself and went to the door. "History can get mighty personal. You best remember that."

The sleigh bells clanged as the door slammed on Birdie, her jail, her precious past.

PART II

THE OLD KINGDOM

11

We would never forget the summer of 1978 when the kingdom of Coweetsee first took notice of Maurice Posey, that same year little Birdie sang in public. August was the season for church homecomings with dinner on the grounds. We went to church for the singing and the sweat the preacher would work up about hellfire and its certainty, but we watched with anticipation the little girl ushered up front, a frail little thing with skinned knees.

She was born Berzilla Mae Wilson on her birth certificate, an old-fashioned name inherited from a great-grandmother on the mother's side. The family album, full of yellowed photos, showed a prim, thin-lipped woman who looked like she had seen the sorrows of the world. Those old-timey names had fallen out of fashion since TV signals brought the rest of America into our mountains. People aimed for better times, better lives, and better names for their broods. No one ever called her Berzilla to her face, except once in grade school, a feckless and freckled Gunter boy had snickered, "Burrzilla, you related to Godzilla?" (The Japanese movie was playing at the Coweetsee that week.) He said it exactly once and she reeled around with a roundhouse that knocked the sneer off his face.

"My name is Birdie!" she said.

Lord, could that girl sing like a little songbird. When she opened her mouth, her voice would make you close your eyes and just about break your heart. Old women dabbed their eyes with tissues and snuffled, thinking of lost loves and youth.

"Amen, amen. Sing it, sister." Though it was impolite and not proper to applaud a sacred song. People's heads nodded and many waved their hands in midair. This was revelation, not entertainment.

After she hit that last grace note, the silence that filled the sanctuary fed our souls. Sundays were so sweet, and the green leaves waving through the tall clear windows beckoned us into Creation. The amen was pronounced by a sweaty preacher. Then the rumblings of hungry stomachs began to be heard. Time to eat.

We filed outside and circled the picnic tables with the feast arrayed on red-checkered tablecloths. The women had laid out their best dishes, eager to best their rivals as far as their cakes would rise and their biscuits would fluff. We surveyed dishes and platters and crockpots of pickled pork, fried chicken, stewed vegetables, opened jars of relish and chowchow and prize-winning pickles, jams and blackstrap molasses, platters of fresh celery stalks slathered with pimento cheese, blocks of home-churned butter, cornbreads and cakes, apple pies and banana puddings, sugar cookies and rolled coconut sweets.

The kids wolfed down their dinners and began to mill about. Some kicked off their shoes, others changed into their denim cutoffs and T-shirts to play in the creek, the same icy waters where they'd all been baptized, dunked to have their sins washed downstream.

Birdie was in her white shift now, having shed her saddle locks and her Sunday dress. She was a delicate little thing, but never acted it. Pleased to be roughhousing like a tomboy, splashing in the cold water with the rest of the young'uns.

Rhonda and Deana Harmon were there too, precocious already with their bosoms. The sisters were rowdier than Birdie and her folks liked, louder voices, pushier. Birdie kept her distance in that instinctive way, respecting the hierarchy of big kids and littler ones, the more experienced and the innocent. The sizing up of your peers, aside from the alien realm of the adults who could boss you about at their own whim.

Rhonda was knee-deep in the water, aiming to baptize little Walter Jackson, whose crewcut skull she squeezed in a headlock. Not much of a contest there, since Rhonda was bigger boned, more the size, say, of that Barker boy, Roy.

Roy had been staring at Birdie since the service. Transfixed by her voice, wringing his pudgy fingers in his clasped hands, fretting about something he couldn't explain, a hollow opening somewhere in the vicinity beneath his Barker-defective heart, stranger to a fluttery feeling that he would always get around Birdie. He stood on the bank with the muddy roots of the trees, watching the horseplay. Girls were still strange, bothersome creatures to him, but he was struck by the sweet voice of this one. Birdie was barely aware of his existence yet. She was hellbent on climbing trees and running barefoot through the grass and catching lightning bugs in a Mason jar during the long summer evenings. Before boys mattered as anything other than to kick or pinch or outrace or terrorize. Before everything shifted and boys became strange beacons.

The young'uns exited the icy water, screaming and splashing when George Sherrill hollered something had slithered over his foot. Wide-eyed, mouths agape, they studied the dark shadows. There. See it. A long, submerged creature darted behind a boulder. Soft, fleshy, and slick to the human touch. A waterdog as the Cherokee had called them and later what the locals nicknamed a snot otter. That rare salamander, a foot long and slick, with monstrous heads that mean boys liked to bash with rocks if they caught the poor things. They were alien, unusual and thus to be feared, instilling the same terror in unschooled children as do snakes, particularly the venomous rattlers and copperheads of these hollers. They had all heard of the Gildersleeve girl, so puffed up with her own petticoats and pride that she wouldn't tell anyone about the copperhead that sank its fangs in her pudgy hand reaching in the hen's nest to collect her mama's egg money that she had been stealing on the side. And for her presumption, her hand swelled up and she died.

The mamas took after the caterwauling children, warned them to quit acting like little savages, but to mind their manners and put on dry clothes lest they get their bottoms blistered, and, "Don't think I don't mean it here in the churchyard in front of everybody, little mister or miss."

๛

Shad Smathers was no stranger to church dinners, and the annual opportunity for politicking and pressing the flesh of his constituents. He could be seen working his way through the crowd, kissing the new babes, rubbing the unruly heads of great-nephews, flirting with the mamas and flattering the shiftless papas.

We all knew Shad Smathers and his people. His uncle had served as sheriff. Smathers clan were anointed as the law keepers in the county, going back to the Civil War. Shadrack grew up the third of the Smathers litter with his brothers Meshach and Abednego, all named after the Hebrew boys thrown into the furnace in Babylon. The Bible story had all the boys walking around with an angel inside the fire, unburned, but life is a little different in Coweetsee than what the King James told.

Never name your babies after the folks in the Bible where all sorts of plagues and bad things happen to the best-intentioned of people, Aunt Zip said. "And the Bible ain't no vacation, regardless of them summer Bible schools. They all want to run and recruit the next batch of plate pushers. More devils than deacons in our parts."

Shad grew up and went off to war. After surveying the shooting at Anzio, Shad came home and started running for office, the high sheriff post that his family had laid claim to since the War Between the States, which was the War Between the Clans, when it came to Coweetsee. The badge was his birthright. His great-grandfather, John Tweed, had been a lawman; he'd been shot dead on the dirt street of Coweetsee in front of the old courthouse. A fallen hero, the story handed down through the generations.

But that old story was about to change, even if we couldn't see it at the time.

At the dinner, a beleaguered woman cornered the sheriff at the desert table where he was heaping spoonfuls of banana pudding on his paper plate. "Shad Smathers! You remember me, your old classmate?"

"Lena Mae Richards, of course."

"Now I'm a Gentry. Have been for ages."

"How's Hal doing these days?"

"Useless as ever and out of work. Crop gone bust with the blue mold."

"Sorry to hear. You talked to the extension agent?"

"Hell with burley. I worry about you, Shad," she said loud enough now for folks to overhear. "My god, you've got the power of life or death in Coweetsee County."

Shad begged to differ. "Hush, you're wrong. I don't wear no robes. I don't pass sentences on nobody."

"The hell you don't. You're the almighty judge. One frown, one smile, a family is flush up in Meadow Fork while young'uns go hungry down on Sneed's Creek. Your dirty money is the only mercy in this damned county."

"You best quit sneaking Hal's moonshine before you come to church." Shad turned away with his plate of banana pudding and nearly ran into a short well-dressed man.

"Shad Smathers? You don't know me all that well. My name is Maurice Posey." He smiled as he shook the long-time sheriff's free hand.

"I know the Poseys well enough." Smathers smirked his pencil-thin mustache.

"Mark my name. I aim to take your badge come the vote this November," Maurice said.

Well-dressed, a licensed civil engineer who could figure the best way to corkscrew a road up a mountain, Maurice was angling his way into politics. He favored tailored suits; some say he went all the way to New York to buy. But here he was on a hot Sunday, not even in seersucker, which men of the hot South used to favor, too stubborn to break a sweat in his double-breasted wool blazer.

Perhaps Shad froze a bit. None of his uncles or grandfathers had faced a serious challenger as high sheriff for a hundred years. He was the law and the lord of the kingdom of Coweetsee for as long as he drew breath and could report for duty.

"We'll see what the voters say, come November."

Everyone remembered Maurice Posey and his people, living out on a few acres by the Laurel Creek. Poor as dirt out in that district where children were skinny, slow-witted, and succumbed to fevers and chills each winter in their breezy shacks. But Maurice was a bright boy. Sharp in arithmetic, he could see that cardinal and prime numbers were the ticket out of losing a finger or an eye to the hard work that is subsistence agriculture. There were higher occupations than managing manure and starving to death on a sloped land when all the best dirt rolled down into the brown river year after year.

He became an electrical hobbyist, building his own blinking stoplight at the crossroads, not that any real tin lizzies came that way, nothing but mule-drawn wagons. He saved his egg money and bought himself a slide rule, able to figure out trigonometry, sines and cosines, the mathematical abstractions of a cosmos beyond Coweetsee. He went down the mountain to the state technical school at age sixteen and became an engineer. With the Korea police action heating up, he volunteered and took the physical, but when the sergeant saw the engineer on his form, young Posey was given new marching orders. While most of his classmates were headed to Hamburger Hill, he found himself wearing a lab coat in a secret outpost over in Oak Ridge, Tennessee. It was all top secret and Maurice never would say much, but he had evidently helped split the hydrogen atom to build a bigger bomb than the ones that flattened the Japanese.

Mustering out after his service, he came home to Coweetsee and worked with the state, drawing up plans for roads and bridges and water lines. He had his slide rule and a head for figures. But Maurice hadn't figured all the angles to getting elected in Coweetsee and deposing the powers and principalities that be.

The election went its usual way, as partisans distributed the political favors in greenbacks. Christmas came weeks early in Coweetsee every election year. More money might have been spent that year, but the votes went the same way. Shad Smathers bested Maurice Posey by thirty votes with the Meadow Fork precinct putting him over the top.

Maurice took the loss quietly, gracefully, like a gentleman, which was a rare thing in Coweetsee politics.

"I tried to get elected constable the honest route, and I couldn't," Maurice said, taking off his horn-rimmed glasses and polishing the specks from the lenses. He held the spectacles to the sun, then replaced them on his broad nose and behind his jug ears. "Won't make that mistake again."

Maurice drove over to Clark's Crossroads Mercantile, an unpainted two-story wooden structure with a tin-paneled ceiling, the last general store in that part of the county owned and operated by three generations of tight-fisted, penny-pitching Clarks. He took the latest proprietor, W. D., down behind the store to the creek for a conversation. Perhaps Maurice laid out his vision for what Coweetsee could become, instead of a backwater with failing tobacco barns, perhaps inviting in jobs with more factories once a decent road could be cut into the mountains. We could join the twentieth century at last and see some of that American Dream. Real money could be made.

And W. D.'s eyes may have widened with that mention of money.

We never knew the deal that the two men struck, the engineer and the merchant walking by the creek behind the store, whose watery rushing over rocks drowned out the conspiratorial whispers. They shook hands.

W. D. would be the first to peel away from Shad Smathers' political machine and side himself with the new man, Maurice. He even turned his store into a kind of informal headquarters for that next campaign, jawing to anyone who walked in and would listen about how changes were coming to Coweetsee, and Maurice was the man to see it through. Nothing like getting in on the ground floor of the new regime.

Four years later, the next go-round at the church homecoming with a new election coming, Maurice and Shad kept their distance, circling each other with the crowd of their would-be voters between them. Maurice had more men now, heavyset fellows, layabouts who loitered on W. D. Clark's porch, men who could hoist hay bales one-handed or topple sleeping cows if they weren't so lazy.

Maurice glad-handed his potential constituents, shaking his head about the sorry state of affairs in Coweetsee, sad to see Shad, a good man, losing his step when it was time for a change. And wasn't it a shame, a black eye and a blight for all decent folks, what had happened with those Harmon girls? That bad seed Charlie Clyde Harmon running over a poor drunk out of pure meanness and his younger sisters married off to pay the legal bills.

The men had faked the matrimony, then man-handled those poor girls. Some said Shad took a turn, as well as preachers, bankers, merchants, the men who wore coats and ties to work, instead of just coveralls red with mountain dirt. They had clean uncalloused hands, more used to fingering documents and deeds and money. We all had our suspicions of who those men were. The sisters certainly would never forget.

The Harmons were no-shows that summer at homecoming, free food not enough to bring them around to the church or the community that had shunned the sisters.

But we did see some new faces that summer. Maurice had brought along a guest, Elder Otis Tomes, Coweetsee's leading citizen of color as the old-timers would put it politely, or some just saying outright the n-word slurs. Tomes pastored the small congregation of Old Neb Baptist, a small, whitewashed chapel in need of a new roof, fresh paint, and more bodies for its creaky pews than the handful of widows, grandmothers, re-formed drunkards, and reprobates who came for the Sunday sermons.

Tomes brought his immediate family, who sat in their white Sunday best at a separate picnic table, eating the food that they had brought. Birdie waved to her young friend, Shawanda, who she'd sometimes played with at school recess. On these summer Sundays, they instinctively understood they couldn't safely socialize under the eyes of their elders. Oil and water, Black and white, no one believed such could ever mix, least of all in Coweetsee with its curse of nothing changing. What Tomes was doing there wasn't clear, other than Maurice had invited him. The old minister stood in the sun with his straw hat, smiling his one gold tooth, and nodding along with whatever Maurice was saying to his would-be constituents.

Maurice conceded that Smathers had been the law for what seemed forever, but that he had failed. People weren't shopping the merchants in downtown Coweetsee but going to the new malls in Asheville. The youngsters were forsaking the fields for better jobs down the mountain, factories and mills and offices in the Piedmont or up in the Midwest. Long-haired people were arriving, buying the abandoned farms as the first families had started dying off.

Once you found us, we were lost. Outsiders would upset the order of things, in the kingdom of Coweetsee.

How did we come to consider Coweetsee a kingdom and ourselves as the guardians?

We had no bluebloods or royalty, only our fair share of folks who thought themselves better than others, thanks to their church attendance or the barns that held their burley, more than the shiftless layabouts in the far hollers from town.

Check your history, and you'll find scores of short-lived republics and independent fiefdoms in Appalachia: the Lost Province, the Dark Corner, the failed state of Franklin. Maybe it was the mountains that surrounded us, hemmed us in, allowing only a few to escape, that dissuaded others from crossing the high ridges. Perhaps it was only a story we told ourselves, that we wanted desperately to believe. That nothing could change in our history, in our kingdom, any more than the mountains could be moved.

Then it all did.

჻

No one really remembers who ordered the strongboxes in the days of paper ballots, long before electronic voting. The ballot boxes were handmade from split oak and branded on the side with a burning iron, thirteen all told, one for each of Coweetsee's townships and precincts. Thirteen marked the Meadow Fork precinct, heart of the Smathers stronghold. Poll workers carried the boxes into the election office late that first Tuesday in November. Both sides of the room were packed with partisans. Guns were laid out on the table as the boxes were opened one by one. The votes were tallied by old men in green eyeshades and rolled sleeves, squinting against cigar and cigarette smoke as they worked adding machines with long tapes.

Last to come in were the Meadow Fork results. The plywood box looked different from the dozen already open on the table. This one was hand lettered with "13" scrawled with a black felt marker. No one said the obvious, that the box didn't match the dozen other precinct strongboxes, an ugly duck swimming with swans. Yet the lock matched the key, so the results were scrutinized and counted.

Strangely enough, everyone voted for Maurice Posey and not a soul in his home township for Shad Smathers.

჻

It was dark out the dirt road that ran by the creek, which fed a larger fork before hitting the river. The November air was chill, and Orion was wandering overhead, his sword drawn from his bright belt, chasing after his dog and the celestial prey beyond.

Two men rode in the Ford pickup. They had their instructions and nodded when asked if they understood. They drove into the November night under the sickle moon, until they found the big tree that overlooked a deep pool by the bank where brown trout still swam, but now lay suspended, asleep in the night water.

They stopped the truck and switched off the engine, which still ticked under the warm hood as they slipped out the doors, the crunch of cold gravel beneath their boots. From the bed of the pickup, they lifted the box and walked it swinging between them toward the bank. One, two, three. They grunted, swung it out into the darkness and heard the splash. The moon glinted on the pool where the box slowly sank and settled.

They got in the truck and drove off from history. Nameless, faceless in the night.

They collected their money the next morning at Clark's Mercantile, W. D. wetting his thumb as he counted out a stack of bills for their dirty work.

"You ever tell a soul, you'll wind up in a box in the river. You hear?"

❧

When Shad Smathers was so unceremoniously unseated, we were shocked, especially at the razor-thin margin, the loss of thirty-one ballots from the Meadow Fork precinct, his own backyard, his stronghold. Shad and his followers swore that the earth-shaking results smelled to high heaven.

It was as if the mountains had moved in the middle of a crisp November night, playing musical chairs, walking about the rim of the kingdom, and settling into new, unfamiliar formations. The saddle of Mount Misery swapping cardinal directions with Big Bald, and the Frozenhead Mountain drifting like an iceberg, shouldering aside Rattlesnake Knob on the southern horizon.

Must have been an earthquake, older folks said, unsure of a world without Shad Smathers and his star. And some swore that a tremor had rocked the county after the polls had closed, although none was measured by any seismometer of the US Geological Survey. Some woke to the crash of framed pictures of their departed parents falling from mantels in their parlors. Shelves of Mason jars collapsed in pantries in the darkness, a bloodbath of canned tomatoes and pickled beets.

Yet neighbors just up the road slept the night through, sound as babies with their mouths rasping open with comfortable snores. Unbothered by the earth opening and closing just as quick. Others said the river itself seemed to have rolled back overnight, at least for a spell. Lester Perkins reported his herd of Black Angus, roused from their bovine dreams, had forded the dry riverbed in a sleepwalk and stood bellowing the next morning on the other side. Beavers built dams of debris and driftwood, pushing the current into new channels. Fishermen said catfish had come up on the sandy banks for a whiskered walk at dawn, shaking their flat ugly heads at the men who dangled hooks in their muddy depths. Rumors spread that a canebrake near Walnut Branch had slipped into the stream and was seen like a primordial giant green porcupine slowly flowing west out of our kingdom.

Many of Shad's faithful voters could not comprehend such a loss, and more than a few contemplated hanging themselves in their leaning barns, while those with alcoholic tendencies went back to the bottle.

Maurice's people were jubilant, certain after decades of defeats and setbacks, hallelujah, that Coweetsee could at last climb out of its calcified devotion to the past, and finally join the twentieth century proper. Better roads, electrification, indoor plumbing replacing outhouses, the extinction of blue mold, no more rheumatism in knees and knuckles, straighter teeth, and fewer cavities with fluoridated water. Colds would become uncommon. Coweetsee would see longer lives, fewer stillbirths, the halt to all rust and rot.

Everything had changed in a blink of an eye—like the Rapture, many roaring red-faced Baptist preachers liked to announce from their plywood pulpits.

Thirty-one votes were all it took, and Maurice was the beneficiary, having bested his adversary. "Guess the best man finally won this time." He allowed himself a shy grin as he pinned the brass star on the broad lapel of his pinstriped suit.

ॐ

We assumed Shad Smathers would run again and reclaim his rightful place. He was aiming to get even with Maurice, the upstart who had claimed his badge.

Votes from dependable precincts were undercounted, and in other parts of Coweetsee, the residents of cemeteries resurrected themselves to cast their earthy ballots on polling day. Looking at the raw numbers, more folks voted in that fateful election than were living souls in Coweetsee.

Shad still had plenty of money, and probably could roust more voters this time around. He had underestimated Maurice. He didn't plan to make that mistake again. He aimed for an even bigger war chest. Inflation perhaps, he needed to raise his voter payouts probably, and money to keep other men quiet. He would need more good old boys strong as oxen, who wouldn't mind twisting a few arms or stomping a few stubborn holdouts. Bare knuckles had their powers of persuasion.

But he never got his chance.

Shad was in his feedlot with that damned plow mule, thinking of his comeback and his revenge. Maybe that was his mistake, thinking too much and not mindful of the everyday dangers. Change comes when you aren't looking.

He didn't hear the mule snorting and grumbling to itself, a hateful creature who hated the harness and the man who had scarred its hide so many years. It reared on its front legs and let out a kick with its hind hooves. Too late, Shad turned his head to catch the blow.

The mule stood over its dead master, trampling on his outstretched hand.

Maurice was beside himself. "How smart could he be to get himself kilt by a dumb beast of burden?"

Showed up after Shad was laid to rest in the Meadow Fork cemetery. He walked into the feedlot at Shad's place. Went right up to that damned mule and pulled his gun from his suit pocket. The barrel against that blinking eye circled by flies, a squeeze of the trigger. The mule buckled and kicked its last in the dirt. The high sheriff walked out of the barnyard and like the rest of us, never looked back. Maurice would run unopposed for sheriff the next election, and for the next six terms and twenty-four years. In the kingdom of Coweetsee, we soon forgot there had been any power other than Maurice Posey.

PART III

THE BARN

12

Birdie drove out the river road, the bright water flashing through the trees, her heart quickening, and then always the surprise in a blind curve, the hidden drive that angled up to Zip's old place, where the first of her people had staked their claim on the hardscrabble ridges in Coweetsee. Last time she visited Zip at Laurel Trace, her great-aunt had been fretting about the house left unguarded. "Cain't remember if I threw the deadbolt on the back door."

"I'm sure it's all fine." Birdie patted the old woman's liver-spotted hand. Surprising it still held such fury. Zip could knock you silly with her small fist.

"No, it's not safe. Somebody could crawl through a window."

"I'll go and check. Don't you worry."

"Promise?" Zip gripped her fingers with a stubborn strength that startled Birdie.

"Promise."

The Sherrill homestead was only a few miles away from town, but it felt a world away in a different century. The house smelled of woodfire and fry grease, of cedar sachets in the bureaus and wardrobes, of an old woman's scented toilet water. The mirrors on the wall were blackened with time and warped your reflection inside the garland of etched flowers. Down the dim hallway came the constant sound of running water. Zip's grandfather had piped the spring and run the cold water into a stone trough set under the staircase. Birdie shivered at the cold taste of that mountain water, drinking from a dinted tin dipper.

But Birdie remembered the house, not for its silences but the songs.

Starting about the age of twelve or so, when boys became a source of some female fascination and their gawkiness grew endearing, Birdie was smitten by the terrible ballads about the troubles between men and women that her great-aunt knew by heart. Zip sang songs Birdie had never heard before on the radio or the TV. Before Birdie got her license, she pestered her parents to drive her out and deposit her on Zip's front porch, so she could learn the words and notes.

"Why you want to hear her old hollering, I'll never know," said Birdie's mother, who believed her daughter would be better served if she played piano or tried the band classes at school.

"Zip feels like the real thing to me," Birdie said, always ready to argue with reality.

"Don't romanticize being poor. We want you to do better," her mother warned.

They passed the usual landmarks. The ratty Scruggs place down at the paved road where the gravel started. The rusted tractor in the rain, the rusted chassis of a Ford coupe by the creek, the barn with its cow shit washing into the brown water.

"Why those people can't pick up after themselves, I'll never know," her mother never failed to remark, though she had passed that sad place a thousand times before. "They act like a bunch of hillbillies."

"Aren't we hillbillies?" Birdie backtalked.

"No, that's a trashy word. You need to have standards."

They laughed at hillbillies on the TV they watched in their '60s brick rancher. Birdie was mortified at how Andy Griffith wore the cuffs of his khaki pants half tucked into his black boots, so sloppy and uncool, or how Jed Clampett struck oil and moved as a millionaire to California, all the silly hillbillies that Americans thought safe to laugh at, the rubes and rustics. Birdie swore she would not be the dimwitted girl with a country accent and wide hips in cutoff blue jeans, though that's exactly how she grew up.

It didn't help that her daddy worked as the county extension agent, always going out in his khakis and a straw fedora to walk through furrows and fields, checking the soil acidity. Their supper talk was of blue mold, cutworms, pests, blights, drought. Her daddy explained how hailstorms would affect

Birdie's classmates, what kind of clothes or shoes they might be wearing to school next fall. "There but for the grace of God." Her mother would frown and shake her head. Birdie's parents were quiet folks, slightly embarrassed by the homespun cloth from which they had been cut.

Zip awaited their arrival on the porch with a glass pitcher of freshly squeezed lemonade, the real thing and not the powdered kind her mother bought at the supermarket.

"You need a new railing on these steps. You're going to break your neck one day." Her mother wobbled on the steps.

"My neck is just fine. See?" The old woman craned her head from side to side.

"All right," Birdie's mother relented. "I'll be back at four sharp. Don't be scaring the girl with too bloody a song, hear?"

"If it don't have blood in it, it ain't an old song," Zip always said.

Once the station wagon pulled away, the old woman and the young girl had the afternoon to themselves. They would march through all the verses of "Barbara Allen," then they went to town on "Pretty Saro."

"What do we sing next?"

Birdie was partial to the heartache songs of poor mothers, the girl left to die out on the snowy doorstep, while Zip seemed to favor the ones where the fool woman got her head cut off and kicked against the wall.

Zip had escaped marriage and children herself, which appealed to her great-niece. Birdie glimpsed the possibility of another life, even as Zip warned against trusting men or true love to save her. Zip was unbeholden to love, she never spoke of it except as a tragic sense, a bad end to her ballads, where men and women did hurtful things to each other in passion's grip.

"When I was sixteen, I thought I was in love, and it made me sick. Sicker than a dog. Pap took me to town to see a real medical doctor and not just the root woman in the next holler. Come to find it wasn't love. It was worms."

Zip would crack her rusty laugh, a joke she'd been telling on herself for years, covering for the fact that she'd spurned all suitors in her youth and spent her life caring for her aging parents. First her father shaken by a palsy into an early grave in the family plot on Frozenhead Mountain, then her heartbroken mother, the way that the knot in her mother's breast had grown into a cancer, putting her in a pine coffin.

Such grief, but Zip had weathered it. The world is hard, and the wind is cold and blows you down the slope if you can't stand your ground. All a woman can do is sing of terrible things and take what solace she can in the sweet song of birds, the aroma of flowers at your doorstep, and the innocence of youngsters like Birdie asking about how life once was in these green hills.

Those summer afternoons seemed suspended in time, in song, as they sang a cappella, competing with the chorus of crickets in the shade trees. The pretty words about tragic events. Birdie found herself rapt, sometimes holding her hand over her blouse to her wildly beating heart.

Too soon, at the appointed hour, her mother never failed to appear.

"Come on, Birdie. I ain't got all day," she yelled from the car, after honking the horn. "I need to get home to fix your father's supper."

"We're not halfway through 'Young Hunting,'" Birdie wailed.

"How about taking home some molasses cookies? I've got some in the kitchen." Zip leaped up.

"Don't be spoiling the girl, Zip. She hasn't had her supper yet."

"Sorry," the older woman apologized.

"Why are you always so mean?" Birdie asked her mother in the car.

"I'm not mean. I'm realistic," her mother said. "Besides, Zip doesn't know how the real world works these days."

Birdie wasn't a fan of the real world. Visiting her great-aunt felt like stepping out of this boring, plastic, commercial time into a more authentic age—or so it seemed to Birdie, who had always been a romantic at heart, rebelling against her own rigid, fearful, fretful mother.

Her mother pursed her thin lips. "Times were simpler in Zip's days. Women must be more careful these days. Look at Rhonda Harmon."

Poor Rhonda Harmon. Rhonda was older by a few years than Birdie, but she had a reputation around the county, running wild with boys, smoking and drinking and dancing all night at roadside bars over the county line.

"I'm not like her."

"But the wrong boy comes along, you could be."

"I'm not stupid." Birdie sat fuming, looking at all the landmarks of her youth fall away, the long ride home, to boredom and normalcy and standards.

"Just remember Zip's not your mother. I am. I always will be."

Birdie never remembered her mother singing, only the tight set of her mouth. It was hard to believe her mother came from the same stock as Zippora and her sisters, women who had built the kingdom of Coweetsee. Her mother had been beaten down somehow. Maybe growing up with such loud and mouthy women, high-minded, or maybe she was worn out with their arguments. She had gone off to a Baptist two-year junior college, finished her education degree at App State, then taught school for a few years. She had given all that up when Birdie came along.

They loved each other dutifully, but Birdie never had the sense her mother really liked her. They talked to each other with such sharp tones, always aggrieved or aggravated. Then she developed the breast cancer that ran in the family, and withered away over one winter. She held her daughter's hand at the end, patted. "Don't cry. You always cried."

It felt more like a complaint, a pushing away.

"She tried. She did her best." Talmadge held Birdie as she wept bitterly.

Why did it feel in Coweetsee like doing your best didn't get you anything but heartbreak?

Something wasn't right when Birdie came up the gravel drive. The pretty postcard view of her childhood had changed. The woodshed and the small barn had vanished behind Zip's house. Birdie looked wildly at the surrounding tree line on the ridge, as if the rickety buildings had walked off and were hiding from her. How could this be? The structures had been leaning precariously for years and would likely collapse someday. But now they were gone. There were muddy ruts made by a truck tire. No, no, she kept saying, running to the house now.

The ripped screen door leaned open, pulled away from the rusted top hinge. Inside, the walls were ripped asunder. The kitchen, so neat and orderly, looked like a stick of dynamite had blasted out the room, covered with plaster dust. Every bit of copper wiring and pipes had been cut out, along with the wainscotting in the parlor and the fancy cherry wood on the stairwell.

Birdie called the sheriff's office but got only a recording in a feminine yet robotic voice.

"You have reached the Coweetsee County sheriff's department. If you have a life-threatening emergency, please hang up and call 911. If you know your party's extension, you can dial it at any time. Listen carefully to the following options..."

Birdie turned in a circle with the cell phone against her ear, mashing it so hard that she could hear her blood drumming in her dizzy head. At the end of the recorded spiel, at last there came the final choice. "If you don't pick an option, someone will be with you shortly."

Birdie was gnawing at her fingertip, her foot kicking at a loose board at the stairwell.

"Hello, Coweetsee County sheriff's department."

"Listen. I need to report a crime. My great-aunt's home has been robbed."

"Your name, please?"

Birdie didn't recognize the voice on the other end. Not local, none of the familiar twang of a mountain-bred native, but a generic TV voice from elsewhere. Yet another newcomer, hired by Cancro.

"I'm Birdie Barker Price."

"And your house has been robbed?"

"No, I told you, my great-aunt's place. I'm here now."

"Is your great-aunt all right?"

"Well, she's safe and sound last I checked at the Laurel Trace. The house is abandoned."

"Address?"

"We're beyond Beaverdam out by the North River Road, then you shoot up the old Sherrill Road to the top of the knoll."

"We need a street number."

Aunt Zip had never had a street number, what mail she got the rural carrier stuffed in a black box a quarter mile down the road. "Everybody knows the Sherrill place," Birdie insisted, though the dispatcher on the other end acted like she was talking foolishness.

"How long has it been since anyone lived there?"

Two winters and counting. The kudzu was creeping up on the outside, and now a worse intruder had come.

"What's missing? Anything valuable?"

Everything. Someone had taken sledgehammer and crowbar to the wood in the barn, the shed, then the house. They had torn out the copper piping that had been added a half century ago to bring a flush toilet inside the farmhouse. Dollar signs in their greedy eyes, they had ripped a hole in time, somewhere where her heart used to be.

"We'll have a patrol car out there shortly."

"Hurry," Birdie said.

But what's the hurry after everything has changed?

She couldn't fathom it. History was supposed to be solid

as the mountains, the facts and dates unchanging. Then they knocked down a few mountaintops to punch the interstate through Coweetsee. Now her childhood memories set in a summer amber glow had been shattered.

13

Clark's Crossroads Mercantile had been a landmark in Meadow Fork for generations. The outside seemed immemorial, the same unpainted wood, the sagging porch. Once a grocery, hardware, and feed store, the failing business showed only the bare bones of its former bounty, the shelves no longer stocked. Anybody needing real food or milk or diapers would likely head to the dollar store out on the bypass.

Roy hadn't been here since Maurice was sheriff, and they drove over to talk to the proprietor, W. D. Clark.

"Son, you wait in the car," Maurice said. "This won't take long."

The screen door swung open and snapped shut with a bang. W. D. in his short-sleeve shirt came out on the porch.

"Let's you and me go for a little walk now," Maurice called, getting out of the car. "Just like the Lord in Genesis, walking in the cool of the evening."

"You quoting Bible these days, Maurice?" W. D. folded his bony arms.

"You and me. We need to talk."

Roy watched the two men go down behind the store, toward the creek.

Maurice might have wanted to give his old friend a fair warning. Clark's had become the go-to for stolen goods. Pull into his gravel lot, and someone would sidle up to your window, wanting to sell you a good mower, or a necklace, or a rifle, which might have just walked off that afternoon from inside a house or barn on the other end of the county.

Why Maurice didn't bust the lowlifes hanging around Clark's was a mystery to Roy. Seemed almost like W. D. had some leverage over the sheriff. Just the tug of an unseen thread in W. D.'s hand, and Maurice's reputation might unravel or his shiny badge tarnish.

Roy couldn't hear the words that the men exchanged down by the creek, but he could tell they were arguing. "Now listen here," W. D. protested in his spitting anger. Maurice's voice remained cool and collected, yet not exactly soothing, more like getting a face-full of creek water that chilled you to the quick. Maurice never raised his voice but lowered it to make a point you couldn't ignore. The worse of all was when he whispered, and everything in his range went deadly still.

After a spell, Roy watched the two men coming up from the creek. Maurice taking his slow and measured steps. W. D. almost running to stay ahead.

"You have a nice talk?" Roy innocently asked.

W. D. spat. He stomped up the steps of his porch and into his store, the screen door slapping loud as a pistol shot in the night.

Maurice got in the passenger side and slammed the door. "Let's go, boy. We're done talking here."

And that was all he ever said on the matter, but Roy noticed the two partisans seemed cold to each other afterward.

Sitting in the gravel parking lot years later, Roy swallowed hard, his mouth suddenly dry. Now it was his turn for a talk. He'd been putting off this stop for as long as he could. Gene had insisted it would be nice now that Roy was running, if he could get the backing of an original Posey supporter like W. D., but he knew better than to get his hopes up.

The store was deserted when Roy slammed the screen door behind him. Not even flies, and the bald man behind the counter, squinting an evil eye in his direction.

"How's business, W. D.?"

W. D. always looked like he was about to spit. The cords in his wrinkled neck twitching. He made a horrible hawking sound in his throat. What came out was a snort, or a nasty laugh.

"Bad. Not enough customers. All my old ones are dying off and the new ones are bad for the five-finger discount."

"Shoplifting is a crime. You could call the law."

"Pshaw. We ain't had no law since Maurice."

"Maybe that's why you need to vote for me instead of this Yankee sheriff we got now."

"You? I don't believe you got what it takes."

"How's that?" Roy decided to humor the old bastard.

"You're not Maurice Posey, nor Shad Smathers. Those fellers had teeth and bellies they couldn't never fill, no matter how many little lives they ate right up. Difference between wolves and rabbits, you might say."

"Wolves all died out," Roy pointed out, finally tired of the old man's fuckery with his mind. "I see rabbits all the time by the road."

"You here to buy something or just waste my time?"

Roy rummaged around the store. W. D.'s business was mainly a few fishermen, so he kept a cooler of bait and worms he could scoop you out for a buck. A pinball machine tilted in the corner. The spring on the plunger was worn, so the ball wouldn't advance far up the shoot, but fell back, a victim of inept gravity, never to reach the flippers and bumpers. A cold Franklin stove squatted in the center, the store's only source of heat, but W. D. was too old and ornery to bother with feeding it any wood.

Roy grabbed a cellophane-wrapped banana-flavored Moon pie from a cardboard box and pulled a pop bottle out of the cooler. W. D. rang him up on the old-fashioned cash register.

"That will be five dollars."

"Awfully high prices."

"Got to compete against the dollar store out on the bypass."

Roy opened his wallet and slid the bill across the counter.

"You been by to see Maurice at Laurel Trace?" Roy asked. "I'm sure he'd appreciate a visit from an old friend."

"We don't have much to talk about these days," W. D. said.

Roy took a long pull on the cold soda. Didn't look like he was getting any political help today, but still he was curious.

"Listen, I remember that time when Maurice and I came by, and the sheriff took you for a walk by the creek. You talked then."

W. D. straightened, the hackles almost visibly rising on his red grooved neck.

"I don't think it was about money or politics. Sounded like an argument to me," Roy said.

W. D. didn't bat an eye, and he didn't say a word.

"Seems to me that conversation came about the time Rhonda Harmon got herself drowned." Roy leaned on the counter, asking the questions maybe he should have asked as a young deputy. "You remember Rhonda?"

"You hear a lot of things in Coweetsee. I heard you had your turn with Rhonda after that pretty songbird bride of yours flew off with that long-haired hippie boy, ain't that right?"

Roy felt his face flush red and hot. W. D. leaned over and lowered his voice. "Some folks say you might be daddy to that little girl that slut had before she got herself drowned."

Roy fired back. "Weren't you in on that scheme to bed those Harmon girls in exchange for Charlie Clyde getting off easy the first time?"

"You're full of shit and don't even know it. Just like that stupid schoolteacher with that fake ballot box down at the jail."

"You leave Birdie out of this," Roy flared.

"You think you can waltz right in here and just ask old W. D. what he knows? You think I was born yesterday? Where are all the votes, where are all the bodies buried? Spit in your hand, that's what all that talk in this county amounts to. Like I'm gonna confess to all kinds of crimes and rumors if you just ask me all nice?"

"I ain't asking you for nothing," Roy said. "Ever."

"Fool with me, and I'll do something to you the devil never done."

"Is that a threat?"

"Naw, just a fact."

W. D. pointed to the other sign on the wall over his bald head.

Management reserves the right
to refuse service to anyone
and/or
to ask anyone to leave the premises.

"You can read?" W. D. said. "Then get the hell out of my store."

When Roy went and sat in his car with his soda, the Moon Pie he opened was stale and hard as a rock, probably sat on W. D.'s shelf for years before any fool would buy food from him.

14

Deana Harmon stepped out for air. The TV blared inside the trailer, mesmerizing her niece. Sometimes, she needed a break from that girl, now as full of sass and trouble and backtalk as her late mother.

She only went so far as the short deck attached to her mobile home, the one they had had such a time delivering. The rig had "Wide Load" labeled on a banner across the rear, barely squeezing down the tight curves of the cove, nearly getting stuck in the creek, then spinning ruts in her gravel drive. The workers dented one wall, jamming the trailer into the dirt bank cut below the abandoned Harmon homestead.

The row of worn rubber tires lined the flat roof. Some fools thought those tires were the same ones that had transported the trailer uphill, little did they know. Deana's other foolish kin thought that it was to keep lightning strikes away or keep the roof on if a stray tornado came this way. She found that a good heavy tire kept the roof from popping or creaking, like a gunshot in the middle of a summer night, or the metallic groans the aluminum braces made on a winter evening. Lord knows, her dreams were dark enough without contributions from cheap factory-made housing.

Deana lit one of her Chesterfield cigarettes, the ones that ladies used to puff in magazine ads, cradling one arm in her elbow, her smoke pinched between two fingertips, a pose of refinement with the worn cardigan draped across her bony shoulders.

She stood in the mountain air, peering down her dirt drive to the paved road that ran nowhere but to town. She should have taken the hint years ago and left this cursed county. But she was a Harmon, and she wasn't going to give the cowards of Coweetsee any satisfaction. Harmons hung in there like pit bulls locking their jaws on a bloody bone.

As she smoked, her free hand traveled to her collarbone where she used to wear that little heart locket on a golden chain, the first pretty thing she'd ever had in her life, given to her by one of the men. He'd put it around her neck and then he'd stretched her on the mattress in that room where they stayed. Whenever the men came to her bed, she wore her necklace to keep from being entirely naked in her mind. As they grunted and rutted and smelled and sweated like the pigs they were, she had placed that locket on her tongue, felt the slender chain across her lips. Her pretty underclothes came off and on, but the gold chain never did until she was unceremoniously returned to her parents' house.

Uphill from the trailer stood the kudzu-draped homestead, windows broken out in the top, the remaining glass glazed over like an old woman with glaucoma, like Deana's mother, who had been blind or refused to see for most of her adult life, not wanting to be blamed for what befell her daughters. Picking the son's life over the innocence of young girls.

Deana hated that house, but still she was enraged when she found Charlie Clyde gutting the place. He had a truck parked outside, loading the bed with scraps of wood, copper piping he'd ripped from the walls of their old house.

"What the hell?" She stormed over.

"Just making a little money. No need letting all this go to waste and ruination."

"Where did you steal this truck?"

"Borrowed it from Junk Jackson. He'll pay top dollar for the wood and copper."

"Get the hell off this property!" she screamed.

He was still her brother, her blood. He always came back. About a week later, he was knocking on the storm door of the trailer.

"Listen, I get why you might be pissed about the house,"

Charlie Clyde said. "Found something you might be interested in."

"Like what?"

"Come see." He coaxed her out of the trailer to his truck out front. He dropped the tailgate and slid out the strongbox.

Deana hadn't seen that box in years, not since she and her sister had hauled it from the creek. She traced her fingertip in the unlucky number cut into the front, the same gesture she'd made touching her sister's coffin.

"Rhonda," she whispered.

She could never forget the two of them, naked and kneeling, wondering what treasure they'd pulled from what they had believed was their secret fishing hole.

They came to fish or simply to sit in their folding lawn chairs and throw a baited hook in the water, fishing for bream, crappie, or even catfish. Something to supplement their meager suppers, but mainly to get away from men and woes.

It had been too hot that day, sweltering even at their elevation, not swampy like the Florida they had dreamed of visiting one day, but a prickly heat. And mosquitoes had migrated with the climate into the mountains. They were slapping at bites on their thighs and heavy arms.

"Good god, I can't bear it no more."

Rhonda was on her feet, kicking off her shoes and pulling her T-shirt over her head and worming out her too tight shorts.

"That little mermaid had the right idea." Rhonda giggled with too much wine cooler. Older now for such nonsense, her breasts pendulous instead of perky, more rolls around her hips, wrinkles around her eyes. Not that Deana was any different, any less weary. They had been girls together and taken advantage of by men, cast off by all Coweetsee.

Deana followed suit, following her sister into the freezing water. She could feel her nipples harden with the cold.

But Rhonda couldn't leave well enough alone, starting to

horseplay and splash water in Deana's direction. Deana grabbed a hank of hair and yanked hard, pulling that grinning face of her sister under the water. Rhonda came up coughing, spitting water, wide-eyed. That should teach her not to mess with a big sister.

Then Rhonda went under again, deeper into the pool. Deana felt a rising panic. Now what was she up to?

Her sister surfaced, gasping. "I found something."

Deana took a breath and dove deep, waved her hands through the water, until her fingers felt a corner. Not a rock, not a stump. She came up, gasping for air. Though the current was about to sweep her away, her toes caught against the flat surface, not sand, not silt, but something solid. She crept her toes along the edge of a box.

Without a word, the two sisters dove down like mermaids, holding hands, hardly able to see in the murky currents, but they found either side, a handle, and kicking and pulling, and not drowning, they wrestled their find toward the bank.

They lay naked, covered with sand and grit, gasping.

"I like to never got all that sand out of my pie," Rhonda would later say after they brought their treasure home.

Rhonda always believed she'd found a real treasure chest. But no greenbacks or jewelry inside, only ballots from an old election. She still thought money could be made, showing off what she'd found to the right person.

Maybe she had been right. And maybe that got her killed.

Her car had been found parked at the fishing hole where they'd first found the secret chest. A few empty pony bottles of Miller High Life left inside her abandoned vehicle and a few more in the eroded bank. Trash bags and snagged fishing line in the overhanging branches, a busted Styrofoam cooler smelling of fish, and a broken fishing rod.

But no Rhonda, and no box either, Deana thought.

Her sister was missing for a full week, her fate unknown, until her body was found down river, snagged in a half-submerged tree that had lost its roots on the bank and toppled into the water.

Maurice had asked around but hung his head when he came to the Harmon trailer to pay his respects, report his findings. He said it seemed an unfortunate accident, maybe self-inflicted.

"Suicide?" Deana asked in disbelief.

"I'm not saying she drowned on purpose, maybe it was just bad luck. I'm so sorry for your loss."

Deana knew that Rhonda hadn't been alone. She had worn her best cowboy boots, the second-hand kick-you, fuck-me Fryes that chafed her thick calves. The shitkickers were left in the Pinto, but the strong box that she had stashed in the hatchback had disappeared.

She wasn't about to mention that missing ballot box to Posey, the one who had stolen his office. He might have been the culprit himself, or certainly knew the perp himself. Never in a million years would Deana ever believed Rhonda had drunk herself silly and drowned. She'd been pushed, her head likely held under, punched. Men were capable of any crime in Coweetsee.

"Poor old Rhonda. She was a card," Charlie Clyde said.

"What do you know about her? You were locked up when she drowned."

"She was my sister too. I know what they made the two of you do, on my behalf. I won't ever forgive the old man or the old lady for what they done to you, but it wasn't my idea. You gotta believe me."

Therein lay her trouble with her brother. He wasn't smiling, that smirk had fled his face. But look into his eyes, deep into their darkness, and you would never catch a light there, just a blankness. She had never trusted him, hell, never even liked him, always smirking and sneaking about, even with those taps on his shoes. But he was still blood, they were bound and chained by DNA and the memories of their parents and their past.

"Where did you find this box?" Deana asked her brother.

"Back of an old barn I was rooting around in."

She lifted the lid and looked inside. Same old scraps of paper Rhonda had thought were so important.

"That might prove that Maurice was crooked from the start."

"You're too late. The Feds already convicted."

"But maybe not for the real crime," Charlie Clyde said. "He framed me for that fire. Who knows if he didn't set it himself?" Who's the law and who's the real villain? She'd watched her brother swear up and down about his innocence and walk away from bad shit with that smirk on his face, his shoes tapping their merry way straight to hell. You couldn't very well blame a red-blooded boy for driving at night. Wasn't it more the fault of Drew Adcock, a known drunkard who didn't have the horse sense not to lay his wet brain in the middle of the road, playing possum, almost begging to turn himself into roadkill with the next passing vehicle?

Charlie Clyde had served time at the juvenile center and escaped being sentenced as an adult. Deana and Rhonda certainly had served their own sentence.

But then all that swearing up and down to be innocent didn't pay when Charlie Clyde was arrested for the arson of that Black church. Another harmless drunk, LeRoy Hubbs, sleeping off his hootch dreams in the pew before he was burned alive.

Charlie Clyde didn't deserve that sentence, but he was guilty of everything else.

"No one's going to believe us if we bring this forward." Deana had closed the lid of the box. "Let me think a bit."

Maybe it was high time that old box saw the light of day, that folks faced the truth of that old stolen vote. Especially now that Coweetsee had a real election coming up again. Roy Barker begging at her door for her vote. That Yankee incumbent would be next, trying to sweet-talk her. Both angling for that brass star, promising high heaven in the peaceable kingdom, but likely delivering more of the same shit for regular folks. That box now might help expose who had hidden it in the first place. Lifting the lid on all those covered-up crimes might be just the trap to catch whoever had killed her sister.

Sighing, Deana snuffed out the butt of her cigarette on the railing of the deck, already weathering from yellow timber into a gray shade. She pocketed the butt in the pocket of her cardigan, then went in.

Angry now, she rushed by the useless Rhonda Jr. watching her shows on that damn TV and went back to her bedroom. There in the top drawer of the cheap dresser, she found the little box and picked up the golden chain. The locket opened with a little space where you were supposed to keep a picture of your true love, but it had always been empty. She placed that empty metal heart on her tongue, closed her eyes hard, and felt the crushing weight of those naked sweaty men.

15

Most mornings, Birdie shimmied herself into her floral tights, unfurled her purple yoga mat across the porch, and proceeded through sun salutation poses that Tal had taught her. Hands in prayer over your heart, then reach your arms overhead. Swan dive to touch your toes, then hop your legs back into a downward dog, more deep breaths. Drop your butt to flatten into a plank position that burns your abs. Down to the mat, then arch your spine to cobra pose. Lift your butt again to downward dog. Hop into your forward fold. Rise up for mountain pose. Then prayer hands again to your beating heart. All the particular postures except for the end. No shavasana or corpse pose for her. She'd break out bawling.

They had done their flow together. Now she worried that her butt was too big, and she had no one to ask, to reassure her.

Not that it did her any good. She hadn't expected to be widowed at forty-eight. Or to feel so middle-aged, her youthful figure no longer so lithe, sag on her backside, her arms and thighs, the same cellulite inherited from her mother. The gravity of age weighing on her. Gray hairs starting to show in her scalp. Time working against her. The scar of her hysterectomy showing whiter against her belly when she stepped out of the shower, glimpsing herself in the half-fogged mirror. Who was that stranger in the glass?

This morning, with her flowery butt thrust skyward, who comes driving up to her porch but Frank Cancro, the appointed sheriff of Coweetsee in his patrol car? Birdie jumped to her feet, completing her sun salutation with her palms in prayer to her heart, mouthing "what the hell' instead of "Namaste."

"Good morning, Mrs. Price." He approached her porch and did a one-finger salute to the brim of his ball cap.

"What's wrong?" For a second, Birdie knew something had happened to Roy Boy, and Cancro was here to break her heart again.

"Nothing's wrong that I know of," the lawman said. "Yet."

Cancro had a loud, insistent New Jersey accent that grated on Birdie's ears. She suspected we all sounded like drawling imbeciles to these outsiders who were moving in, developing Coweetsee's choice ridgelines.

"You found who tore up my great-aunt's house?"

"We're keeping our eye out for any scrap sales. There's been a few reports we're following up." He seemed all business, too much in a rush, not sure how to do small talk.

"It's not just my aunt Zip's house. I was driving by and saw that the Drucker barn out Snook's Creek Road just disappeared. I believe you've got a ring of poachers ripping off old places."

"We do regular patrols, but I've not heard any reported incidents," Cancro said.

"What do you know about Charlie Clyde Harmon back in town?"

"Who?"

"The man that Maurice arrested for burning down the Black church. You ask anybody. Charlie Clyde has always been a terror, a one-man crime wave."

"We got databases now, computers, and we're aware of all the felons in Coweetsee. We're keeping an eye on everybody."

"I just want you to arrest whoever trashed Aunt Zip's home."

"Sooner or later, we will. Meanwhile, I'm hoping more residents like yourself will do the community watch program."

Under Cancro's regime, the county now had signs with an unblinking blue eye along the roadways, warning would-be burglars and thieves that we were on the lookout for evildoers.

"Don't be afraid to report any suspicious activity. Law enforcement only works with the support of the public."

"Sounds like a man running for office." Birdie folded her arms, jutted her chin.

"I know I'm probably not your top candidate for sheriff."

"Actually, I don't vote."

"Not even for your ex-husband?"

"I don't believe in choosing between two evils," Birdie said.

"Coweetsee has had way too much corruption in its past," Cancro said.

"You should come see our latest exhibit at the museum. We go into all that history with a ballot box from the '82 election."

"I'm not much for history. I'm more focused on the future."

This man had no clue what he was up against in Coweetsee. Birdie couldn't see any local voting for this Yankee, aside from Rhonda Jr., who was only trying to antagonize all the adults in her life.

Cancro stepped across the porch and squatted by her swing, reaching into the ash tray to pick out a half-burned roach.

"Mrs. Price? I hope this is not what I think it is."

Birdie's heart began to race. "I enjoy some. Is that such a crime these days?"

"Well, technically yes."

Birdie started to lie. "This is part of Talmadge's old stash. It really helped with calming the chemo and helped with the pain."

"Both you and your late husband were drug users? You just helped him smoke it?"

It was probably a bad idea to bring up Talmadge's death to the sheriff, who seemed suspicious of how quickly Talmadge Price had succumbed to his terminal illness.

"I hear that New Jersey has approved medical marijuana. Maybe you ought to focus on real crimes, like whoever stole all the wood and fixtures out of my great-aunt's house."

"Consider this a warning," he said quietly. "I can't turn a blind eye."

"Thanks for dropping by, Sheriff."

Birdie didn't wave as she watched the cruiser ease down her drive crunching over the loose gravel. Was he on to her? What if he knew what she had done? Birdie still felt guilty that she had agreed to Tal's plea. If only her husband could have been stronger and not put her into that terrible role as the angel of death.

Birdie went inside and rummaged through Tal's desk. The Shaker box they had bought at a Southern Highland craft guild fair sat on the corner. He'd loved intricate woodwork, admiring how straight strips of cherry could be soaked to shape into an oval, pegged and fitted with a matching lid. Inside were his ashes in the plastic bag she'd brought from the crematorium up in Asheville.

Talmadge, whittled away by his cancer, losing twenty pounds, insisted on cremation, his body being burned. "It's more ecological friendly. And no funeral, I mean it. All those strangers lying about how much you meant to them."

But what about me? Birdie thought.

She was the only one left to mourn him, to keep his memory alive. His folks were long gone. Birdie had met them once when Tal took her to his childhood home in McLean, Virginia, on the outskirts of the capitol, for Thanksgiving. They likely thought she was Sadie Hawkins, a snake handler from way back in the hills who had put a charm on their boy.

Birdie had been hoping to stop in the Mall later to see the art in the National Gallery, but after that dry turkey and the tsk-tsking of his mom, Birdie was ready to hightail to the hills again. She had outgrown her angry youth, rebelling against her mother's fatalism, forever asking, "What's wrong with you people?" Now away from her mountains, she began to hear the accusation turned against herself—"What's wrong with your people?"

Mrs. Price had a habit of holding her hand against her breastbone over her sweater, as if catching her breath, or telling her beating heart to still.

"Talmadge says you know old-fashioned songs from your region," she said. "Perhaps you could favor us with one."

"No one wants to hear me holler about murder."

"No really," Mrs. Price insisted.

"They aren't pretty songs, that's for sure. They're kind of

wicked and wild, and the women used to sing them when the men were off in the woods or off to town."

Birdie sat on the edge of the loveseat, knees tightly touching, with her hand clutched below her brittle clavicles, the posture she'd always practiced with Aunt Zip. She picked a love song that left the lovers apart on either side of the ocean, but at least the boy hadn't thrown the girl in the river. No bloodshed or murder, just heartbreak. It wasn't one of Zip's favorites without the violence, but it had stuck with Birdie, who savored its sadness.

My true love she won't have me so I understand,
She wants a freeholder, but I have no land.
I cannot maintain her with silver and gold,
Nor buy her all the fine things that a big house can hold.

If I were a poet and could write a fine hand
I would write my love a letter that she'd understand.
I'd send it by the waters where the islands overflow,
And I'd think of my darling wherever I go.

When she finished, the only sound in the room came from the grandmother clock ticking on the mantel. The Prices sat transfixed, as if Birdie had shot them between the eyes, and all the blood had drained from their proper corpses. Only Talmadge was smiling at her.

"My, oh my," his mother said.

Talmadge's father clapped briskly. "That was really something, wasn't it?"

Talmage leaped up and hugged her hard. "What did I tell you? She's something else!"

❧

Birdie sat alone in their cabin, gazing into a lost time. Absentmindedly, she had unlatched the cherry box and opened the plastic bag inside, running her fingers through the fine white ash, all that remained of Tal.

Death had cheated her of her love. She still felt his last wishes were unfair. She had wanted him to lie with her in the plot next to her momma and daddy side by side in the sloped cemetery behind the Grassy Fork Baptist, which has some of the best views down the valley and the hills beyond Coweetsee, a nice place fenced off from the grazing cattle to while away eternity.

Imagine carrying that nice cherry box down to the river. Sprinkle your true love on the water. He would rise like a cloud and fall over the currents, and he'd be forever gone, swept away through the hills and toward the sea.

She couldn't let go just yet.

16

Roy hated to visit nursing homes. His own folks, thank god, had died before they had need of one, keeled over before their time, a loss, yes, but not that grinding grief that Birdie had to contend with watching the slow decline of a loved one.

He always unconsciously held his breath, passing between the automatic sliding doors of Laurel Trace. The ammonia and cleaning chemicals, the lavender room-freshener sprays, could knock a man down, barely masking the odor of age and death, piss and sweat, lurking in the recirculated air. Laurel Trace smelled of the grave. He crept down the hall, looking in at relics and skeletons, gibbering in their second childhoods, throwing tantrums or humming church hymns, awaiting the inevitable, the unknown.

At last, he found the shell of his old sheriff, propped up in bed. Maurice's mouth hung open, his head leaning back so Roy could see the gray thickets of nose hairs, the skin loose over his hard skull. For an instant, he worried that the old man had given up the ghost. But the rap of his thick knuckles at the half-open door roused the sheriff.

"Come on in, son." Maurice waved. "Pull up a chair."

"Didn't mean to disturb your nap."

"That's all right. Sleeping's about a fulltime job here."

"Sorry I haven't been by all that often," Roy said.

"It's all right. Old folk homes always gave me the willies. And lo and behold here I am. But Laurel Trace sure beats Camp Butner. They tell you when to eat but they don't lock your door." Maurice chuckled.

Roy looked around. Pastel pictures on the wall, anonymous as a hotel room, biding its time for the next resident. "Nice and quiet around here."

"Only when them women aren't hollering bloody hell next door."

"What's that?" Roy raised his eyebrows.

"Zip Sherrill next door and her great-niece, your ex," Maurice said. "They can't converse like civilized folks. They want to sing them morbid ballads."

Roy had to agree. Birdie had a sweet voice, but he preferred the Baptist hymns he'd heard her sing in their childhood. The ballads were something she took up again after she ran off with the hippie. Lord, they could raise the hairs on the nape of your neck.

Maurice continued his complaint. "I hear your ex is putting some old ballot box on display at the jail, like it proves my '82 victory was stolen. You know about this?"

"I begged her not to, but she gets into her mind that she's right, then Birdie gets all hellbent."

"Nothing wrong with that vote, other than it was too close for any comfort," Maurice said. "That box sounds mighty fishy to me."

Roy readily agreed. "That was what W. D. Clark told Birdie when he went by the show. Said it could be a forgery."

"Old W. D.," Maurice mused. "Hadn't heard from him all the time I was away, and we used to be thick as thieves."

"Went by his store the other day, looking for his support," Roy said. "He was as cranky as ever."

"And he didn't even ask how I was doing?"

"Sorry, no." Roy wavered.

What about that strange visit years before when he drove his sheriff over to the old fixer's store, the strangled conversation they had had down by the creek? Roy still wondered what had happened between the two partisans.

"Some say it was W. D. who ratted you out to the Feds."

"We have our history, but W. D. knows how to keep his mouth shut."

And the old man fixed his lips in a tight frown as if following his own admonition.

The silence grew long, then awkward. They had never been much for face-to-face heart-to-hearts. They had said more when they were driving, looking at the sights instead of awkwardly into each other's eyes. Roy's gaze tended out the window, at that rough rock cliff only a few feet away from the rear of the building. Maurice seemed to be looking at the door, maybe wishing he could up and leave his bed behind.

"Oh, guess who's back in town, out of the pen, our old friend Charlie Clyde."

"Word gets around. I heard that colored girl talking to your ex in the hallway." Maurice reached over to his nightstand and picked up a cigar. They didn't trust him with matches and the oxygen tank, but he still loved the taste of a good Cuban on his tongue.

"Best keep an eye on that old boy. There will be mayhem soon enough, something burned down or broken into, or god forbid, some poor girl floating face down in the river, and you can bet Charlie Clyde will be smirking somewhere nearby, mark my words."

"I talked to him the other day," Roy said. "He's still singing that old story he was framed for the church fire."

"Never met a felon who didn't claim he was always innocent," Maurice said.

Including you? Roy thought, but he kept his mouth shut. Maurice had taken a deal and pled guilty to the federal charges. If he was innocent, why had he not fought it out at trial?

"How goes your campaign?" Maurice asked. "You getting out the vote, pressing the flesh, kissing the babies?"

"This running for sheriff is an awful lot harder than I thought."

"I thought you had yourself some advisers. Gene Hooper and the other deputies."

"I do. But you could be a mighty big help to me winning this thing," Roy said. "We could get Coweetsee back to itself."

"I'm an old man fixing to die. Not sure how much help I can be."

Roy's shoulders sagged. This wasn't what he wanted to hear. Maurice took the cigar from his mouth and studied the chewed end. "Still, you want to know what I think?"

Roy perked up again. "I'd be much obliged."

"Somebody's trying to piss on your election is what I think."

"What do you mean?"

"That ballot box down at the jail. It gets people all nostalgic or churned up about the good old days or how bad it was. Muddies the water. Makes it harder for you to stand out when you're up to your ass in shit."

"What can I do about it?"

"Learn to swim in it, son."

❧

Birdie was climbing out of her little VW in the parking lot when Roy came out, able to breathe as he hurried away from the smells inside Laurel Trace. They exchanged awkward hellos.

"You been visiting the sheriff, I reckon," Birdie said.

"Yeah, just ran some campaign strategy by him. You come to see Aunt Zip?"

"We like to sing our ballads. Makes her happy. Me too."

Roy chose not to say what Maurice thought of that hollering next door.

"Sounds like you've been doing good business at the historical society. Drove by the other day and you had a crowd."

Birdie brightened. "Folks are mesmerized by that ballot box, politics of the past and all. I wouldn't have believed it."

"People care about politics. I've been telling you that for years," Roy said.

"Listen, Roy. I've been thinking. Gene Hooper might be right about one thing."

"What's that?"

"Hanging out with Maurice might not help you as much as you think."

"What do you mean?"

"You drove that old man to town and watched him suck up

all the air when he opened his mouth at the courthouse."

"Maurice could always give a good stemwinder," he argued.

"You're the one running now, not him. You need people paying attention to you."

"You could pay more attention to my campaign."

"If it helps, I am offering voter registration forms to anyone coming to see the exhibit," Birdie said, but it seemed she wasn't going to pick a fight with him.

"But it sure as hell doesn't help when you're showing off that ballot box and riling everybody up about stolen elections."

"People need to know the truth, no matter what they want to believe," she said.

"You don't believe I can win this race." He bristled.

She rolled her eyes, that familiar dismissive look. "I'm just not sure that being sheriff is what you really want or need."

"What I need is to get going." Roy got into his jeep and slammed the door. "Give my best to Zip. And Maurice would appreciate it if y'all didn't sing so damn loud."

17

Her mama would never directly say who her daddy was. Rhonda Jr. could remember no father in her short life, only vague memories of a man on the riverbank, who refused to take off his wet boots. A man who never lifted her up, or acknowledged her, but was a presence muttering to her mama. A dark current passing overhead as she splashed in the water, slapped her pudgy hands in the water, her diaper full of sand and her warm stool.

Their rendezvous was by the river, the shady places under the overhanging sycamores and shag-bark birches, where they unfolded their lawn chairs, wedged the aluminum frame in the sand, maybe her mama would kick off her flip-flops, dangle her porky toes in the cool currents. They watched kingfishers flash over the waters, and sometimes an eagle could be seen winding its noble way along the river bends.

They sat in their shallows and drank beer from aluminum cans. They kept their counsel, their company, kept away from the scolds and gossips, the stone sober deacons and the frigid church ladies, grim-lipped and fish-eyed, the rest of Coweetsee.

Sometimes they came home with a cooler of fish in the melted ice, strings of blood dribbling from their gaping mouths. Her mama would clean and scale the catch in the sink, pulling out the guts. She'd fillet the best and soak it in Sprite soft drink, her secret ingredient, then batter the fillets in cornmeal and seasonings, and fry the fish in the cast-iron skillet until the smell of grease clouded the kitchen.

Rhonda Jr. missed that taste in her mouth.

There were other tastes from childhood, like the clay she dug out in the clamminess beneath the trailer. She tried to feed her baby doll the little mud pies she made, but the doll wouldn't open its painted lips no matter how hard the girl smeared the mud there. She sucked on her fingers, tasting the earth, the worm shit, the rich life itself.

She sang in made-up language, plucking one by one the polyester blond strands from the doll's plastic scalp. She'd gotten the doll for Christmas at the Elks Club, when her mama had taken her to a toy drive, along with a pair of shoes. "Charity!" Aunt Deana would grimace, but her mama argued there was no honor in depriving a young-un of a little joy in a wintery world. Sometimes when the adults weren't around, she went snooping for clues, for answers to her questions. In Aunt Deana's chest of drawers, she found frayed panties, rolled socks, a strange device she would only realize with a shock years later was a vibrator. In the jewelry box, cheap rhinestone and mismatched hoop earrings, but also a slender gold chain and a little heart-shaped locket with what looked like a bite mark in its finish.

She still had the muscle memory, the shooting pain in her arm snatched up, her backside blistered by Aunt Deana who had suddenly appeared. "Don't you ever mess in my things again. Don't you ever!" she screamed. "Don't you be crying like a baby now. I'll give you something to holler about."

In her keepsakes, Rhonda Jr. treasured the strip of film from the mall photo. They used to go and walk around the mall, its stores full of jewelry and manikins posing with clothes she had seen only on TV and in magazines. They wedged into the booth for their shots, her mother and her making wild eyes, sticking their tongues out, smushing their similar faces together, their flesh one flesh in that tight space, for both of their warm bulks. She took after her mama, she knew, with her heavy thighs and small breasts and a fat low neck with a fold of flesh around it. The photo and her own flesh now the only reminders of her mother. And her name.

Then came the day Aunt Deana herself was crying, terrible tears on her ravaged face, sobbing silently, her shoulders rack-ing up and down, but the girl could see no one beating on her.

"Where's Mama?" she dared ask.

"Baby girl, your mama ain't coming home tonight. She loved you with all her heart, you know. You're the spitting image. It's like she's here with me in you, girl."

When she went back to school, Aunt Deana was calling her Rhonda Jr., instead of her middle name June. But she had the distinct sense that Aunt Deana didn't particularly like her as she grew older. The refrain became "don't you be like your mama, hear?"

Her mama had been to blame for getting herself pregnant, for even having a baby like Rhonda Jr., certainly at fault for hanging out with those unseen men, for getting herself drowned.

"Remember you can't trust or turn your back on anybody but blood kin. You're your mama's baby girl. A Harmon to the bone," her aunt kept harping at her.

Love was a hollow word to the Harmons. What passed for sweet affection in this family felt like a harrowing she could not escape. Yet a part of her remained alone, aloof, a diapered girl splashing in a creek or crawling in the dirt beneath the trailer, putting rocks and figurines in the cavities of cinder blocks that held up her whole world.

She dreamed of buying a bus ticket or just sticking out her thumb for a ride, headed to Atlanta or Charlotte for waitressing, or modeling, maybe singing. She could see herself on the small stage of a honky-tonk, wailing about no-good men. Or throwing a baby off the Tallahatchie Bridge. Her voice, her looks would hook the eye of a handsome fellow, who would buy her drinks, buy her rings, buy her happiness.

She would put this trailer, these mountains, this life far behind her. She could change her name, change her life. Anywhere but here. Anyone but Rhonda Harmon Jr.

When Aunt Deana had had one too many of the PBRs, her head lolling on the worn loveseat set in front of their old TV, her mouth parted with her stale breath and the whiskers on her upper lip began to tremble as she snored. Rhonda Jr. studied her closest kinswoman with a hateful satisfaction. Never turn your back on or trust anyone other than your blood.

What would it feel like to take that embroidered cushion "Love is the Home" and smother her auntie's face? Rhonda Jr. sometimes imagined her mother's face from the photo booth, her head being held underwater, under the river until the struggle was over. Her arms quit their flailing, her legs their kicking, and she was free at last to float on down.

All rivers fall to the sea, headed forever out of Coweetsee at last.

18

One morning, Roy drove out to Sycamore Shoals, some of Coweetsee's finest country—fields high with corn, cattle grazing the hillside pastures, cicada choirs shrieking from lush shade trees along the banks of the creek. He wasn't just sight-seeing but working up his nerve to knock at doors, trying to get someone, anyone to vote for him, come the first Tuesday in November.

Meanwhile, he had his window rolled down, his free arm propped on the sill, letting his hand float in the warm air. He jerked the wheel to avoid what looked like a puddle of oil. The rough surface of the tarmac sounded funny beneath his tires. He slowed and pulled off onto the shoulder.

Roy stepped out and slowly walked back up the road, following the cracks in the asphalt. In the west lane near the solid yellow line, the fissures converged on a black hole about the size of his fist, like a pursed mouth or the blowhole of a whale. He thought he heard the echo of dark water below. Felt like he stood atop a beast about to buck him off.

He returned to his jeep and fetched a couple of flares, set them on the road, then stretched yellow crime tape across the way.

Jerry Lee drove up in his battered truck and rolled down the window. "Whathup?"

"Sink hole up there. I just saved your life."

"Damn." Jerry Lee kept fiddling with his mouth.

Roy thought it was a mite early in the morning for his buddy to be hitting the hard sauce and slurring his speech. "What's your problem?"

"Bad toof," his adviser said and smiled his crooked incisors.

"Best turn around and take the long way around."

"You coming or not?" Jerry Lee finally got his hand out of his mouth.

Roy had a campaign meeting scheduled at the McDonald's on the bypass. The coffee would be cold, and Gene would be all hot and bothered about something, mainly money but Roy had promised to listen.

"I'll be there directly."

"Gene's counting on you. We're all counting on you, Roy. I hope you know that."

At least that's what Roy was able to make of Jerry Lee's spittle-flecked muttering.

"You better get those dentures."

He fished his cell phone from his pocket and called dispatch. "This is Roy Barker. I'm out by Meadow Fork and I've got the road blocked. Tell Frank he better get his ass out here. We got a sink hole looks like it could go at any time."

Coweetsee had seen buckets of recent rain. A tropical depression from the Gulf had swelled the creeks all red with clay and runoff, sweeping a couple of cows out of pastures. No more than the usual flash flooding that afflicted the county's tight coves and steep slopes. But after things dried out, the damage made itself known. The ground grew uncertain underfoot, perhaps not even solid earth, but a thin shell scarcely able to bear your weight.

Roy stood guard, ready to wave away passersby. It put a dint in the day's campaigning, but it might play to his advantage. Maybe the weekly newspaper would run a story: *Barker Discovers Dangerous Paving, Demands Answers*.

No sirens coming down the road. Cancro sure was taking his sweet time. Maybe he had some serious jaywalking or parking tickets to write in deserted Coweetsee, maybe he had gone over to Mass. They say he was a devout Catholic, believing all that papist stuff, robes and communion wafers and a shot of cheap wine every damn day to stay on the straight and narrow. To each his own.

Roy had given up on church long ago. He knew his place in a

Baptist pew, but the dogma didn't touch him. He didn't believe nor disbelieve. He mainly relied on what he could see with his own two eyes. Maurice had confirmed those initial doubts in his impressionable mind. But that didn't mean Roy couldn't get a shiver of superstition prickling the nape of his neck, like now. Strange how this hole had popped open on the same stretch of pavement where Charlie Clyde had his run-in with poor Drew Adcock, smushed his drunken gourd under his tires one dark night. Maybe Drew had been lying where that crater was now, as if the road remembered the very spot where Charlie Clyde had started that collapse, that hole in the heart of everything we wanted to believe about Coweetsee.

Cancro pulled up in his patrol cruiser. The new car had a shotgun rack and computer and all the accoutrements of modern law enforcement. In the trunk, probably a full armor body suit and perhaps a bazooka from the Department of Homeland Security to handle most any crisis. The Yankee appointee had wanted to professionalize local law enforcement, so first thing he did was bill the county for patrol cars. Each was painted with his version of the seal of Coweetsee, a logo with a mountain behind a courthouse topped by Lady Justice and encircled by the legend *Pledged to Serve*.

Suit yourself, Roy muttered. We all had watched the new patrol cars and the men Cancro hired from outside the county to wear the uniform. They would ride the roads and turn on their sirens and make dogs howl whenever they went flying by in the night. Coweetsee was turning into a police state.

Cancro got out, hoisting his gear belt under his neat abs, adjusting his polarized aviator sunglasses. Roy was reminded of the X-ray glasses advertised in the comic books of his youth, next to the muscle-building schemes to thwart the bully kicking sand in your face.

Roy waved from the yonder of the fluttering yellow tape.

Cancro ignored the warning, yanking the ribbon overhead to pass under.

"You're blocking the road here, Barker."

"I'd watch your step, Frank," Roy warned. "You don't want to fall in a sinkhole."

Roy had an image. The road, the earth, Coweetsee County eating this outlander whole, swallowing him right up. Putting Cancro out of contention.

The new sheriff kicked at the hole, and sure enough a chunk dropped off beneath his boot. He jumped back.

There could be a joke here how Cancro couldn't tell his ass from a hole in the road, but Roy couldn't come up with the punchline to land on his opponent. That was what his advisers kept telling him, that he needed to be quicker on his feet. He was a wrestler at heart, slow, down on all fours and pushing his weight around like a bulldozer.

"I already saved Jimmy Lee's life from driving his pickup right over that."

"How did you get over it then?"

"Guess I was just lucky."

"Why'd you call? This looks like a Department of Transportation issue."

"About the time a widow drives her old Buick into a hole in the road that wouldn't be good for business."

"I'm not running a business. I'm a public servant."

"Better do your job while you got it. Before the public demands a debate," Roy said.

Cancro had brushed off Roy's requests for a one-on-one live debate, a chance for voters to size up the two men, the native and the outsider.

"Your pal Maurice Posey never debated Shad Smathers. He just stole the votes that weren't going his way, didn't he?"

Cancro had obviously been talking to someone about local politics or maybe he'd seen Birdie's damn exhibit at the historical society. Gene was right. She had discovered a new world of troubles with that old ballot box.

Cancro went and sat in his car with the door open, with his

boots on the pavement, radioing in a message to get DOT out here with orange traffic cones, get this stretch of asphalt on the endless list of road improvements that Coweetsee needed.

He wasn't taking Roy's report all that seriously, and Roy could feel the nape of his neck getting hotter. The man didn't respect him for doing the right thing.

Roy yelled, "Hey, Frank, you know anything about Charlie Clyde Harmon getting paroled?"

"I might have seen some paperwork. Why?"

"He's a bad one with a long history."

"I know. I was just at your ex-wife's cabin. She mentioned Harmon to me."

"What are you doing, talking to Birdie?" Roy panicked. He hadn't expected this move on his opponent's part.

"Following up her complaint of vandalism at an abandoned homestead."

"Sounds like you might have a crime spree on your hands. I hear about barns full of chestnut lumber just disappearing. Old wood like that is worth twenty-five dollars a board foot."

"We're on top of it," Cancro said. "We'll handle it."

He walked over and stared at the hole, then at Roy on the other side.

Roy crossed his beefy arms. "I aim to whip you fair and square come November. That's all you need to be afraid of, Frank."

"May the best man win, but that will be me," Cancro said, readjusting his sunglasses.

"We'll just have to see." Roy angled for the last word, then bit his tongue. Poor man didn't know the curse of Coweetsee, that nothing really changes.

19

Two girls wandered the empty streets of Coweetsee, waiting for their real lives to begin, hoping someone someday would love them, buy them things, give them a big house and pretty things to wear, would worship them and make them worthwhile, forever waiting for something to happen in their wasted lives in this podunk place they couldn't wait to leave, but didn't have the drive to make that move.

They were primed for disappointment as they ambled along the abandoned sidewalks from the vape store to the boarded-up mercantile, then turned at the intersection past the jail and strolled out to the bridge, the river beneath their Doc Martins as they perused their phones, eyes downcast as always.

Rhonda Jr. halted in her tracks, stopped by the post that flashed on her screen. With the rage of adolescence, and how unfair life is, and how stupid and mean people can be, even your own supposed best friend, who had sexted a selfie of her bared breasts, offering to give a BJ to Rhonda Jr.'s supposed boyfriend Donnie Gunther, and in his hormonal excitement, the idiot Donnie had accidentally forwarded the shots to Rhonda Jr.'s spangly phone. That unfairness overcame her since Melody's breasts were somewhat bigger, perhaps more desirable than hers.

"You dumb skank!" Rhonda Jr. screamed.

She grabbed the expensive suede jacket that Melody had found in a Goodwill store in Asheville. She wore it on a too hot day, like a cape over her shoulders. Rhonda was swinging it by one arm and flailing her cheating friend with it, before flinging the costly coat over the rail into the river.

"You stupid bitch!" Melody shrieked. She bloodied Rhonda's nose with a sucker punch she had learned keeping her brothers at bay. They were pummeling each other's painted face, pulling dyed hair and screeching to high heaven on the bridge.

Birdie heard the commotion, coming back from Shawanda's studio. She saw the two girls precariously close to the railing, as if they were going to jump or push each other, screaming and cursing each other as hellcats. With two youngsters acting outside the bounds of good sense, her teacherly instincts kicked in. Birdie ran, hollering, "Stop, stop. Don't, don't!"

Birdie pushed in between them, their bodies perfumed and sweating and crying, flailing punches at each other, looking for purchase on each other's hair, raking skin with their broken nails. As she grabbed Rhonda Jr.'s arm, Birdie caught an elbow hard in her ribs, but she separated them at arm's length.

"What's wrong here?" she cried.

"She threw my coat over the side," Melody wailed.

Poor skinny Melody with her thin arms, and only a tank top, a kind of sexy lace bustier. Birdie remembered the young girl without breasts, shivering on the playground, without a mother to make her wear a coat to school.

They watched the suede jacket, floating downstream.

Rhonda Jr. said, "Stay away from my boyfriend, you slut."

"Your mama was the slut," Melody hissed.

Rhonda Jr. roared. She started throwing roundhouses with her fist, fighting like a boy. Birdie's nose caught a glancing blow.

They froze at the short squawks of a siren. Sheriff Cancro jumped out of his cruiser.

"What's going on here?"

"Nothing, Sheriff, nothing at all, ain't that right, girls?"

Bloodied, crying, sniffling, with their heavy mascara smudged. They were silent.

"Looks like you're bleeding, Ms. Price."

Birdie touched her finger to her nose. My god, how red blood is. "I'm fine. We're all fine. Just a disagreement over a boyfriend. Girls will be girls."

"I'm not going to have street brawls in downtown Coweet-see, male or female. I could write you up for disturbing the peace, assault and battery." Cancro went through the list of possibilities, but he really didn't want to be bothered.

"Just a misunderstanding. No harm done," Birdie repeated herself, trying to keep from bleeding all over herself.

"Move along then." He gave them his sternest glare, and then a quizzical hook of an eyebrow. He walked over and bent down. "What's this?"

A plastic bag, a quarter pound of fresh sinsemilla, Shawanda's latest crop, spilled across the concrete, dropped out of Birdie's tote bag.

"This looks like a drug deal."

"No, Sheriff. These girls were just fighting over a boyfriend."

"Then whose is this?"

Birdie swallowed blood at the back of her throat. "That's mine. I can explain."

"I'd save all that for your lawyer."

Cancro piled all three in the backseat of his cruiser and hauled them to the detention facility. They were buzzed into a tight room where a magistrate sat behind a plate glass and explained the charges. Birdie Barker Price was ordered to appear in district court on misdemeanor charges of marijuana possession.

At least she didn't have to post a cash bail, but was released on her own recognizance. Not that she recognized herself. Mortified. About to die from shame and all the blood rushing to her face, her nose, until she was able to staunch the flow with wadded tissues.

Cancro was gentlemanly enough to deposit them downtown again. But he had confiscated her pound of dope. At least she hadn't snitched on Shawanda.

"We're fine, aren't we, girls?" Birdie shepherded her former students off the bridge.

They weren't speaking to each other but parted at the intersection beneath the courthouse where the blindfolded Lady with Justice weighed the scales with a bird nest. They would get over it. Girls and boy problems. They didn't have anyone other than each other. They would find new friends, they would make up, maybe not.

Birdie had done much the same thing when she was their age. She once gave a black eye to Teresa Honeycutt, who was flirting with Roy Boy by the water cooler in high school. Birdie hadn't hit her but was more subtle. She tripped the skank and Teresa stumbled into the corner of the water fountain. Roy was flustered. He had seen the move, and stared in horror at Birdie, who smiled sweetly at him.

Cruelty, indeed. She still remembered that flush feeling, the satisfaction. Teresa on the floor and the shock on her face. Girls can be so mean. Men can treat women badly, but women can wound each other worse.

Now sitting on the swing of her front porch, smoking a doobie to calm her jittery self, Birdie couldn't shake what she had seen this afternoon. In the water, the jacket floating down, somersaulting like a ghost though the summer air to float on the river current. The arms filling with water, then sinking in the cold rushing water, like a drowned girl glimpsed beneath.

20

Birdie's mouth was dry as she climbed the steps to the Harmon trailer. She swallowed again her pride, then rapped her knuckles against the screen door, calling into the dim interior as if into a dank cave.

"Hello, anyone home?"

Deana Harmon appeared behind the screen. A hard glint to her eyes. No makeup but still a beauty to her high cheekbones. Men would have called her a looker in her day.

The women sized each other up through the ripped wire mesh.

"Thought I best come by and explain what happened the other day," Birdie said.

"Wondered why it took you so long." Deana held the door open, inviting Birdie inside.

The girl, Birdie's new nemesis, sat on the sofa, the TV reflecting a makeup commercial in her blank eyes.

"Hey," Birdie said, but the girl said nothing.

Birdie wrinkled her nose at a faint odor from the kitchen, maybe the bathroom. The front room was not particularly tidy, a sweatshirt balled beside the cushion of the couch. Rhonda Jr. didn't bother to lift her feet from the sofa. Yellow shag carpet. Ashtrays full of Deana's cigarette butts. The vinyl recliner likely belonged to Deana. A stiff-backed ladder chair that no one ever sat in. That was the chair that Birdie took, the hot seat. She cleared her throat and dove right in.

"I need to apologize to you and Rhonda here for getting her in trouble. She's totally innocent. That was my marijuana that we were caught with."

"Everybody knows that," Rhonda Jr. snickered. "Nobody but a Boomer would mess with leaf shit these days."

"Hush now. Let Ms. Price talk."

"Just saying." Rhonda Jr. flounced her hair, streaked with purple this week.

"Girl gets herself in trouble all the time, but it's nice to hear you say it wasn't her fault for a change," Deana said.

Birdie tried to explain what would happen. They had been all released without having to front any bond money, but the court expected them to show up for their hearing. "That's not something you can miss," she warned the girl.

"We know all about courts," Deana said.

Birdie went on. "I'll probably plead guilty since I technically am, but I'll certainly vouch for Rhonda and her friend Melody."

"That little bitch. She tried to steal my boyfriend," Rhonda Jr. cried.

"Hush, girl," Deana said. "Your elders are talking here."

She faced Birdie. "Law's the law. People get framed all the time in this county, like my brother."

Birdie wasn't going to argue with Deana, but the Black church had been burned down with the deacon sleeping in the last pew. Charlie Clyde had run a man over in the roadway when he was a teen. He was not innocent.

"I know what happened to your sister and you when your brother first got into trouble," Birdie said. "I heard the story."

"What do you know? You heard only the stories everyone tells behind our backs."

"I'm sorry. I didn't mean it that way." What she was trying to ask, what Birdie had always wanted to know: What really happened, and how did you feel? Your innocence traded for your brother's guilt.

"Tell me then." Rhonda Jr. leaned forward on the couch, her thick arms on her bare knees. "You've never said much about my mama, other than I shouldn't be like her."

"You're taking after your mama in the worst way and it's scaring me. Maybe it's time you heard the real story."

Deana lit another Chesterfield, blowing smoke into the close air. Birdie tried not to wrinkle her nose, but sat still as a church mouse, listening with her hands wringing in her lap. Rhonda Jr. snapped her gum, her fingers tapping the vape pen against her knee. The women sat in the gathering gloaming, the autumn sun casting long shadows across the darkening holler below the rim of the cursed kingdom of Coweetsee.

"Say you're just a young girl and you don't know any better." Deana's voice grew quiet as she waded into her darkest memories. "Wrestled a few boys in the barnyard maybe, seen how the dogs and farm critters mount one another. You understand the mechanics, but not old enough to know how it all feels.

"Then one day Mama comes in all quiet and says, 'Put on your pretty dresses. Y'all are big girls now and it's time for y'all to act like women. The men are coming to marry you.'

"And soon we sat side by side in the back of the men's shiny car, in our Sunday dresses, saddle lock shoes and bobby socks. Rhonda had a bandage on a skinned knee and held her baby doll in her lap. She was only fourteen. The men in their jaunty fedoras sat in the front. They eyed us in the mirror. 'You gals like music?' They turned up the radio. 'Y'all going to have such fun.'

"They drove us to the river, to a nice house with views and shiny Christmas lights strung on the porch all year round. They showed us upstairs. In two separate bedrooms, pretty dresses laid out on the soft beds. There were phonographs with all the records for us to play and dance on the porch, spin around in fancy flocks. Chocolate and plenty to drink. We were warm and well-fed and called pretty little things by men who were as old as our daddy but smelled way better than that old hog farmer.

"That party went on a while. But miss that time of month, then the next, and the men notice that maybe we're getting fatter than the food we're eating. Back in the car for a long drive down to South Carolina to see a doctor, clean up all that business. Party was over.

"We were riding home again, Rhonda staring out the window. She didn't have her baby doll with her anymore. I didn't have the heart to ask her. I tried to hold her hand, those once pudgy fingers she had, but Rhonda pulled away, clenched her fists tight.

"The men dropped us off at the house and sped away, gave the old man a few folded bills. But not a word was ever said. Mama pretended the less said, the better. Nothing said, then nothing had happened. The old man, he kept moaning and crying and feeling sorry for himself. Weeping for his poor, lost daughters, like we weren't there."

Birdie interjected. "I thought you got married."

"That's what they told everyone. But there never was a preacher there saying vows, there were no certificates or licenses."

"But those men? Surely you remember their names. How could you forget them?"

"Most of them are dead now. What does it matter? Water under the bridge."

Maybe as a schoolteacher, or as the director of the historical society, Birdie felt obligated to offer an apology on the behalf of the whole county, all the church ladies who had whispered the rumors, or the men gathered on porches or by hunting fires, joking about the loose Harmon harlots, all the terrible stories that followed the sisters.

"Here's the thing about old men. Take off their coats and ties, drop their pants, they all look alike, big old white bellies and little dicks." Deana laughed bitterly.

"Why didn't you say something? Good Christian folks would have helped you," Birdie wondered aloud, trying to make sense of the unspeakable.

"Like we have good Christian folks. No one in Coweetsee is going to help a Harmon. I grew up knowing that."

"I'm so sorry. You were so young."

Deana snubbed out her cigarette in the ashtray. "All I want to know, the one man whose name I don't know. The one who drowned my baby sister."

"I'm so sorry." Birdie kept repeating herself, sounding foolish to her ears. "I wish there was something I could do for you."

"Well, you are. That's why I brought you that old ballot box. It was high time Coweetsee faced the truth about the powers that be."

"W. D. came by the society the other day. He insisted that ballot box was a forgery," Birdie said.

"Did he now? That old liar."

"That's exactly what he said about you."

"W. D. didn't mention getting that box from my sister?"

"No, he said he bought it from Junk Jackson, then had it stolen from his barn."

What Birdie didn't say was she wasn't sure who to believe about that ballot box. Believe the women. The men are all silver-tongued devils as Zip would say.

"But how did you find it?"

"It's more like it found us. My sister and me, in the creek years ago," Deana said. "Rhonda thought it was worth something, and she went to sell it or blackmail somebody. She wound up drowned in the river, and I think it was about that box."

"You waited all these years and didn't say a word?" Birdie pondered this unlikely story that made so little sense on the surface. "Why come clean now?"

"Because I was busy making sure that this child had a roof over her head, and clothes and food to eat. You don't do that, and I knew the social services were just waiting to snatch that baby girl away, put her in a foster home, just because she's a Harmon. She's all that's left of Rhonda. But now that she's growing up into a woman, I didn't want her to make her mother's mistakes all over."

"Do you know who my daddy is? Do you think he killed my mama?" Rhonda Jr. whispered.

"I don't know, but I aim to find out," Deana said.

The story was out, the silence had fallen on them. Birdie was crying, they were all weeping. That could have been her, could have been a thousand women. The Harmons weren't going to hurt her. They wanted her help. We are all Harmons, we are all harmed, she thought.

"It never changes. It never does." Deana sighed.

It was the same sad voice Birdie had heard in her own aunt Zip. While men are off to war, or hiding in the woods, deserters and soldiers, deputies and barn poachers, women are left in the kitchen to cook the food, raise the children, to keep the world alive while men are so damn busy tearing it down. Women sing the murder ballads, tell the legends, they tend the home fires and the histories. "If you sing it, means you survived it," Aunt Zip used to say.

Birdie had an idea. She turned to the teenage girl. Mascara running down her face, she looked for all the world like a forlorn raccoon.

"I know you like to sing, and I've heard your voice out on the sidewalk."

"Yeah?" The hard suspicious face softened. A little girl hid beneath all that bravado, behind the dyed hair, the goth mascara.

"If you teach me how to vape, can I teach you some old songs?"

21

R oy was sadly right. Coweetsee was seeing a crime wave. Widow Jenkins over in Sycamore Shoals found the glass busted in her kitchen door, her pantry rifled through, the mattress in her bedroom upended, someone looking for her loot. Jimmy Lee up in the Yonah community had someone break the padlock on his metal shed and make off with $5,000 worth of tools. From Beulah to Beaverdam, and the townships in between, folks locked their doors with loaded shotguns set by the threshold.

Cancro and his men came out and dutifully filled out reports, but no arrests are made. The likeliest suspect had not been caught red-handed. Yet.

Charlie Clyde was no longer thumbing rides along the river road and up the ridgetop curves. Some had seen him barreling about in a Ford pickup, the bed piled with scrap wood, timbers hanging ten feet out the tailgate with a red bandanna nailed all legal to the end, as if to ward off the evil eye of state troopers and Cancro's clueless deputies. None of the proper authorities thought to stop that good old white boy to inquire about the legitimacy of the load. No one bothered to inspect the lumber, chestnut felled a century ago and hand-hewn, invaluable to certain connoisseurs of the Appalachian authentic, the American Grain.

But Charlie Clyde's long shadow could be a bright spot for Roy's campaign, Gene kept saying. Folks would come to their senses and vote in someone like Roy. Four years of an outsider was a long enough mistake. Time to put Coweetsee on its right track, restore the kinship of the old kingdom. Common sense and decency. Not a police state, and high-handed manners. Instead of busting anyone for break-ins, Cancro had pinched poor Birdie Price on a trumped-up possession charge.

"I warned Birdie about that weed. I ain't getting in the middle of that mess." Roy wagged his chin.

"Cancro's pissing off everybody. And that doesn't pay in Coweetsee," Gene said.

Roy sat with his campaign crew at the Mickey D's for the latest update and strategy session.

Their financials weren't looking good, compared to the competition.

Dylan figured that Cancro had amassed a war chest already of at least $10,000, gauging from all the roadside signs. Roy was tempted to pull over and yank a few out or plug a few holes in the "o" of "Cancro" with his pistol, but he resisted the temptation.

Advertising was a new wrinkle for local politics. Used to be in Maurice's time, elections were waged by word of mouth and dollars changing hands. It was bad form to put a man's name out in front of your house, same as if you put your church denomination on your mailbox. Exceptions were made for those insistent and troubled souls who wanted to nail Jesus Save signs on the trees, next to the No Trespassing posts.

"Who can afford ten grand?" Roy cried.

"Cancro can, sitting on that big nest egg up in his mansion, looking down on all of us," cried Cutworm.

"Money talks," Gene added. "Too bad, you couldn't get W. D. to weigh in on your side."

"I'm not begging that old buzzard again."

"But he's the kingmaker, the man with the money," Dwight said.

W. D. hadn't been afraid to sell off his birthright, as that ridge overlooking Meadow Fork had gotten him a pretty penny when the developers bought it and turned into the second homes for the rich.

"I hear W. D. might be in the market, swapping up lots and lands along the interstate. That old buzzard knows when the next new thing could line his pocket," Gene explained.

"Shame to see all those barns and farms go by the wayside," Roy said.

"We can't afford nostalgia now. Fact is, the future's coming hard at us, and there's money to be made soon," Gene said. "Whoever wins this next campaign can damn well make sure that some of that new money gets into the pockets of regular folks and not just the few."

The future and its uncertainties intimidated Roy. He could grasp the past and its politics when Maurice effortlessly campaigned by riding around the county, just jawboning his constituents. Politics ain't for pussies, Maurice used to say, but then again Maurice didn't have any organized opposition for four or five elections, only write-ins for Jesus or once for Charlie Clyde, ballots he kept in his desk drawer and pulled out for laughs from his deputies.

Now the old man lay staring at the ceiling of his room in Laurel Trace, seemingly unwilling to lift even a little finger to help his chief deputy continue his legacy in Coweetsee. How unfair, Roy thought.

"Seems a shame we can't just hand out money like in the old days," Cutworm said.

"Shame is you couldn't keep your mouth shut around an Atlanta reporter," Gene hissed.

The pretty blond reporter had sashayed into town as sweet as she could be, just wanting to do a "color piece" on quaint Coweetsee and its notorious non-stop voting. She'd stopped in Cutworm's feed store, asking his opinion on how dollars were distributed before every local election.

"Folks generally appreciated a little folding money around the holidays. Why I recollect the election seasons when candidates stood right yonder on the courthouse steps and took bids just like it was an auction."

"Do tell," she said all innocently, quickly doing her prim shorthand in a flip notebook. "And how do you spell your last name.

"M-A-B-E, first name Carl, but folks here call me Cutworm."
Cutworm had not realized the reporter was going to repeat his every word for readers across the civilized South. She
returned to hot 'Lanta, wrote a front-page Sunday story on
corruption in Coweetsee, the worst case of vote buying since
Chicago, according to the district US attorney.

History had caught up with the kingdom and wrote an end
to Maurice Posey's long reign.

"Remember how politicians used to do their politicking at
church dinners?" Dewey said.

"Not as many folks going to church these days. Sad to say."

"How about an old-fashioned pig picking?" Jimmie Lee
suggested.

Everyone looked shocked that Jimmie Lee had come up
with a solid idea.

"What?" Jimmie Lee said. "Who doesn't like barbecue?"

"That's not a half-bad idea," Gene said.

"Can't buy their votes no more," Cutworm said. "Nothing in
the law says we can't fill their bellies."

"We can put out tip jars for donations."

Dewey said he would check on the rental from the Ruritans.
Jimmy Lee would enlist the cooks to roast the pig. Dylan would
start printing out the fliers to nail to posts and slip under windshield wipers of the cars and trucks parked at the dollar store
on the bypass.

"Make the case for your candidacy. Tell them why you're the
best man," Gene said.

"People know me," Roy said.

"But here's your chance to say a few words to close the deal."

"You mean, like a speech?" Roy blanched at the idea of public speaking. He wasn't Maurice Posey, who could talk until the
moon waxed full and waned dark.

"Yes. Doesn't have to be long. We can find other fellers to
sing your praises."

"How about some music?" Dylan asked.

Cutworm reckoned he could find some fellers to pluck banjo and bow a fiddle.

"We'll need more than that." Gene abruptly snapped his fingers. "I know. Suppose you get Birdie to sing. Remember how folks used to tear up over that sweet voice of hers?"

"I don't know if she'll want to help. We are exes after all."

Gene groaned. "You want to win this thing or not?"

"I'll talk to her," Roy said, but he wasn't looking forward to the conversation, and another argument against him running for high office. They hadn't really gotten past that blow-up about the ballot box. Now he'd have to get into it with her again.

"We're all set then." Gene had his tight-lipped smile now. "Maybe we have a chance after all."

22

Birdie was hurrying down the hall at Laurel Trace, so much on her mind these days, not paying attention, when she nearly bumped into the man closing Maurice Posey's door.

"Watch where you're going," W. D. Clark said, startled himself.

They sidestepped each other cautiously.

Birdie rushed into Zip's room and closed the door quietly behind her, suddenly shaking. "Speak of the devil. I just saw W. D. Clark coming out of Maurice's room."

"Thought I heard someone over there talking to the sheriff, but I couldn't make out what they were saying. First thought it was Roy. He comes by occasionally, but I usually hear them laughing."

Birdie took her usual chair. "Wonder what those two are up to?"

"No good if you ask me. But I'm sure it's about money."

Zip told how W. D. Clark had been a lifelong bachelor, too cheap to marry a local girl and provide for a family, though he had taken his pleasure where and when he wanted. All of Coweetsee believed he must have a fortune stashed somewhere in his barns or buried in his many fields.

"They say now he's buying up all the lots around the exits on new highway." Birdie shared the gossip.

"Lord, just what we need. More of them chain restaurants. Home cooking's going to go by the wayside in Coweetsee," Zip said.

"W. D. still gives me the willies. He came by the historical society and just about called me a liar to my face."

"He was always an ornery man. I wouldn't pay him a bit of

mind," Zip said. "You came to sing, didn't you, not just talk?"

"What are you in the mood for today?" Birdie asked her aunt.

"We ain't done 'The Twa Sisters' in a while."

They started with a hum to find the right key. "No pitch it higher," Zip reminded her. Starting too low would drive you down into a hole, until it sounded like gargling gravel deep into your throat. Then they would set off, pulling the words and the song between them. Zip first, and then Birdie repeating the couplet, taking turns with the refrain.

A farmer he lived in the West Country,
And he had daughters, one, two and three.
And I'll be true to my love
If my love'll be true to me.

As they were walking by the river's brim,
The eldest pushed the youngest in,
And I'll be true to my love
If my love'll be true to me.

O sister, O sister, pray give me thy hand
And I'll give thee both house and land,
And I'll be true to my love
If my love'll be true to me.

I'll neither, I'll neither give thee hand nor glove
Unless thou give me thy own true love,
And I'll be true to my love
If my love'll be true to me.

Birdie couldn't believe the words they were singing, how men could act so cruelly toward their girlfriends, bashing them on the head and throwing them in the river. It was even worse when women turned on each other, all over the love of a man. Like Rhonda Jr. and Melody the other day, or her and Teresa Honeycutt ages ago.

The song kept going. What kind of sister throws her blond sibling into the river, even if she did steal the handsome knight?

The verses wended onward—how her body floated to shore where two minstrels found her. They made a harp from her breastbone and strung the terrible instrument with her blond hair. Then they played their morbid instruments to guilt the dark-haired sister in her father's castle. "In terror sits the black-haired bride." That line wormed into Birdie's brain. In terror, she sat these days, not black-haired as before, no longer a bride. She was a widow accompanied only by her darkest fears.

They were between songs, catching their breath, a chance to catch up on life, which never seemed to stop for a history museum director or a Laurel Trace nursing home resident.

"Something eating you today, girl?"

"What? nothing." Birdie had been lost in the rock face out the window, searching for the two chipmunks scurrying among the moss and weeds.

"You done forgot half the words. I'm supposed to be the old one here, losing my memory."

Birdie had been dreading this moment when Zip would see through her, and she would have to come clean.

"Something bad happened. I did something bad."

"It ain't like when you painted my cat green?"

Once when she was six or so on Zip's porch, entertaining herself while Zip was in the kitchen, she had found a brush and a can of housepaint and wondered what old Tom the calico might look green. Cat wasn't pleased and hissed, but Birdie kept slinging paint onto his fur, until the poor creature looked more like the Grinch than the Cat in the Hat in Birdie's Dr. Seuss readers. That was also the one and last time that Zip blistered her bottom, though it was likely only an angry swat or two at her backside.

"No, I got arrested."

"Lord, girl. What were you doing?" Zip wondered.

Birdie relived the whole shameful incident, blow by blow. She kept her head down, confessing her guilt, wringing her hands raw in her lap. She just wanted her great-aunt's forgiveness, but knew she was not worthy.

"Shoot, girl, ain't the end of the world." Zip was grinning.

"But no one in our family's ever been arrested."

"You had great-uncles and great-aunts too that showed their asses sometimes. More than a few Sherrills ran afoul of the sheriff when it came to corn liquor. Marijuana, if you ask me, is more natural than moonshine."

"I did go apologize to the Harmons for getting Rhonda Jr. in trouble."

"It's a wonder Deana didn't bless you out."

"She was very decent about it. She did fill me in about what had happened to her sister and her with those men. That poor Rhonda Jr. just sat there, about to bawl."

"Those girls were treated badly." Zip nodded. "Shame how they all turned out."

"I can't believe Cancro is making me go to court, plead guilty to the whole shebang."

"Did you talk to Roy Boy? He might could get you off."

"He's mad at me about that old ballot box," Birdie said.

"Good Lord, girl, y'all used to be married. He owes you something, doesn't he?"

"Roy says bringing up all that history, he says might mess up his campaign for sheriff." Birdie shook her head. "It's always politics. People getting hurt."

"You take after your daddy," Zip said. "A sensitive soul."

As county extension agent hired by the state, her father had tried to steer clear of local power struggles. "The rain falls equally on the just and the unjust. It ain't political if the creek comes up and washes out your land." Blue mold didn't care if a tobacco farmer went for Shad or for Maurice.

But being neutral was not an option in the kingdom of Coweetsee, and Maurice had had enough sway that soon enough, Birdie's father found himself sharing office space in the Ag Extension building on the bypass with a young cousin of the Posey's, a callow youth who hadn't even been down to the State University, but who was soon throwing his weight around, handing out copies of *Progressive Farmer* and hawking fertilizer and pesticides from a favored contractor. Urging them to clearcut their timber, sell off the land, if they could, for top dollar and new tract housing of shoddy drywall and brittle two-by-fours. "When they get that new interstate open, it's going to be a killing and you don't want to miss out."

Boy didn't know about runoff, soil erosion, much less blue mold. You didn't hear about blue mold since tobacco went by the wayside with the settlement.

It about killed her daddy, seeing how Coweetsee couldn't raise a decent crop of anything but corrupt weeds it seemed. He died of heartbreak at age sixty-four, forced out of his career, just shy of retirement.

Birdie couldn't keep from biting her knuckle.

"But that's not all, is it? Tell me the rest, child."

"What do you mean?"

Aunt Zip kept pressing. "You haven't been yourself in quite a while, not since that man of your heart passed."

"Oh god." Birdie let herself go, her face in her hands, her shoulders heaving.

Birdie often felt herself choking since Talmadge had— Since Talmadge, oh Talmadge… She couldn't say the final, fatal word aloud, much less admit into her rattled mind the fact of his death. She had lain with his cold body and knew in her marrow that he was truly gone. Dead, dead, dead. But then she had forgotten, at times calling into the next room to share a tidbit she had unearthed in her endless research, before catching herself, furiously shaking her head, squinching her eyes against any tears, as was the habit of the hard women in her family. Now came the time for the truth.

"He didn't just die on his own."

Zip was rubbing her hand. "It's all right. It's fine, girl."

"He asked and I helped."

"Of course, you helped. You're a good girl."

"Zip, I killed Tal," she wailed out loud, a confession that sailed out the open door and down the hall for anyone in Laurel Trace to hear.

"No." Zip gripped her hand. "Keep your voice down, girl."

"I killed him. I killed my husband."

"Hush now." The old woman took her sobbing niece in her scrawny arms. "Hush now."

When Birdie could collect herself, she wiped her eyes with the backs of her hands until Zip handed her the box of tissues at her bedside.

"Now tell me what you did," the old woman ordered.

She went into the details, the extra doses of drugs that Shawanda had been able to secure for her, how they had drank that last bottle of wine, and she had given him the final overdose, how Sheriff Cancro had come by, somewhat suspicious of the circumstances, why Talmadge hadn't been in the hospital but conveniently died in his sleep. People were talking about her. She was guilty.

"Listen to me, honey. The cancer killed your man. You were only helping him, relieving his pain. There's no crime there. I did much the same when it came the time for my daddy."

"No," Birdie said. "Really?"

"Morphine." Zip nodded. "It's hard, but you're not the first, and you won't be the last."

The old woman reached over, her liver-spotted hand patting Birdie's hand.

"I do have a favor to ask of you," Birdie said.

"Name it, girl."

"I told Rhonda Jr. that she should learn the old ballads you taught me. Do you mind if I bring her by, even if she is a Harmon?"

"She don't bite, does she?"

"She punched me, but she didn't get her teeth in me," Birdie said.

"If you think it's a good idea, bring her by. We'll see how she does."

"Thanks, Zip."

Kezia knocked softly at the half-open door. "You'uns doing okay? I don't hear much singing today."

"Guess we ain't in the mood," Zip said.

"Maybe a nap then. We don't want you to get too tired out," Kezia said.

"That might help her." Zip hooked her crooked thumb in Birdie's direction. "She forgets all the words."

"I'll do better next time," Birdie promised.

After Birdie said her goodbyes, she found Kezia loitering in the hallway, waiting for a word with her former schoolteacher.

"Ms. Price, I'm worried about my mama. You need to go see her. She was all upset the other night when she called and said there had been a problem at the church."

23

Shawanda? Are you okay?" Birdie crept carefully into the studio, almost afraid of what she would find after Kezia's warning.

Sitting amid her fabrics and pieces, her hands useless in her lap, everything scattered around her, her friend stared off into a middle distance, lost to herself.

"You look like you seen a ghost," Birdie said.

"Charlie Clyde," Shawanda said, her voice echoing in the old classroom. "You won't believe it. He came to the church last night."

"Oh my Lord." Birdie took a seat, and like Aunt Zip would do, reached across the table and held her friend's hand, laced her fingers, white into black. "Go ahead. I'm here. Tell me what happened."

"I can't believe he came to the church, not after what he'd done."

Birdie squeezed her hand.

Shawanda shook her head, the beads clattering in her beautiful braids, but she began to talk.

Wednesday nights, we look forward to a chance for us to sit and cool our tired dogs, after another week of chasing after grandchildren and babies who need feeding or money or a good whipping, always needing us. My fingers get so pinched and tingling from poking that silver needle into swatches all day, it feels like my hands are on fire.

But Wednesday nights I can flip through those thin pages of my auntie's old Bible and rest myself. So can Rowena and Lucille and Minnie and Claudine. We close our eyes and pray Jesus, Lord Jesus. The new church, the one we built after our old sanctuary was torched, was a million-dollar miracle, as our pastor likes to say. With no insulation, the old church was a freezer in the winter and hot as Hades in the summer. Now our new place hums with warmth in the bitter months, and then clicks over to air-conditioning to cool off women of a certain age. And the windows, what wonderful windows. Instead of those warped, cracked panes we used to have, where all you could see was the meanness of Coweetsee County, we installed a nice gold pebbled glass, like you could see into the foyer of heaven.

We're studying on Black women in the Bible. In the book of Ruth, how the Moabite woman would become the double great-grandma of King David and later Jesus. Moses married an Ethiopian. "I'll bet she could cook." "Do Hebrews eat biscuits?" "Are biscuits unleavened bread?" "Maybe cornbread is." "Mmhumm."

Just us women sitting and learning and sharing with each other a bit of the peace that you get sitting in a good solid church. Minnie who always wears that handmade fabric blossom on her big bosom, a sign that her life is still blooming and good, even though she has diabetes now, and is going blind with glaucoma, but not before she saw her man run off with a loose woman and her sons sent off to prison. She's seen a hard life, but she's kept the faith.

And the doors open and tap-tap-tap in comes you know who. Charlie Clyde takes a seat in the last pew, spreading his arms out like wings along the wooden back.

"Can we help you? We're having our prayer circle."

"Then you don't mind a guest now. Door was open. I could use a prayer or two."

"Why, welcome then." That was Minnie.

No one says what was on our minds, a young white man fresh out of prison coming to pray with a room of old Black women (and me, I was the youngest). Minnie had touched my hand. "Where were we now?"

We go on with the reading, like that terrible smiling white

man ain't there with us. That was the longest hour we spent in prayer, and I could hear every page turn of the onionskin Bibles, like it was our own skin shedding, and the goosebumps went up my flesh. What was he doing there? Would it be Christian to ask him to leave? Did he have a gun, did he aim to kill us? And if I thought hard, maybe he would simply set fire to our church once more, burn us all up.

That was the longest Bible study I ever sat through. We say our prayers as usual for our kids, our country, for the county, going through the long list of the afflicted, and those in need. And when we pray, I keep my eyes open and Charlie Clyde sitting there, with that smirk on his face, looking straight at me.

Amen, prayer answered. Time we get the hell out of there.

"See you Sunday. Have a good week."

Charlie Clyde holds the door for us to leave, and I'm at the last of the line, fishing the key out of my purse to lock up.

"Listen, can we just talk?" he asks. "In private."

"I'll be all right," I tell the ladies who drifted down the steps to their cars in the parking lot, leaving me and that monster in front of our sanctuary. My hands are shaking as I turn the deadbolt in the door.

It was my turn to unload on that monster. "How dare you come here? This place is holy."

"I didn't mean to scare you ladies none."

"After what you done to LeRoy?"

My uncle LeRoy was bad to drink and even as kids, we caught a whiff of the whiskey on his breath when we went to hug him. He'd sit and smile and laugh on the front porch, and I never saw him tip the bottle. He kept that out in the car. He was family and the women all wagged their heads over him. But he loved us all even if he didn't love his own life. It was likely a coincidence and not any judgment he passed out in that church pew.

But no man, even dead drunk, deserves to be burned alive.

"Look here, I'm sorry about that deacon, but that wasn't my doing."

"You did the deed. You had a trial," I tell Charlie Clyde.

My cousin, Alyssa, testified at the trial. She had been working at the Gas 'n' Go out on the bypass that summer night when Charlie Clyde came in. He bought his usual, an RC Cola and a pack of roast peanuts, gave the Black girl a leer and the usual guff. "Hey, good-looking, how tricks?"

Alyssa gave him his change, but kept silent, waiting for him to leave. There was a pay phone outside the convenience store. Maurice was able to get the good folks at what was then Ma Bell to trace the 911 call that came at 10:07 p.m. from that very location. Caller used the N-word, said our church was on fire. It was too late when the trucks got there, and LeRoy's remains weren't found in the ash until the morrow.

"I was framed." Charlie Clyde's hot breath is in my face. "I'm telling you it was Maurice Posey."

"Why should anyone believe you and your record?"

"Exactly. That made me the perfect pasty. Think about it. Why would I go and burn up a church for free?"

"I'll tell you the hard truth. You torched my church. You murdered my kin. You deserved what you got. And you're not welcome here."

I walk away. I have my car keys in my hand, ready to gouge his eyes if he follows me to the car. Least I didn't hear that tap-tap-tap of his shoes coming after me.

After Shawanda finished her story, the two women both took a deep breath.

"Did you call the law?" Birdie said. "Report him?"

"And say what? There was a white man at our church?"

"I can't believe he's never once changed his story in all these years. Even his sister, you know what happened to her the first time Charlie Clyde got into trouble, even Deana insists he's innocent."

"You can't trust a one of those Harmons. We all know him, what he's done. Trying to turn the blame on Maurice."

"But I mean—Maurice—he didn't turn out to be exactly a saint, now did he?" Birdie said. "He did plead guilty and go to prison."

"Maybe so, but Maurice was the only one who looked after our church. Everybody thinks he stole the election. Nobody remembers he got Black folk to vote for him."

Shawanda shook the long braids of her hair, the bright beads in the weave, clattering their disapproval. "I tell you if Shad Smathers had been in power, they wouldn't even have bothered to arrest anybody white for the crime. At least Maurice made sure Charlie Clyde served time."

"No, you're right," Birdie conceded. "I'd still say something. You might need protection at the church."

"I talked to Minnie after. She said we just need to pray, but she always says that." Shawanda bowed her head, the braids falling across her face like a black veil. "All I know is, praying ain't going to bring back LeRoy."

"That was so sad," Birdie said.

"Sad ain't the word. It was unjust, unfair. It was just wrong. LeRoy never hurt a soul. He just drank too much."

And Shawanda rubbed her eyes with the heels of her hands, trying to wipe away the angry tears.

"But it's supposed to be God's will, and who am I to argue with the Almighty? Pastor says all things work out in the end, but I don't believe that. I have hate in my heart, and I can't forgive the man who burned up LeRoy asleep in the Holy of Holies. I just pray that Charlie Clyde will leave us all be."

"Amen," Birdie said.

24

As the election drew closer, Roy kept making his campaign rounds, knocking at doors, asking for votes, like the old days with Maurice. Few folks answered the doors or seemed very receptive. "Good talking with you, Roy" was as far as many would go. After the conversation, going down the steps, climbing into his jeep, Roy was never sure if he had their vote or not.

He had a habit now of driving up the gravel lane to Birdie's cabin. For what? he wondered, other than to make sure no one other than himself was snooping around, someone like Charlie Clyde. He'd heard about the commotion at the New Nebuchadnezzar Church when Charlie Clyde had crashed the Bible study and terrorized those poor church ladies.

Birdie was never home but down at the historical society, showing off that damn ballot box, as if that proved something about past politics. Roy still fretted that tainted history would cast a pall over his campaign, his bid to restore the rightful law and order to the kingdom.

Roy sat uninvited on her porch swing, the chains creaking under his guilty conscience. He lifted his boots from the floorboards and felt himself glide through the afternoon air.

It was so pretty up here. Roy could see the two of them sitting side by side on the swing, maybe having an iced tea, admiring the valleys to the far ridges and the sun making its way down. And the crickets would come up and the clouds would float by, and the world would be all right. They wouldn't have to say a word to each other, they would know how blessed it is to be breathing this mountain air.

He shrugged, shook off that fantasy. Birdie had made her dream life with Talmadge, not him.

They had tried. They grew up together, childhood sweethearts playing house in that bungalow always in need of paint, set hard against the road with the cracked concrete steps. A starter house for a broken home.

He had been so busy, patrolling the county with Maurice, and she was dog-tired teaching young'uns. They would both come home and collapse in front of the TV, too tired to say much to each other. They'd wrestle beneath the sheets, taking out their frustrations with their bodies on each other, mistaking that for love.

Told her too much when they were married. Maybe listening to his worst fears was more than their marriage could bear, those vows to love and protect and cherish, under the weight of all that's wrong in this world. Bringing the worst dregs of humanity home with him whenever they worked a killing or car crash. Coweestee didn't have the crime of big cities but he still saw some rough things that would haunt any thinking man. He would bring that bad news home, like he had stepped in a big pile of shit and tracked it right into the house.

Then one day, it seemed out of the blue, she turned to him and said what he didn't know he'd been waiting to hear. "This isn't working out between us, Roy Boy."

Roy couldn't argue. Pinned to the mat, you can only slap your hand and surrender, walk off with your head down while the cheers go to the other guy.

Still, it was nice up here, this place she had made into a dream life with the hippie. Solar panels on the roof, they could go off the grid, never have to pay another bill to the rural co-op.

He looked down the long slope. Last time he was up here, that redbud had been in bloom, the first sign of spring. Bright scarlet, like blood against the bare trees, it still stabbed his memory. Now the trees showed that tired overgrown green of late summer. The first colors of autumn were still weeks away, but the weather was uncertain these days. The seasons getting later or earlier, less predictable. Even the climate was changing in Coweetsee, they said.

Her lawn needed mowing. More of a meadow. Looked like

it hadn't been touched since Talmadge had passed, losing his fight against the cancer. Snakes and the like could creep right up to her.

Roy opened her work shed, nothing locked up. He checked the riding tractor, a vintage John Deere. The key, of course, left in the ignition, an invitation to any thief or trespasser, including an ex-husband. He sat on its bouncing metal seat, probably last warmed by his rival's skinny backside. Reach down, set the choke, turn the key. Nothing. He got off and checked the battery cables, tried again, and it roared to life.

Off he went, across the gravel, then lowered the blades, the green smell of slaughtered grass shot away in the wake of the mower. It would take a few passes; the grass had grown so high and tall, it nearly choked the blades, which probably needed sharpening, but he mowed on.

There is something meditative about machinery. Roy had never been a farmer, nor his people, but he could see the attraction, riding up and down, going back and forth, on the slope of the hill, careful on the turns. Easy enough to tip the tractor on top of him. Roy had seen more than a few good old boys, maybe a little too liquored up, make that fatal mistake.

But this was just a riding mower, not a full-fledged harvest machine. He should be able to manage. Maybe Birdie would appreciate the gesture.

It would also signal to anyone else that Roy was here, that her house was not unguarded.

Even with the vibrations of the engine below him, Roy couldn't shake the sense that someone or something was circling Birdie. He worried about her up here all by her lonesome, a target for the likes of Charlie Clyde and other men whose eyes squint and their brows furrow when they see a good-looking woman. They scheme for her favors, whether they come consensually or by the merciless hand clapped over her screaming red mouth.

Someone needed to protect Birdie, to have her back, when she didn't even know how easily someone could sneak up on her.

In his mowing mediations, he kept going over his worst fears and old regrets. Too bad he couldn't help her out of her drug charge. He'd made things worse between Birdie and himself when he'd arrested Talmadge Price on the exact same charge.

Roy had been patrolling Meadow Fork out past Clark's Mercantile, when he saw the VW Beetle parked off the road, near the creek and the sagging bridge. At least the boy was bright enough not to have driven across this half-rotted timber, lest his little tin bug had fallen in the water.

He had parked and walked over the bridge into the field, the cicadas singing August heat. Sure enough, that long-haired fellow was rooting around the stalls and corn cribs of the abandoned Newell barn.

"Hey, you know you're trespassing, don't you?" There were no signs posted to that effect, but the fields were owned by W. D. Clark, who disliked anyone messing in his business.

"I was studying the architecture. They don't make 'em like this anymore."

Roy liked arguing with him, just for the hell of it. "What you like so much about barns? Not one of these fellers putting one up would think it was worth all the trouble you're making about them. I never did see anybody take a picture of their barn and put it on the wall next to their great-granddaddy."

"They might when they're all gone," Talmadge countered. "And look what I found inside."

He was hauling out a wooden chest with the No. 13 on the side. At the time, Roy didn't pay it much mind. He was more concerned with making Talmadge Price pay.

"This ain't finders-keepers. You best put that back where you found it and go home."

Roy waited for him by the VW, as Talmadge came out slapping at some mosquitoes or chiggers. Any fool that goes on wearing shorts in an uncut meadow is going to get his ass eaten up, and it was fun to see him in discomfort.

"You give my best to Birdie," Roy said.

He waited until Talmadge got into the car and switched it on.

"Talmadge, this ain't personal, but I'm going to have to ask you to turn off that engine and step out of the car. You've got something suspicious in that ashtray."

Talmadge squinted. "I'm not sure this is exactly a legal search." Roy sat down behind the wheel and pulled out a roach and clip. "And this sure as hell ain't a legal substance."

&

Maurice arched one eyebrow when Roy marched his handcuffed prisoner into the office and back to the lockup. "Sure you want to be doing this, son? I understand entirely but I'm not sure your ex will. I wouldn't want to get on her bad side if I were you."

Talmadge called from the payphone with the quarter that Roy gave him. Everyone in the office could listen to the awkward conversation.

"Sweetheart, you need to come get me. Roy says it's a hundred dollar bail if I don't want to spend the night here."

Birdie stormed down and shot daggers at everyone inside the office, but saved her fiercest fire for her ex.

"What's your problem? Can't you leave us alone?"

"Just enforcing the law. Can't look the other way just because we used to be married, you know," Roy explained, but even as he said it, he knew it sounded lame. So he had to add: "What do you expect hanging out with a hippie?"

"Maybe he's more interesting a man than you ever were," she fired back.

Roy knew that Talmadge was a trust fund baby, never had to really work a day in his life, so he didn't feel like he was hurting Birdie financially when she had to pay the cash bail.

Talmadge was court-ordered to perform community service and spent a month of weekends wearing a fluorescent orange vest on the side of the road, stabbing bits of foam cups and emptied beer cans from the ditch alongside the main highway.

Pickups flying by would leave hoots and hollers or throw another can or two out the window for Talmadge's collection. Birdie burned with shame for her husband, but Talmadge proved nonplussed. "Paying my debt to society, such as it is, in these parts." He kept trying to develop a drawl.

Thinking back, Roy winced. He felt like such a small and petty man at times.

After about half an hour, the meadow looked more like a lawn, scalped in places, but at least the march of weeds had been slowed somewhat. He rode into the shed and cut the engine. Roy's ears rang, and his buttocks still vibrated when he dismounted the seat.

All that bouncing around up and down, his stomach had not sat well with his lunch, a greasy hamburger, Carolina style with chili and slaw, down at the diner. Suddenly, now urgently, he had to go. Birdie's house was locked up tight, and it wasn't like he had a key.

He made like a bear ambling down through the woods. Nature's call.

After he finished his business, cleaned himself with leaves, making sure it wasn't poison ivy, he went on downhill, hoisting his trousers, tucking his shirttail. But the slope was steeper than he suspected, and he was going faster than he wanted, then a tree root reached out, and he felt his ankle roll and something snap and down he went, rolling down the hill, yelling. He rolled off the bank and onto the gravel road.

He lay on his backside, tears in his eyes, a sudden sick feeling in his gut, shock as his consciousness swam to and fro.

Then Birdie was leaning over him, shaking his shoulder. "Roy Boy. What're you doing in the middle of my drive?"

Birdie was a wiry woman but more bone than muscle. She couldn't lift him. He sat upright and with his good leg pushed himself, scooting on the seat of his pants through the gravel to the passenger side of her tiny VW Beetle, then lifted himself, kicking his injured ankle against the door as he maneuvered his heft inside. He nearly vomited with the searing pain.

She drove him out of the kingdom of Coweetsee over to the urgent care in Asheville that everybody went to when the injury was dire. Roy blushing red, ashamed that Birdie had found him, grateful that she was helping.

Birdie was exasperated. "You'd think a grown man would know better. What were you doing here?"

"I dropped by to ask you something. Thought I'd mow your yard while I was waiting."

"No, I mean, how did you wind up face down on my road?"

"Um, slipped and fell. Clumsy me." Roy didn't want to get into the intimate details of his bowel distress, how he'd lost his balance on the slope, trying to get his pants up.

"Thanks for mowing my lawn, but no one asked you." She gripped the wheel, stared straight ahead. "I thought you were mad at me, about the ballot box, about everything, you know."

"No, I'm not mad," Roy lied.

Mad, angry, hurt—those weren't the right words. Betrayed is what he felt, about her and Talmadge, a long dull resentment that wore at him every day for the past fifteen years, since she gave up on him and their marriage.

"Water over the bridge." He waved his hand and looked out the window.

"Under the bridge. The saying is water under the bridge."

"Over, under, whatever."

"Sorry," she relented. "It's the schoolteacher in me."

Why, oh why did this woman always want to argue with him, point out his every mistake? They remained the same people as they were twenty years before, still fighting the same battles. They rode in a frustrated silence.

"You mentioned a favor," Birdie remembered. "What is it?"

What he'd been dreading the whole afternoon from the time he drove up to her cabin to busting his ankle on the slope to riding shotgun in this tiny clown car in this whole shit show. How he hated asking for help.

"We're planning a campaign fundraiser at the Ruritan Hall. Gene thought it would be nice if you sang something, maybe one of your ballads."

"Gene thought that, huh? What do you think?"

"Me?"

"Good god, Roy, why is carrying on a conversation with you like talking to a doorknob?" She glared at him. "Do you think it would be nice if I sang?"

"Lord, Birdie, you know I've always thought you had the sweetest voice. I'd love it if you sang for us."

Yet this didn't feel like a regular sprain, and the pain was getting worse. His whole foot seemed to be swelling like a pink balloon in his brogan. He made the mistake of trying to adjust his weight in the tiny seat and managed to kick the floorboard again with his injured foot, sending a shooting pain through his leg, and he cried out. "Why you driving this little clown car, anyhow?"

"Reminds me of Tal," she said.

"Hippie-mobile. Made for midgets." He fumed but she only smiled.

"Hold on, we'll get you looked after." She patted his thigh, almost friendly like, then removed her hand as if she thought better.

He appreciated that small gesture, that moment of mercy for a man in all types of pain. His spirits rose a notch or two, even if his foot felt like the devil himself was turning that limb on a rotisserie in hell.

X-rays showed more than just the sprain he was praying for.

Orthopedic doctor said that he had torn some ligaments and broken the bones in his ankle and foot, and they put him into a thick black boot. Roy wouldn't be able to put any of his two-hundred-eighty pounds on the delicate bones for a while. He wasn't supposed to drive, since he couldn't really feel the gas pedal or brake, let alone the clutch of his jeep.

"But I'm running for sheriff."

"No running, no walking. Stay off that foot if you want to heal," the doctor ordered.

Roy was off the campaign trail for a spell, laid up at the house. Gene and Dylan dropped by with updates on contributions, yard signs, the occasional calls at their headquarters. Plans were progressing for the big fundraiser at the Ruritan Hall.

"We're not licked yet," Gene insisted. "We may even get the sympathy vote. Everybody's heard about your bum foot. They feel sorry for you."

"I don't need any pity," Roy fumed.

"If pity gets you elected sheriff, then you'll be dancing a jig on that bad ankle come Christmas," Gene said.

25

Coweetsee was looking mighty different these days. More landmarks had simply disappeared. Driving home, Birdie had seen a hole in the landscape where the Newell barn seemed to have collapsed overnight and then been cleared, even without a recent wind or bad rain.

She climbed her gravel grade, parked at the porch, and turned the key. The VW engine promptly cut out. Impulsively, she pulled her phone from her tote bag and dialed the sheriff's department, asking for Frank Cancro. There was a hold and then that Yankee voice came on: "Cancro here. Can I help you?"

Birdie launched into a tirade about missing barns, and that as a concerned citizen with the community watch program that Cancro himself had instituted, she thought it was her obligation to report what seemed like a series of crimes, and of course, it was his sworn duty to deliver some semblance of justice.

"Do you ever drive around this county? Patrol, I mean. If you did, Sheriff, you'd see there are things going on. Barns don't just walk off in the middle of the night."

"If you see something suspicious, please do call and we'll be more than happy to come out and investigate." Then that damn Yankee sheriff hung up on her.

Furiously, she unbuckled her seat belt and slammed her door and stormed into the empty house. She went straight to Tal's former darkroom, now stacked with the cardboard boxes of all his research, journals and photos documenting Coweetsee's thousands of barns.

Talmadge's journals—college-ruled composition books, sewn, not with those tacky cheap wire coils. Inside, his tight penmanship, terribly neat and precise, the Boy Scout, A-student achiever he had always been, despite his rebellious demeanor.

Talmadge Price came to Coweetsee in the early wave of hippiedom, with his Stewart Brand catalog and Foxfire books. She had daydreamed that Talmadge would whisk her away from this poor mountain life to a glamorous Big City. They would sit in coffeeshops, listening to acoustic music, Joni Mitchell tunes about love and regret. They would save the planet, recycle, hug trees, live at peace with all people, protest perhaps injustice and racism.

Instead, he wanted to stay put in these remote mountains, in love with the old ways.

Tal turned out to be a true Barn Believer, in love with the American Grain, and not against it, only the greedy politics that broke his soft heart. A rural romantic, he saw the care and the craft of simple men who could fell timbers, plane them smooth, and raise them into sturdy structures. He saw the poetry of chestnut-raftered cathedrals, naves filled with the folded brown wings of burley, like rows of roosting angels, and made his notes carefully.

She traced her finger along the lines of his fine handwriting, pretty cursive script, better than most of the students she'd taught. Talmadge's No. 2 pencil stub sketching out the particulars:

D. Nelson Anderson Bull Face Tobacco Barn (early 1900s). Out the Laurel Road, three miles from state line. Unusual placement bridging a steep swale. Ground brown and powdery with old tobacco. Timbers from nearby ridges, chestnut before the blight killed the most common tree in the 1920s. Used to store Bull Face tobacco, also called dark tobacco, with its dark green curly leaves. Smoke-cured by building a fire on the dirt of the barn. Fire often fed with apple culls or cherry bark for flavor. Sold as twists of chewing tobacco

Besides the notebooks, he had boxes filled with sheets of negatives and stacks of his darkroom black and whites, aiming to be the Ansel Adams or Stieglitz of Coweetsee barns.

Talmadge had talked of a coffee table book, a photographic

essay honoring the agricultural architecture, as fine in its rough-hewn way as the ancient wooden temples of Japanese Buddhist monasteries. And Birdie thought of pitching Tal's archives as a fundraiser for the Coweetsee County Historical Society, perhaps something they could sell at the old jail for more income. The old photos still caught her eye. They spoke to her of him, how he had swished the proofs in the chemical baths of developer and fixer. She could see where he had dodged and burned, brushed away shadows or focused more fiery light, trying to bring out rusted tin, weathered grain, even the tobacco dust hanging in the empty air.

Sometimes she saw his bucolic love affair as silly. What if she had gone to his native Chevy Chase and admired the architectural genius of two-car garages? Barns were one thing, but too bad he had never been good at shooting people.

They had once tried to shoot some nudes, but Birdie was dismayed at the results, his still lives of her breasts and hips and thighs, all the comely parts he said he loved. Loved like autopsy results, she thought. His lighting had made her look like a corpse. He had destroyed those proofs and the negatives, now to her terrible regret.

She'd lost the love of her life. She couldn't afford to lose all that he had loved.

That last night with Tal, sitting side by side on this porch swing, drinking the last of the chardonnay.

"What can you do? But go with it, I guess," Tal said, hunched over, his voice rasping.

"Or not," Birdie said more insistently, more loudly than she had intended.

Tal let go a long sigh, like he'd been saving up his last breath for hours. "You can't fight forever. I can't."

Birdie had kept her stubborn silence, biting at her thumbnail. Why would he give up so easily?

He was still trying to win her over.

"Why not go with the flow, with what is?"

He picked up the bottle of wine, studied the label in the porch light.

"A good year." He tipped the bottle toward her glass. "Let's finish it off."

"Easy for you to say." She was fighting back tears, a sob, wailing out into the night.

"No, it's not, babe. Not at all."

She sat alone on her porch swing, smoking her doobie, trying to treat her own rising anxieties. But the weed wasn't working as before. Birdie Barker Price couldn't forget. No mellow buzz in her forehead, but like an abyss opening below her abdomen, a falling sensation in her gut, her heart frantically beating faster.

She fretted over the Talmadge's beloved barns. In her dreams, those looming, leaning structures stood in fields, like lone elephants, their timbers weathered gray and grained like the hides of the great African animals she had seen in zoos and circuses, poached nearly to extinction, on heartrending TV commercials. The barns like those endangered beasts, who never forgot.

Now everyone was forgetting the barns, all but Birdie.

Tonight, that moon, how horribly bright, like a spotlight trained on the benighted world, the kingdom of Coweetsee. This would be the perfect night to steal away with a barn.

She could call Cancro again. I'm worried about the barn. Have you seen anything suspicious? No. I just can feel it.

Men were of no use.

She had to help Talmadge toward his own end, free him from his pain. She'd had to rescue Roy from her gravel drive after he tumbled down the slope and nearly broke his neck, but certainly busted his ankle. Who was going to rescue her, let alone the barns?

Zip had always warned her, "Worrying is but a prayer to the evil of tomorrow. Pick your blooms today before the frost and blight that's bound to be. One day you wake up, all dried out, a crone like me, all the juice of a full-hefted woman sucked right out of you, usually by the useless likes of menfolk."

Birdie gnawed at her knuckle. She'd better do something herself.

&

She found herself, driving down the gravel bend from her cabin, her tote bag packed and bouncing on the passenger seat. She didn't believe in premonition, signs, omens like Aunt Zip did—that a chicken laying an even number of eggs was a danger sign or that a broom that fell over as you walked by was bad luck. But she had an intuition she couldn't shake. Her gut was telling her something she couldn't ignore.

The Anderson barn, a cathedral of wormy chestnut, the high rafters, the smell of the ancient tobacco leaf, the powdery dirt in her memory, along with the shape, the heft, the warmth of Talmadge's naked body laid over her own. She could not live to see that place lost or defiled. Tonight, it was at risk.

She drove along the Laurel Road, past the log bridge that crossed the stream. She parked in the next bend and walked up the road. The moon bright overhead, showing her bruised face, all those craters and lunar dips two hundred thousand miles away from the lost and lonely kingdom of Coweetsee.

She hurried along lest a car come catch her in their headlights. What would Birdie Barker Price be doing out in the middle of the night, all by her lonesome? She broke into a run, then slowed in the shadow of the trees, working her way over the bridge. She hurried through the high field. She had put on blue jeans and boots, a sweatshirt to protect herself against briars. She went up the knoll behind the barn, to the tree line where she would have a view of the moonlit field.

She was not alone, she heard things in the sharp shadows. She froze when a roosting turkey flew up in the darkness, a great rush of wings that about stopped her heart.

Birdie settled with her spine against the rough trunk of a hemlock, cradled between the knees of its roots. She rubbed her hand against the deep-grained bark. She couldn't believe she was here, that she was doing this.

She nibbled nervously at a chocolate bar and sipped a diet soda she'd brought in her bag. A little caffeine to accompany the adrenaline. She didn't want to fall asleep; it might be a long watch ahead through the wee hours.

She'd closed her eyes, maybe for a second, when she heard the crunch of tires across the plank bridge. A truck and a car were coming through the field, with their headlights off, under the spotlight of the unbelievably bright moon. Four men stepped out on either side, leaving the doors open. They spoke quietly, but the drawl of their voices, their sharp curses carried across the field. She could hear tools clattered from the pickup bed.

Men maybe afraid of an honest day's labor, but more than happy to skulk around in the night, carrying off reclaimed wood, which could fetch a pretty penny on today's antique markets and house construction trades.

Birdie dug in the bottom of her knapsack where she had once carried her textbooks and lesson plans. Her palm wrapped against the dimpled grip of Zip's heavy snub nose revolver. She aimed the barrel into the darkness and pulled the stiff trigger. A shot at the stars, an explosion in the night that echoed against the ridges.

"Leave my barn be!" she hollered at the top of her lungs.

The men were running now, cursing, jumping in the truck and the car. She aimed at the truck and fired. The taillight went out. The car and the truck roared over the bridge and up the road, engines revving, tires squalling, getting the hell out of there.

Those men wouldn't likely be coming back tonight and the next, if they knew there was a sentinel, a shooter in the woods.

Her heart was racing behind her thin ribs. She felt fully alive, no longer afraid but exhilarated.

The night resumed, the crickets their midnight chorus.

Shouldering her bag with the warm gun, she thought she heard the groans of the timbers settling in the barn as she walked past, headed for her car and home.

PART IV

ELECTION SEASON

26

At the county's west side, two creeks flowed down opposite ridges and met in a confluence to create Meadow Fork, a long valley filled with pasture and homesteads, one of the prettier places left in Coweetsee until the developers bulldozed switchbacks up the tallest mountain, clearing and grading lots for a new gated community.

Many folks stretch a sturdy chain across their dirt drives to keep out hunters, but Mountain Meadows boasted a ten-foot-high security fence wrapping the whole hillside. A uniformed security guard manned a glass hut at the entrance, lifting and lowering the zebra gate for the luxury SUVs of the owners.

Who the hell would build atop a ridge where there was no spring and the wind battered your windows, your exposed roof begging for a bolt of lightning, five hundred feet above the rich bottom land along the creeks and streams? Certainly not farmers or factory workers with a lick of common sense, but newly arrived, highly credentialed professionals with soft hands, hard hearts, and fat portfolios. Coweetsee's latest arrivals.

≈

Sheriff Frank Cancro stood on the back deck, drink in hand, talking with his fellows as the sun was setting.

Million-dollar views. On clear days, they could count the ridges rolling like blue waves to the horizon. Only occasionally was their richly purchased peace and quiet interrupted by random gunfire and chainsaws from the hollers below.

"Debbie never gets tired of that view. It would be paradise if it weren't for the people, eh?" Bob Quattlebaum, a semi-retired venture capitalist, rattled the ice in his single malt. "Need another, Frank?"

Cancro held out his empty tumbler.

"Follow me then."

"Nice woodwork." Cancro ran his palm over the richly grained paneling by the bar in the study.

"They don't even make wood like this anymore. My builder said he got it from an old barn."

Cancro's neighbors were already remodeling their palatial homes built on acre tracts up and down the ridge overlooking the bend of the river. Their dens showcased reclaimed barn wood, elegant but authentic, bringing the best and priciest of the Appalachian spirit. Columns of river stone and chestnut rafters, harvested more than a century before, adorned their game rooms and foyers and outdoor decks.

"A barn, you say? Do you know where?"

"Local, I suppose. I could ask the contractor," Quattlebaum said.

"Oh, don't bother."

Cancro had been getting an earful almost daily from Birdie Barker Price down at the historical society. "Did you know what wormy chestnut wood is worth? Someone's cashing in on abandoned barns," she insisted.

And he kept saying he'd investigate, but until a property owner filed an actual report of larceny or trespassing or vandalism, anything that was on the books, there was little he could do, he tried to explain.

Besides bitching about the barns, the Price woman kept pestering him about the local lowlifes, namely one Charlie Clyde Harmon who had evidently paroled after serving time for manslaughter/arson committed at the county's only African American congregation.

"Unless and until he breaks the law, I can't do anything, Mrs. Price."

The only way he had shut her up was busting her for simple possession when the schoolteacher had spilled her stash on the bridge in some altercation with two underage girls.

Cancro had to patiently explain to the law-abiding and the

lawbreakers alike how things would be done under his watch. "I'm not Maurice Posey. You don't have to worry about that." Not that that seemed to reassure any of these yokels. What the hell was wrong with these people? Living in another century, locals didn't see the harm in passing out money for a vote, no more than it paid to know someone in power if you were going to be a schoolteacher, or an accountant, or hell, run a gas station out on the highway. Graft was a given. Maurice Posey had been the de facto mayor, county manager, chief financial officer, yet the county budget on the books was thin as a broken shoestring. Tax collections were meager, most were in arrears, and Cancro had arrested more than a few for not ponying up their back taxes.

Cancro drifted around the high-vaulted room, smiling and chatting up his friends, more at home with his kind of people.

The Quattlebaums were hosting a fundraiser cocktail hour for Cancro. Invited were the couples who could write off a thousand-dollar check, the limit of campaign contribution. These men made that much money each hour of each day from their hedge fund investments, their real estate, their offshore factories. Each pass of the second hand on the face of their golden Rolex watches and their profits piled up in numbered accounts and deep vaults. Cut these boys and they would bleed gold.

But they understood law and order. They needed to make sure the local methheads weren't breaking into their second homes when they were away for the winter. They wanted to make sure the place stayed civilized and that slow-moving farm tractors didn't get in the way of their luxury sedans, coupes, and SUVs winding along these scenic mountain roads. They wanted the county to clean up the eyesores. Trailers shouldn't fly Confederate flags, conjuring bad mojo for tourists. Nor did they want too many Jesus Saves signs littering the roadside.

"God's country, or so they say." Quattlebaum was getting tipsy with his scotch.

With fresh drinks, they were still considering endless blue views of the world's most ancient mountains. God, it was pretty here, yes, God's own country, if you didn't count the people here. You weren't a local, but always an outsider even if you've been here fifty years. If your family wasn't an original hillbilly, folks looked at you squinty-eyed.

"Talk to the locals, they act like this is their kingdom," Cancro said.

"How medieval."

"And they say Coweetsee comes with a curse."

"Whoo, how scary." Quattlebaum hooted. "What's the curse?"

"That nothing changes."

"Well, the rubes may be right about that."

Cancro was surprised. "How so?"

"Money." Quattlebaum beamed, warm with his single malt. "That never changes, not in America, not even in Coweetsee. Whoever has the money makes the rules, isn't that right?"

He playfully punched Cancro's arm. "Don't worry, Frank. You've got money on your side. We're going to win this thing, and you're going to whip this place into shape."

Cancro smiled.

The locals seem to have come out of their shock with former deputy Roy Barker running against him in the country's first contested election in ages. Slow was how he would describe Barker, a big shambling fellow, probably well-meaning, but just so damn slow. It took forever for the words to fall out of his slack-jawed mouth, while Cancro was straight to the point, crisp, all business.

Tax base was rising. State transportation was starting to patch and pave more of the road work, which hadn't seen any. A few more cell towers were slated for location and activation in the coming year. Coweetsee looked to be joining the modern world, after subsisting for so long in its nostalgic coma. Another term or two, and this county might be a normal place. Hell, they could even attract tourists to the local sights. Or maybe just more regular people would move in from the rest of normal America, and the indigenous freaks and inbred clans could finally die out. Though Sheriff Frances Cancro would never say that out loud in our earshot.

We had our own argument with Sheriff Cancro and his kind, who were never bashful about telling us our business, how it all should be done properly. Noise only goes uphill in these parts. Down below, we never heard the tinkling of ice on crystal, the soft jazz, the laughter of rich women, those outlanders looking down their long noses at the rest of us in the kingdom of Coweetsee.

We felt the weight of their high judgments on our heads.

We woke up every bright or foggy morning with the inarticulate feelings stuck in our dry mouths. Bubbling up like a coffee pot percolating its bitter brew on the stovetop, the daily regrets rose in our gorge, inarticulate rage and sorrow and guilt, the sense that our best days were fled from us, the good old times long gone.

The kingdom collapsing like the tobacco barns besieged by the invasive kudzu, the fields laying fallow with thistle and broom straw, none of the white-sheeted tobacco beds. Our sole cash crop now blamed for all the cancer deaths. Our last livelihoods abandoned when Uncle Sam yanked the subsidies for burley. Left to fend as always for our lonesomes.

The politicians came along our unpaved roads, posed for pictures on our sagging porches, promised prosperity or at least chickens for our iron pots. Then came the interstate, torn through the hills. Family farms sold off to the developers to be subdivided, the trees cleared, like an outbreak of blight killing the hemlocks these days. Fancy houses popping up like pimples on the ridge lines. Rich outlanders flocking in, looking down on us as always, as poor benighted people who just didn't know any better.

They thought of us as barefoot and long bearded, slouch-hatted ignoramuses bent on feuds and incest, Li'l Abner with his big brogans and patched jeans, or shiftless Snuffy Smith, always with the brown jugs marked with Triple X Mountain Dew. Or maybe we were throwbacks to Elizabethan England with our unsullied speech, we talked like four hundred years ago. Secret sodomites, monsters lurking in the mountains. Myths, all told on us, and made up of course.

They were all laughing at us, the rest of the country chuckling at our expense. But we didn't think the joke was all that funny. We could feel their condescension raining down on us.

They'd found us all right, living here back of beyond, and they had the gall to believe that we were the ones lost.

We only wanted to know who to blame for losing our kingdom.

27

We were all looking forward to Roy's pig-pickin' and politickin' extravaganza, the biggest community-wide gathering Coweetsee had seen in years. The Roy Barker for Coweetsee Sheriff campaign had rented the Ruritan Hall, which stood empty these years, all the farmers who once paid their dues dying off, our civic spirit slowly draining away. Like the old days, we brought our best cakes and pies, casseroles, pickled pork, deviled eggs, potato salads, gelatin molds, platters of buttered corn on the cob, crockpots of greasy beans, collards stewed in fatback, corn muffins and buttermilk biscuits with slices of salty country ham.

Gene had hired Shawanda's cousins to cook the pig, a quartet of stout Black men who once anchored the front line of Coweetsee High's football team in its single championship season. They had been out all night with the smoker, basting the suckling over the coals until the skin glistened and then crackled. They brought out the cutting boards and the heavy cleavers and went to work with a rhythmic chop. "Make that piggy all itty-bitty." The juice ran everywhere, and the smell was heavenly.

"Lord, there's enough food to last a man till the next election." Jimmy Lee showed his new set of overly white and straight dentures, a beaver grin aimed to do damage to the tables arraigned to his appetites.

"Great turn-out, Roy Boy," said Junk Jackson.

Roy's old sparring partner had at last put on a shirt and sported some suspenders with the Confederate stars and bars to keep his jeans up on his thin hips and under his paunch.

Big gallon jars for campaign donations stood at the head of every table. Junk peeled a dirty bill with a wetted thumb from a bankroll he carried in the hip pocket of his jeans and made his contribution.

"No one pitches into an empty jar." Junk grinned and poked his sharp elbow into Roy's ribs. "I might even vote for you."

"Thanks, Junk." Roy was swinging like an orangutan on his crutches, holding the black boot before him like a perpetual punter frozen on the gridiron.

"I think we're in business." Gene was sipping from a cup of coffee, probably his twentieth of the day. "Go shake some more hands, kiss some babies. We might win this thing after all."

Dylan had borrowed a sound system from the First Baptist. It whistled feedback and screeched in the autumn air. Cutworm brought his Martin guitar and two boys from one of the school's Appalachian Jam programs, tow-headed and acned teens who could strangle passable sounds out of a fiddle and a cheap banjo, because what was a barbecue without a little music to enliven the air? The impromptu trio took their time tuning, and when it sounded like it would make no difference, they began to play. They sawed and hammered away at the old tunes. Couples took to the floor to waltz while a few chunky gals in cowboy boots did a little shuffle.

Charlie Clyde tapped his way out onto the plywood as the fiddle fought with the guitar and the banjo battled all. He swung his arms, and his shoes began their tat-a-tat-tat on the wood. Who would have known that old heel could kick up his heels?

He jigged his way over to the edge of the plank dance floor and motioned for Birdie. "Care to join me?"

Birdie couldn't believe his audacity. "My aunt Zip stuck a gun in your ear when you tried to molest me on the sidewalk two blocks down when I was just a girl."

Charlie Clyde smiled. "I've had a lot of people stick a gun in my face."

"I know it was you," she said. "The other night."

"Me?" He kept shuffling his feet, shaking his head, bending closer to hear what she was saying.

"At the old Anderson barn, trying to steal that wood. I fired at you."

"Good thing you're a bad shot." He grinned, shuffling his feet to Cutworm's fiddling. He pointed his index fingers at her, like little fleshy six-shooters, then blew the imaginary smoke off his fingertips.

Junk Jackson pushed her from behind. "Go ahead and dance with the devil."

Birdie was exposed, out on the floor. We clapped our hands, and now she was too embarrassed to retreat before Charlie Clyde and all of Coweetsee.

Cutworm's fingers flew over the taut strings of his guitar. The fiddler began to saw his bow harder and higher at the bridge of his fiddle. Beet-faced now, Birdie began to kick her heels slowly. Whenever Charlie Clyde approached with his tapping shoes, she retreated. When he grabbed for her hands for a doesy-do or a promenade, Birdie would twirl away like a leaf or a feather, her toes softly wiping the plywood dance floor. We hollered and yodeled and clapped along.

Finally, Birdie waved both hands, surrendering to the applause. "Get me out of here." She walked off, her face flushed.

Charlie Clyde was left alone, and he began to spin as his feet flew and the taps sounded on the plywood, and he was at the center of Coweetsee, like a little tornado come to town, our own dust devil, kicking up his heels. We all applauded when the music stopped.

Cutworm mopped his glowing brow with a red bandanna. "I'm tuckered out, but we've played all we really know and some we could fake."

The sound system did a wild whistle that about burst our eardrums. What was next?

"Birdie should sing."

Who said that? Folks looked around. Charlie Clyde was at the back with that bright smile that couldn't melt butter.

"Birdie. Birdie. Let's hear Birdie."

She took the stage and shook out her long hair. She closed

her eyes and tapped her foot, humming to herself as if to find the key.

"You go, girl," Shawanda called and waved from the crowd of cooks by the smoker.

Birdie said she would sing an old ballad she'd learned from her aunt Zip. "Usually in a ballad, bad things happen to poor maidens, who get drowned or beheaded or abandoned to freeze to death. But there are some where the men get their comeuppance like in this song called 'The Willow Tree.'"

Birdie's small voice began to climb and swell and fill the still air.

Her song concerned a cruel youth who lived by the sea.

Six little maidens he drowned there
By the lonely willow tree.

As she sang, Roy stood by the steps to the stage, swaying slowly on his black boot planted in the good Coweetsee dirt, lost to himself and his running thoughts.

And Birdie's song melted something inside, not just in Roy Boy, but inside us all as we stood transfixed, hanging on the sad notes that kept climbing out of her throat.

The verses went on: The cruel boy orders the girl to drop her clothes, which he plans to steal before he drowns her. But the blushing maid talks him into turning his head while she disrobes.

But then suddenly, Birdie quit singing. For an instant, we weren't sure if she had forgotten the old words, whether she would go on.

"Hang on." She started to cough. "Sorry." She took a swig of water from a plastic bottle.

Men were looking at her. W. D. Clark with his hard scowl, Junk Jackson with his leer, and Maurice Posey with his slowly wafting halo of white hair, smiling beatifically. Poor old Roy in his black boot and his cronies, Gene, Cutworm, Jimmie Lee.

All these men, all too often with one thing on their mind when they eyed a woman in Coweetsee.

Deana and Rhonda Jr. stood side by side, their hips cocked, their thin arms crossed, the family resemblance unmistakable, while Charlie Clyde kept to himself at the edge of the crowd. The Harmons always on the outskirts, keeping their own company.

Birdie started again.

The last maiden brought thee a wooden chest.
That pretty girl had seen all its secrets inside.
But to your horrid crimes you would not confess
What happened to her and the chest, you lied.

No one had heard that verse before. Had she made up her own on the spot?

It sure sounded different. What was she singing? What was she saying?

Lie there, lie there, you false-hearted man.
Lie there instead of me.
For if that first maiden you have drowned here,
The last maiden may have drowned thee.

Men began to drop their gaze and shift their weight and shuffle their feet as if their boots suddenly fit too tightly, or they may have felt hot coals underfoot.

"Now I'm done." Birdie wheeled off the stage.

Gene rushed up to the microphone, clapping a bit, trying to encourage some applause. "That was a ballad from our own Birdie Barker Price. What a sweet songbird. Now let's hear from the man of the hour, a true native, and your next sheriff of Coweetsee County. Let's have a big hand for Roy Barker!"

Roy lumbered forward on his big black boot. He stood unsteadily, rubbing the heel of his hand into his eye socket, betrayed and blinded by the suspect wetness in his eyes. He blinked at all of us gathered before him, the people he'd known his whole life, folks who had come out to eat the barbecue pig, to dance to the bad music, to listen to his ex-wife sing her heart out. All our upturned faces, with our warts and wens, our lazy eyes and crooked teeth, weak Gudger chins, Ledford jowls, the long beaks of the snooty Cornetts, the thick beetle brows of the Mabes, the jug ears of the Sheltons. The lanky Burlesons who looked over the heads of the short-legged Hensleys. The well-fed big bellies of the Bares, and the raw-bone Honeycutts whose women all had blue veins in their porcelain skins. All the familiar genes of generations who have stuck here in the hollers and never left, even when it felt like all Coweetsee was being left behind. We all had voted for Smathers and Poseys, fought for the Confederates and the Union a century and half before in a war that was only half-forgotten, the blood coursing through the black earth along the river, never washed away.

We were his people. But Roy didn't seem to know what to say to us.

"Y'all know me. I'm Roy Barker. I know all of you since I was a young-un at Spring Creek elementary. You remember my daddy who was the best principal. You know Birdie too. I appreciate her singing."

"Roy Boy, whooeee!" someone hollered, liquored up already.

Roy froze on the stage. "Please vote!" He fled the stage as fast he could with his crutches and black boot.

Gene jumped onstage, clapping his hands, eager for an ovation. "He's a native, all right. Before we dig into that heavenly hog. Let's get Elder Tomes up here to say a blessing."

"Who invited him? I thought he was dead," Roy whispered to Dylan.

"Uncle Gene did. Diversity isn't bad. We could use the African American demographic if we're hoping for a good result," the young number-cruncher said.

The elderly pastor giggled in his little bow tie, his gold tooth and his thick spectacles gleaming in the light. He fumbled around looking at his scuffed shoes, as if he'd forgotten how blessings go, or prayers in politics.

"You'ns all know what happened to my little church, how it burned down. So sad."

Tomes was rusty. He'd been out of the ministry business

a while, forgetting his scriptures, speaking in tongues, not of angels but Alzheimer's. He hung his head, then he looked up with a bright thought. "But thank the good Lord for insurance! And thank God for Sheriff Posey for signing the policy!"

He pointed toward Maurice, his white halo of hair, sitting at the picnic table. Maurice smiled and waved to the applause.

Roy whispered to Gene: "Did you remind him that I'm the one who's running, not Maurice?"

"Hang on. He'll say something," Gene said.

"I am reminded of scripture now," Tomes continued, seemingly unaware he'd been sent up here for a quick blessing and not a sermon. Stomachs were beginning to rumble, but the old pastor was not dissuaded. His eyes flashed behind the thick spectacles, and you could see the gleaming gold tooth in his smile. His giggling ceased as if the Spirit had descended upon him, and he found his old baritone pulpit pitch.

"Yes, I am reminded. When our church was put to the torch, I cried out, 'Oh Lord, why Nebuchadnezzar Baptist, why this fire, why me, Oh God?' And then I recall all the fires that test men's souls. Remember those Hebrew boys in the book of Daniel? They won't bow down before the golden gods of Babylon and the king throws the three into a fiery furnace. Now, you know their names, Shadrach, Meshach, and Abednego. You know what happens next. Ol' king looks in the furnace and Shadrach, Meshach, and Abednego are strolling around in the flames and there is someone with them, a man made of fire, and he holds their hands in the heart of that terrible holocaust. King tells them to come on out, and they walk out the furnace door, Shadrach, Meshach, and Abednego. Not a hair of their young heads singed. Not even a bead of sweat. They were tested and they were not burned up. They came through the fire, holding the hand of that man made of fire."

We stood there, wondering where this Black preacher was going and what this had to do with who would be the next sheriff of Coweetsee County or when we could dig into that pig on the smoker.

"What happened to Shadrach, Meshach, and Abednego has happened here to our church, to you and me. We all have been tested by the flames. The king of Babylon has looked in on us and we are not burned up with hatred, we are not sweating despair. We came through the fire, holding each other's hand." But Tomes wasn't through by any means. "We have a man here today, a guest. We all know who he is. We all know what he's done. But I can't be no king, judging this man. I cannot see if his heart is black. I can only see that my own heart is not burned with hate. I forgive you, Charlie Clyde Harmon."

Charlie Clyde stood there, but that ever-present grin on his face was gone. His teeth were wet and not smiling now.

"Goddamn, I don't need your forgiveness," he shouted. "What's wrong with you people? How many times do I have to tell you I didn't do it?"

He turned and walked through the crowd, which parted for him, scuffing across the asphalt. He was walking so mad he almost made sparks with the taps of his soles.

The Holy Spirit that had filled Tomes' empty head and touched his silver tongue and his gold tooth had fled. Poor preacher was left muttering, "Thank the good Lord for insurance. And thank God for Sheriff Posey."

Shawanda Tomes had been shaking her head. She rushed onstage to grab her old pastor by the arm, leading him away.

Gene fumbled toward the microphone with its earsplitting feedback. "Amen," he cried. "Time to eat, folks. Remember to vote for Roy Barker."

Later that afternoon, Deana Harmon sidled up to Birdie.

"Sorry for that scene with Charlie Clyde."

"You don't need to apologize to me," Birdie said.

"Mighty nice song you did." Deana was holding a paper plate and gnawing at a fried drumstick. "I like how the girl drowned the knight, rather than the other way around."

"That's very kind of you," Birdie murmured, embarrassed at

the easy praise. Her own voice sounded tremulous and pitchy in her head. She was almost glad that Zip was at Laurel Trace, and not here to hear Birdie butcher one of her favorite ballads. "I appreciate you teaching Rhonda Jr. them old songs. She seems to like it."

"She's a good student. Zip says she's learning fast."

"If she can stay focused. Girl's gone boy crazy, I'm afraid." Deana nodded in the direction of her niece cozying up to Dylan who was showing her something on his laptop.

"She could do worse than Dylan Caldwell. He's got some brains, at least."

"I still keep my eye on her." Deana tipped her chin toward the picnic table by the stage. "Then there's those two."

W. D. Clark had sidled over to Maurice who sat on the bench beside his oxygen tank. Birdie still resented that old stick-in-the-mud of a man stalking through her historical society, lying about that old ballot box, accusing her of telling lies about the real history. Who did he think he was? A man with secrets, with buried treasure, plenty of cash in the bank or stashed under his mattress, a man who always thought he would get his way.

W. D. bent down and was saying something into Maurice's big ear. The old sheriff's eyes widened, and he shook his head excitedly.

Deana grasped her arm and was hissing into Birdie's ear. "Watch. Look at them."

And the two old men began to laugh, sharing likely a lewd joke between them.

"Never mind," Birdie said to Deana. "Let's go get some pie."

But Deana was already storming over. "My Lord, if it ain't Maurice Posey back from the pokey."

Maurice smiled and squinted. "Do I know you, dear?"

"I was but a young'un at the picnic when you first challenged Shad Smathers. You took the badge away from him. You've got the power of life or death in Coweetsee County."

"You may be confusing me with someone who once mattered." Maurice tried to wave her away. W. D. stood like a scarecrow, looming over the old reprobate, leering at Deana.

"You know me." Deana wasn't backing down. "Don't you act all high and mighty like you don't know me. Biblically. Especially old W. D. here. You remember, don't you?"

"Ms. Harmon. Deana," Maurice insisted. "That wasn't my doing. That happened under Shad's watch."

Deana turned to the crowd, calling on all Coweetsee as her witness. "Look at these men. They can bed little girls and say we're their wives. They can steal elections and pretend it's all a democracy. They can burn down a church and blame my brother. They hide a ballot box in the creek. Then they drowned my sister when she brought them that box."

"Hypocrites!" She raised her voice and pointed. "Liars!"

"Harmon Whore," someone muttered in the crowd, but most of us were thinking it, if not saying it out loud.

"Let's calm down now." Roy stepped in. It looked like they were doing an awkward dance—Roy hobbling on his black boot, holding Deana's thin arm until she shook him loose. Gene and Jimmy Lee were standing back, none of them daring to touch the screaming woman.

"Don't you be touching me. Don't none of you touch me." Deana was fierce, likely to haul off and hit anyone who crossed her.

Then Rhonda Jr. was at her aunt's side, tugging at her arm, imploring her to stop. "They're all watching us."

Deana relented. "You're right. Damn their eyes. Let's go."

The crowd parted and let the two women pass to the parking lot.

W. D. finally broke the terrible hush that had blanketed what was supposed to be a joyous time, a community fellowship. "Them Harmons. They would start a food fight at the Lord's Supper in a Baptist Church." He spat in the dirt.

Later, after the bones were picked clean and the crowd was

gone, Birdie looked for Roy. She found him sitting alone at the picnic table with his crutches propped to the side and his boot-ed foot stretched on the bench. He looked defeated already, she thought.

"No, don't get up." She sat beside him. "Nice turn-out, Roy. Thanks for inviting me."

"Glad you could make it, everybody helps."

"Maybe not the Harmons. That was quite the scene with Deana."

"Least, no one got shot—yet," Roy said.

"There's just so much bad blood." Birdie shook her head, then she added, "Whose idea was it to have Elder Tomes for-give Charlie Clyde? I don't think he saw that coming."

"None of us planned that. Gene thought having a blessing from the pastor would help get out the Black vote."

"I did see Shawanda and her cousins, though I didn't get a chance to talk to her."

"I just wish Maurice would have gotten up there and said a few words himself," Roy said. "That was the plan, but when I went to pick him up at Laurel Trace, he said he was feeling poorly, that he would have to pass." Roy felt himself start to complain, to feel some self-pity the more he talked. He had no one else he could share his self-doubts with.

"Roy, I'd be careful if I were you. Maurice is in cahoots with W. D. Clark again. I saw those two talking."

Roy knew what she was saying was true, he'd fallen into an old habit. Their ancient arguments, one always trying to be right for the other. She was likely right, though he was loath to admit it. He shifted his burdensome weight; his ankle was starting to ache inside the stiff black boot. If he couldn't change her mind, at least he could change the subject.

"You sang awfully sweet. I appreciate you agreeing to do that."

Birdie hesitated. "Not sure the crowd liked it."

"Hadn't heard that ballad before."

"I kind of got lost, made up some words," Birdie lied.

"Funny. Sounded like you were accusing someone of lying about that ballot box."

"Let's not argue about that box again."

"Still I'm glad you came and performed for us," Roy said. "I remember that picnic at the church when we were little, when Shad and Maurice were fighting each other. I saw you then."

"I remember you too."

"You always could sing so sweet."

"You're sweet yourself." She edged closer to buss his cheek and squeeze his hand.

The way she was looking at him, all soft-eyed, it seemed possible to Roy that Birdie might just kiss him again, kiss him hard, like the way he always wanted to kiss her.

But then she let go his hand, and the electricity of the moment fled.

"Thanks again. I've got to get going." She stood. "For what it's worth, Roy, I hope you win this election. This county has got to change for any of this to count for something."

28

Birdie, in her blue jeans and boots, fluorescent orange safety vest and county-issued work gloves, toiled under the late September sun along the bypass. Armed with a spike pole, she ambled along, stabbing stray papers and Styrofoam to place in her garbage bag.

She faced four weekends of community service, a total of twenty-four hours as ordered by the district judge, not any native of Coweetsee, but one of the white-haired eminences in their black robes who drove up from Charlotte each quarter to hear the caseload and dispense justice.

On the appointed day, the court-ordered volunteers had made their appearance at the new county detention center's parking lot. Their full Christian names were officially marked off on checklists as they climbed on the short bus with the grated metal windows. An orange-vested misdemeanant was deposited every quarter mile, armed with a trash bag and a spiked stick, given strict instructions to stay out of the road and keep moving along the shoulder. The bus would circle back, collect the stragglers and relay them ahead. They had ten miles of unkempt roadside to properly police.

Everyone in Coweetsee got wind of Birdie's criminal ways, drivers waving and honking their horns as they blew by in their trucks and SUVs. She could feel the hot wake on her forehead. She was getting thirsty, but she had another quarter mile to go before the guard would offer her bottled water.

Lord knows, enough trash out here to keep her busy. Tons of flotsam and jetsam from pickup beds, tall boy beer cans, quart-sized plastic foam Giant Gulps from the bypass convenience stops. Why some folks were so trashy, she never knew, but it was too common in Coweestee. Drive anywhere in the county, you come across signs on the back roads: No dumping.

Many had grown up burning or dumping their own wastes. Go by a creek, you're likely to see tires and a junked car or two, more than a few times a body.

Since there was little reliable municipal trash collection, Coweetsee's sole sanitary truck only made the rounds every couple of weeks, leaving a wake of flotsam along the road shoulders like swathes of artificial wildflowers.

The day was unseasonably warm for early autumn. Birdie wore a bandanna around her neck for the sweat, and to keep the nape of her neck from wrinkling. She prided herself on being no literal redneck, those furrowed lines she saw at the nape of too many tobacco farmers, like rivulets run through raw red clay.

Walking up the road, poking trash and stuffing it in her bag, her face burning with shame, Birdie wondered how it had come to this. Her life could have been so different.

She could have left Coweetsee. While most settled for high school diplomas, Birdie aimed higher and enrolled at App State in Boone. She was dating Roy, who had started his career with Maurice and was working toward an associate degree in criminal justice at the regional community college. She came home every weekend with her novels and poetry and tried to study in her childhood bedroom.

She lay belly down on the bed, her ankles crossed behind her, dreaming of the love children in California, or the folk singers up in Greenwich Village, anywhere but here in this holler. If Coweetsee refused to change, many of its residents decided to change themselves. People had been moving out for the past century, over to Texas and out west, over to Nashville with their guitars, or maybe just down the mountain for a job in a furniture factory, a decent wage, and a house big enough to keep young'uns warm and healthy and not poster children for LBJ's Appalachian War on Poverty. Teacher or nurse, educator or healer—about the only things open to a woman even at that late date.

But Birdie had stuck.

Damn James Dickey, that's all she could say.

Birdie and Roy had made a Friday night date one summer to see *Deliverance* at a drive-in. Roy Boy drove his daddy's Nash Rambler. Birdie didn't tell her beau, but she had a crush on Burt Reynolds in his leather jerkin, how he drew that bowstring with those fine biceps. She winced at the hillbillies, those plainspoken, unpretty women at the film's end. They had the faces of Aunt Zip and all the other old women she knew in Coweetsee. At college, she met the author himself after a reading, drunk on the cheap white wine set out in jugs by the lobby.

"You wrote about my people," Birdie said.

"Hey, little darling," he said, with a leer. "How about I give you a private reading? I bet I can make you squeal like a little piggie."

The poet patted her behind. If it had been any of the boys Birdie grew up with in Coweetsee, she would have punched his lights out. But he was famous, and she was intimidated. Birdie gulped her white wine and excused herself that evening and never forgave herself.

Damn James Dickey. He wrote some wonderful poems about kudzu, but he did Appalachian folks no favors, making us out to be monsters sodomizing Atlanta suburbanites in the woods.

But Birdie knew there were real monsters, not just movie villains.

Like Charlie Clyde, running over a drunk just to see what would happen, setting fire to a Black church, burning up another drunk. God didn't exactly look after drunks and young children in a place like Coweetsee.

But here was her place, her home. She was stuck now, exiled to a stretch of scrub grass, red clay, crumbling asphalt, and all the litter from careless drivers. Stab cup, place in bag. Stab beer can, place in bag. Stab burger wrapper, place in bag. Jesus, is that a condom?

She was going through all her regrets. What could she have done differently?

She married at her first chance, desperate to flee her mother's clutches. Roy Boy was her childhood pal, then high school sweetheart, if not her real soulmate in the end. They hitched up to do what comes naturally to teenagers in rut. Birdie had always thought she wanted children.

She had spent her teaching career wading through a crowd of kids, other women's babies. She hadn't made their bodies, but she molded their minds. They were hers in a way, not blood but what they would make of themselves, she hoped. Best part, she let them go at the end of the day, sent them home to their mommas to feed them, put them to bed, sew and wash their clothes, nurse them through their fevers and measles and mumps and the illnesses that most kids pass through.

She still missed the touch of her fifth graders' heads, her hands lighting on their heads or their shoulders, how they mill around. The girls playing hopscotch on the sidewalk, the boys roughhousing, but sweet as can be once they caught the sharp edge of her schoolteacher voice. You could spot the girls who would be trouble and the ones who would follow devoutly in their mothers' worn footsteps, marrying and breeding and becoming inhabitants, finally, of Laurel Trace.

The truth came at the end of her marriage to Roy Boy. They had been pushing at each other to have a baby forever, going at each other with a ferocity and a hunger for something other than themselves.

They drove from Coweetsee to the real hospital at Asheville, like driving into the future with fluorescent-lit waiting rooms and clean examination rooms, and the muffled noises next door as they sat, waiting for the doctor to come in with the test results. They said nothing to each other, scared of what was happening.

Turns out the cramps she was getting were not normal. They had found a growth. The future died right then and there, the dream that she would be a matron, a mother and grandmother, all her little babies in her arms. But something even deeper inside her didn't want to die, not leave this life behind. The doctor recommended a hysterectomy, the long white scar on her belly. It matched the white scar on her ring finger. Once, cutting up a winter squash from Zip's garden, Birdie nearly took off that fingertip with her great-aunt's big kitchen knife. "Law, it was like you were trying to butcher a hog." Aunt Zip marveled at how the blood sprayed across the kitchen.

Birdie had seen those white cuts on the skin of girls in class, ones who were doing that on purpose, in the privacy of their bathrooms or bedrooms of their small lives and houses. Girls trying to hurt themselves, to let that hollowness ease out of them from beneath their ribs, told so often that they were left-over rib meat from Adam's side, no more than cutlets in that Old Testament version that put Eve down. A good reason that Aunt Zip and other women put so little stock in what red-faced preachers hollered from their pine pulpits.

At least she had the childless Zip as a role model. Women didn't all mature into mothers, grandmothers. At least she didn't have to repeat the mistakes of her own mother.

Roy Boy said he didn't care, but she didn't believe him. She had let him down. No progeny, no kids. Looking back, she had left him before he could leave her.

Not that they ever talked about it. They stayed worlds away, sitting side by side in the cramped little room of their first and only house, watching the one channel that broadcast its signal over the ridges and into the hollers of Coweetsee.

They signed the divorce papers the week before her thirtieth birthday, parting on amicable terms. She could never hate Roy Boy, nor could she give him her heart and soul.

Birdie had found the love of her life in a long-haired boy. She made her escape with Talmadge, and then he had left her behind too soon. He was gone, but not really. She sensed not his presence now, but that sense that he had just left the room. Stepping out on her porch in the mornings, she would hear the creak of the chains on the swing, the gentle sway as if he had just gotten up and walked around the corner of their cabin. Gone but just a moment.

Since she'd admitted her complicity to Aunt Zip, that she was guilty of helping her husband take his own life, something had shifted inside her. Maybe she had only done what had to be done, nothing heroic nor heinous as the old woman saw it. Not that she felt any less shamefaced or grief-stricken or angry at herself, but somehow the weight on her had lifted, what once had pressed so hard on tight ribs, her heart and lungs, her life. She found herself able to breathe more deeply, more freely. She felt it this morning, swinging on her front porch. She was still here, still alive.

ॐ

"Hey, good-looking!"

The truck pulled up beside her and stopped. Charlie Clyde leaned out the passenger window. Junk Jackson was behind the wheel.

"If it ain't my old dance partner," Charlie Clyde said.

Birdie kept her hard gaze down, avoiding his jeering face. "Leave me be. I'm busy."

"Heard you were selling weed to underage girls. How's it feel to be a convicted criminal, paying your dues to society?"

Birdie stabbed another piece of trash for her expanding bag. "Least I'm not lying about being innocent," she said quietly.

"You're doing a mighty fine job." Charlie Clyde tossed a Big Gulp foam cup on the shoulder. "Be sure to get that for me."

The truck roared up the road, tailgate open with timbers hanging out back, tied with a red bandanna according to state law, so as not to get a stop from a nosy trooper or one of Cancro's deputies looking for an easy citation. Likely for that busted taillight on the passenger side. Maybe the same one she'd shot out the other night protecting Talmadge's treasured barn.

Ahead on the bypass, the pickup stopped alongside Rhonda Jr. dragging her sorry self and her garbage bag along the shoulder. Birdie could see her talking to them. Then Charlie Clyde stepped out and held the door as the girl climbed in.

"Hey, you can't leave. You'll get yourself in more trouble," Birdie yelled and waved.

They still had another couple of hours of court-ordered community service and roadside tidying and local humiliation. They weren't free to go just yet.

Charlie Clyde grabbed the trash spike and hurled it like a javelin in Birdie's direction. He jumped in, slammed the door, and the truck roared away.

"Wait! Don't! No! Stop!" Birdie ran up the road too late to save that silly, silly girl.

29

Charlie Clyde and Rhonda Jr. had themselves a family reunion, catching up as they rode in Junk's pickup. "Last I saw you, you were but a wee girl. You don't remember but your mama and me used to take you fishing at the creek."

She had dim memories of a shadow man at the creek, laughing over her head as she patted her pudgy hands in the sand. Her uncle?

"Didn't you run over a drunk and burn down a church?" she asked.

"I didn't do all that they said, but I might have done some things no one ever caught me at, ain't that right, Junk?"

"You're a slick one, all right," Junk agreed.

"You were a bad seed was all I ever heard about you," the girl said.

Charlie Clyde cackled. "But like they said, I didn't fall far from our tree. You and me, we're the same blood."

Here was her blood and kin. She could see the likeness in Deana and Charlie Clyde, the knife-like noses, the keen profiles they gave to the world. She took more after her mama and the maternal side of the family, pudgier, fleshier, shorter.

"I liked your ma too." Junk grinned. "When we saw you on the side of the road, I said, 'That looks just like Rhonda,' and we just had to stop."

The girl was feeling somewhat flattered by the attention of these older men who had known her lost mother. Better here with them, than picking up trash on the side of road. She'd just as soon keep going and get the hell out of this peckerwood place.

"Where are we going?" she thought to ask.

"Wherever you want, little darling," Charlie Clyde said. "But first we ought to unload all that wood in the back."

They headed to Junk's house. Charlie Clyde jumped out and started stacking the dusty timbers off to the side.

Rhonda Jr. marveled at the amount of scrap and debris and junk scattered across the yard. The Confederate battle flag hung limp at the corner of the porch. And the signs on the outside read: *Ask a Real Redneck. Trespass at own Risk.*

"Are you the real redneck?" she asked.

"Just a side gig of mine," Junk replied. "You'd be surprised how many folks will stop by for real world advice."

"What do you tell them?"

"Whatever they want to hear, mostly. Long as they ante up in the tip jar." Junk patted his pot belly, taunt over his loose khaki pants. "You must be thirsty. You want something to drink?"

She followed him into the house. He went into the kitchen to fetch a bottle of rum and tall glasses. He put on some music, dropping the needle on an old-fashioned vinyl LP, sound suddenly blaring through the hi-fi speakers, the technology of the analog age. Here was a man who knew how to party on a summer afternoon, how to treat a girl.

"Do I know you, mister?" she said with all the sauce of her family, a shake of her hair, even when she was wearing a fluorescent, tacky vest.

"Not that I know of. I just like to be helpful to a girl out on the highway," Junk said. "I liked how you were cleaning the road of all that litter."

"Not my idea of fun," she said.

Through the window, she could see Charlie Clyde still unloading the wood scraps from the truck bed. "He's working pretty hard. Shouldn't you help him?"

"Naw, Charlie Clyde's got his own way of stacking it, says I just get in his way," Junk observed. "That wood is worth real money to some folks. He finds the best wood and I find the best buyers."

Rhonda Jr. took a sip of the rum and looked around. She didn't see much sign of money, only junk. This could get boring even with the liquor. "So what do you do for fun?"

"Come back here. I have something that might interest you." In the bedroom, overcrowded with antiques, he opened the closet door.

The closet was full of vintage dresses, from ancient proms, weddings, dances, events that the girl had only glimpsed in magazines and Instagram posts. Flapper dresses with sparkly beads, sleek sheathes that she wouldn't worm her torso into, off-the-shoulder drapes, and '80s-issue gowns with linebacker shoulder pads. Tulle and tuft, silk and satin, lace, organza, chiffon, sequins, folds, pleats galore.

"Take your pick," he said.

"Really?" she said.

"I just want to see you put it on." He slid out and closed the door behind him, for her privacy.

How would someone as gross as this Junk Jackson collect such snares to catch a woman's eye? She imagined herself winning the attention of all the men if she were to come into a room, or walk down the street, garbed in such glamour. Imagine that Donnie Gunther all gape-mouthed, or even that cute Dylan despite his acne. She imagined herself not just desirable and desired, but even loved.

She tried on a couple of dresses and spun around, wishing for a full-length mirror so she could capture the full effect instead of squinting into a smudged dresser glass.

"Let me see." Junk knocked softly. "Oh my, you do have taste."

Rhonda whirled around in a flapper dress, 1920s vintage with glass beads and fringe, frail and glamorous. The music was louder in her head, as she hummed along.

"You're the spitting image of your mama, you know."

"Did you know her?" The girl stopped in her spin, even though the room kept swinging somehow.

"Your mama and me were great friends back in the day. We used to go down by the creek and let you splash around while we watched and talked and drank a bit."

Was this the shadow man in her memory, the masculine presence looming over her sometimes in her dreams? Why hadn't her mama said something?

"You want another drink, my dear." Junk winked. "The party's just getting started."

Charlie Clyde hollered from the other room. "Where y'all go? Better behave yourself, Junk. That's my niece, you know."

They came back into the cramped and crowded parlor, Rhonda Jr. spinning in her glittery dress. "Look what Junk has in the back."

"Ain't she pretty?" Junk beamed. "Now this is a party. Hang on."

The Real Redneck went into the bathroom and returned, carrying a chipped plate of pharmaceutical pills like party favors.

"Take what you want."

"What are they?"

"Little items I traded for with some of my customers. Special K, they call it. Feel good pills, maybe horse tranquilizers. They won't bite you."

Both Charlie Clyde and Rhonda Jr. picked a tablet, smiled, placed them on their tongues that they stuck out at each other. Then they swallowed.

The rest of the afternoon turned into a liquid blur.

She remembered Charlie Clyde grinning, getting awfully mellow on the couch, as he leaned his head back and stretched his black denim legs out on the coffee table, the dulled metal taps showing on the scuffed soles of his shoes.

His mouth dropped open, his eyes widened, and he fell into his private world.

The hours paraded by like slow dray horses, clip-clopping their huge hooves moment after moment. Rhonda was hypnotized by their slow progress. What girl didn't love horses? But what was loaded in the wagon they pulled behind their gleaming backs, their straining flanks?

Rhonda Jr. made her uneasy way into the kitchen where she was trying to mix another margarita, pretending to be civilized, a Housewife of Some City, like you see on TV, and not some poor hick growing up in Coweetsee.

Suddenly, she felt someone behind her. Junk nuzzled the back of her neck, the stubble of his unshaven chin making her skin crawl. She wheeled around with the butcher knife she was using to cut the limes. Junk's eyes went wide, and he went "omph."

And he was holding her hand on the knife handle now, looking down at his pale belly as if to ask how the hell did that get there.

She rousted Charlie Clyde who had zoned out on the sofa, staring blankly at the ceiling, listening to the loud music. "We got to go. Now."

Junk stood in the doorway, holding his belly, with red stuff oozing through his fingers.

"What the hell!" Charlie Clyde jumped to his feet.

"Get that girl out of here. She's just like her mama, nothing but trouble," Junk cried.

"Dirty old geezer. Tried to sneak up on me and cop a feel," the girl cried.

Charlie Clyde looked baffled, torn between allegiances, his best cash dealer and his own blood kin.

"You're bleeding pretty bad there, partner," he said.

Junk studied his red hands. "Seen worse. Little bitch didn't stick me too deep. Go on. Git."

Charlie Clyde was ushering his niece out the door now, even though she was still dressed in the flapper dress. They jumped into the pickup and tore out of there.

Rhonda Jr. was shaking and crying. "He kept coming at me. I didn't mean it."

"Shut the hell up." Her uncle dropped her off at Deana's trailer. "Don't say a word to anyone."

Junk Jackson tried to tape himself up, but the world was getting woozy, and he slid down on the floor, getting closer to it, to the end. It wasn't as bad as he thought. He probably had some herbs and roots, healing plants he'd got down in Big Cove on the Qualla Boundary, collected by granny women who knew the old ways and the proper formulas.

Junk prided himself on keeping his blades razor sharp. He could make short work of ribs or a pig he sometimes cooked whole out on his smoker. A man needs an edge he can count on. He hadn't counted on some fool girl poking his belly with the point.

Spitting image of her mama, he kept thinking. Like she was resurrected out of that water again. He just wanted a little dance, to touch her soft skin, so much like the drowned woman.

There was a hand on his neck. He opened his eyes wide.

"Roy Boy," he muttered. His old friend, of all people, shaking his cold arm.

"My god, Junk. What have you done?" Roy said, trying to get a pulse.

"I didn't mean nothing," Junk said, the words slurring out of his mouth, the blood from his belly sticky around his fingers. "I didn't mean to."

Last thing Cancro needed was a sensational case that had all of Coweetsee talking, especially this close to Election Day, an October surprise could swing the vote in weird ways. Cancro was none too pleased that his opponent Roy Barker had discovered the crime scene.

Barker had gotten a phone call, a tip from his ex. He found his old high school wrestling buddy wounded and drove him straight to the hospital.

Not that anyone would call that trash peddler Walter Jackson a pillar of the community, though everyone seemed to have traded with him at some point.

A day later, Jackson was sitting upright in his ICU bed and joking about how he had the worst luck with women, young ones at that, which the nurses didn't exactly appreciate. He was already posting pictures of his incision on Instagram, winning hearts and emojis from his many followers.

Cancro quickly centered his suspicions on Charlie Clyde Harmon, and took him in for questioning. Harmon, a recent parolee from Department of Corrections, admitted to picking up his niece and driving over to Jackson's. "Harmless fun. We had some drinks, maybe, played some music, talked."

"Underage drinking, contributing to the delinquency of minors. So you and Jackson got into a fight or something," Cancro pressed.

"Wasn't me. I was taking a little nap on the couch when the girl came and said, we got to go. You best ask her."

Cancro drove to the Harmon trailer. The girl met him at the trailer door, sobbing out her confused confession. As far as Cancro could determine, it seemed more self-defense and bad luck on that underage girl's part than any premeditated crime.

But the story wasn't ended yet.

Junk Jackson had returned to the hospital only a couple of days after he was discharged. Somehow, the wound had not healed but turned septic. The pictures he was putting on Instagram were more dire, the colors turning purple and a greenish yellow as his belly began to swell. He took a turn for the worst, and a week later he passed.

Birdie Barker Price felt herself a party to the guilt. After all, she had set off the strange chain of events that put Rhonda Jr. picking up trash on the highway and making that wrong turn in her young life.

Birdie followed up on her protégé at the Harmon trailer, knocking at the storm door.

Deana had stepped out on the deck, closing the door behind her, as if not to disturb the poor girl within. Rhonda Jr. had been vacant eyed and morose, traumatized, but at least she wasn't facing any charges.

"She'll be all right. She didn't do anything wrong if you ask me."

"Self-defense, that's what the sheriff said," Birdie agreed.

"I knew something was up when she came in crying, still wearing that glittery dress. Took a while to get the truth out of her."

Birdie said, "She's still got her life ahead of her."

Deana crossed her arms in her sweater, drawing its thin wool tighter about her bones in the chilly afternoon. The Indian summer was gone, and winter could be felt coming down the mountains.

"My sister had her secrets, but I've always had my suspicions."

"What do you mean?" Birdie asked.

"I'm afraid that Rhonda Jr. might have killed her own daddy. Maybe that's a fitting judgment."

30

Come October, the leaves were brilliant in their golds and scarlets along the river. Birdie hadn't crossed the bridge in a while to visit her friend, Shawanda, to sit a spell in her warm studio. So much to talk about, the upcoming election, poor Junk Jackson and what happened with Rhonda Jr.

Shawanda was, as always, hard at work, her glasses perched on the end of her nose, pulling the thread taut with a silver needle through the colorful patches.

"You've been working on that forever." Birdie considered the quilt in Shawanda's lap.

"Patience."

"You have more than me." Birdie giggled, but Shawanda was serious about her sewing, not very talkative today.

"I know you told me, but I forgot. What did you call that pattern again?"

The seamstress spread out the pieced fabric. "The Drunkard's Path," she said.

And with its curved ovals and strange geometry, it looked like the wayward tracks of a man stumbling, swaying to keep his balance, bleary eyes looking at the doubled vision of his trail, back and forth, a spread that would cover some rich Atlanta lady's king-sized bed.

"We could certainly use something that pretty for the historical society—" Birdie said.

"You couldn't afford my prices." Shawanda cut her off, and folded her work. "You come for a little pick-me-up?"

"Sorry, no. I've been vaping now. Rhonda Jr.'s turned me onto e-cigarettes."

"You too good to smoke the natural stuff now?"

"It's a trade. I told her me and Zip would teach her the old ballads. She's picking up on the verses. The girl's got a good head on her shoulders if she could just stay focused."

"How's that poor girl holding up?" Shawanda asked.

"Shell-shocked. It's a shame what happened between her and Junk Jackson. Evidently, she thought he was hitting on her."

"No surprise there when it comes to men in Coweetsee. At least she stood up for herself and put a blade into his belly," Shawanda said.

"Deana insinuated that Junk might have been Rhonda Jr.'s real daddy. If that doesn't beat all?"

"Too late for a paternity test now."

"Rhonda made the rounds back in her day. I was always worried that Roy may have been the baby daddy," Birdie said.

"No, I'd bet on Junk, that old scoundrel," Shawanda said.

"Pity, what happened to him. Last I saw him alive was at that fundraiser for Roy Boy. At least he was wearing a shirt that day."

"With Confederate flag suspenders," Shawanda observed.

"It was just an act, his redneck routine for the tourists." Birdie felt the need to explain. "He was just a good old boy."

"But he was not a good man. White people are always going on about their history and leaving out all the worst parts."

Shawanda seemed awfully prickly today, Birdie thought. "I'm trying to change that with the new display about the election. You should come on over."

"You don't have any of my history in there now, do you?" Shawanda narrowed her hazel eyes.

Now that Birdie thought about it, her friend Shawanda had never walked the bridge over the river and visited her at the historical society. It was always Birdie coming to her studio and talking and buying her dope. As Birdie roamed her mind and memory over the exhibits, the   black-and-white photos, she couldn't see the hole in the history.

"I'm sure that's an oversight." Birdie wondered what had gotten into her old friend. "Is something wrong?"

"You grew up same as me in Coweetsee County, and you're

asking is something wrong?" Shawanda sighed in exasperation. "There's a whole history to things you don't even know, like this quilt, this pattern, Drunkard's Path.

"You heard of the Underground Railroad? Bet you didn't know it ran through Coweetsee. Where Black slaves had driven herds of pigs and flocks of geese down the old turnpike down into Cracker land and the plantations, Black families and escaped slaves started retracing that old road.

"We melted into the mountains so they couldn't find us, made our way in the dark of night, by the moonlight on the river. And along the way, a few women would hang quilts like the Drunkard's Path and Bear Paw, showing them the way, signs that safety was just over the mountain. Most of those folks crossed over the state line into the Union friendly counties. But plenty of us stuck around. There is such a thing as Black hillbillies.

"There once was as many Black folks in Coweetsee, plowing crops, cutting timber, washing little white babies, as there were white folks who had bought them. After the Civil War and the whites who owned all the Blacks families had lost their property, let them meet in a clearing out in the woods, down by the creek, for their whooping and praying and Black feelings to all come out. Not that they were welcome to sit with white folks in their pews."

"I didn't know. Why didn't you clue me in?" Birdie asked.

"You never asked," said Shawanda, "and because you're not curious about Black folk. You've got your old ballot box, think it was all forged and faked, but maybe you don't know half the history of what happened in that '82 vote. It was Black folk who made Maurice Posey. Nebuchadnezzar Church turned out for him, the whole congregation, Elder Tomes praying up a storm, saying change was coming to Coweetsee, and righteousness and justice, even for Black hillbillies like ourselves. I was just a little girl. All those church ladies and the sober deacons in their suits marched down to the polls that Election Day, nobody stopping them with evil glances or poll taxes or literacy tests, making anyone say the Pledge of Allegiance, or name the capitals of fifty states. Maybe Maurice didn't have to steal no votes, maybe he just found folks who hadn't ever voted for a white sheriff."

"I'm sorry. I don't know what to say." And she truly didn't. The best Birdie could do was sit there and take her truest friend's complaint to heart.

"Girl, I know you mean well, but maybe that's the problem. My history is not your history. Coweetsee doesn't change, especially if your skin is dark. My cousins show up and cook the pig for Roy's fundraiser, but they still ain't been paid for their labor."

"I'll ask Roy to check on that," said Birdie.

"And you need to ask him whose idea it was to get Elder Tomes up there," Shawanda said. "They should leave him be. He don't hardly make any sense these days with the dementia. Tells you old sermons he once gave, but he can't remember your name most of the time. Then he gets up there, mentions that insurance policy on the church, and all the money we got, and something doesn't make any sense."

So Shawanda went digging in the Old Neb Baptist archives, which was a fancy word for the storage closet and the cardboard boxes stacked inside with old papers, baptismal records, deeds, deacon rolls, certificates of appreciation for long-dead pastors.

"It was a mess in there, but I found the paperwork. What I don't understand was how our little church could afford that policy in the first place. Monthly premiums were five hundred dollars, and we were lucky to get twenty-five dollars a week in the collection plate."

"That does sound funny," Birdie agreed.

"But then at the bottom, I see the signatures. That policy was signed by Elder Tomes, and witnessed by Sheriff Maurice Posey, not more than six months before that fire."

"You think Maurice was behind that?"

"I don't know, but I can read the black and white on a damn

insurance policy. We got us a million dollars for damages. But that policy said it would pay two million dollars to the beneficiaries. What happened to the missing money?"

"We need to get to the bottom of all this," Birdie said. "We need to know the truth."

"Then what? It's not like you can put that truth on display at your museum."

Shawanda was trembling now with rage or sorrow; Birdie couldn't be sure.

"Maybe that's our curse after all," her friend told Birdie. "Not knowing the history. Lying to ourselves about what really happened."

31

Roy Barker lost the orthopedic walking boot first, then the limp as his bum ankle slowly healed, and he didn't shamble about like a clubfooted bear anymore. Soon, things would be different.

Once he had won the seat fair and square—no cheating, no slipping envelopes of dirty dollars to voters, or opening the back of a store with pints of store-bought liquor or cartons of free cigarettes—the election on the up and up. Once he was the law, and everyone had forgotten about Maurice, when righteous order was restored to Coweetsee and everybody knew where they stood…

Then what?

No one would ever call him boy again but Sheriff Barker or just sheriff, the title and badge that Maurice had worn so proudly on his pinstripe lapel for so long. He would be the king of the mountain, lording it over the kingdom of Coweetsee.

And just maybe Birdie would forgive him. Roy hadn't forgotten how he'd lost her love and she'd run off with Talmadge Pierce and found happiness. That was a betrayal.

But then even after they had split, Roy felt somehow like he was stepping out on her when he went out a few times with Rhonda, and even once with Shawanda, but in the light of those remorseful mornings, he was always gazing at the hills on the horizon, waiting for Birdie to fly back.

But sometimes, staring up at the dark of the ceiling at three in the morning, with the sound of the creek roaring down the mountain, carrying it all down, a sound like weeping. And the pillow next to his, fluffed and high and empty like his suspect heart.

Roy just wanted someone at the end of the day to talk to. Maybe not even talk, seeing as how they knew the other's thoughts. Someone to sit silent with on the porch in the cool of the evening. A presence.

Sometimes, he stared at the blank screen of his smart phone, waiting for her text to flash across. *Come on over. All is forgiven. I love you.*

What he wasn't expecting was a call from Shawanda Tomes out of the blue.

"Roy, I need your help. I need to tell you something that's weighing on me."

"Go ahead. I'm listening."

Roy drove to Laurel Trace the next afternoon and sat in the parking lot, listening to the tick of the jeep's engine after he turned off the key. He got out and gazed up at George's Gap, that high road out of the county where he used to sit and look over the kingdom. What he would give to be up there, or anywhere but here.

He went through the sliding doors and nearly bumped into Kezia, Shawanda Tomes' daughter, who was wheeling one of the elderly residents out for some sun and fresh air.

"Hey, Mr. Barker. Good to see you. Guess we'll be calling you Sheriff Barker now, won't we?"

"We'll see," Roy said. "Hope I'm getting your vote."

Kezia chuckled. "We'll see. My mama says to always vote for the devil you know."

"Well, you and your mama know me," Roy said. "How's the old man today?"

"Resting, I think. He's not had much company these days. He'll be glad to see you."

Roy wasn't so sure about that, not with the news he was bearing.

Down the hall, there came the sound of women singing, a rhythmic keening. Birdie and Aunt Zip with their murder ballads. And a third voice, more hesitant. Birdie had said she was trying to get that Harmon girl to learn the old songs.

Twisted, strangled voices, pitched high, singing of daggers and death, bodies thrown in rivers and wells, a cuckolded king who kicked his wife's severed head against the wall of his castle. But Roy wasn't here for the old songs and stories Coweetsee had always told itself. Maybe the truth had been in plain view the whole time and we were all too afraid to see it.

He knocked at the door. Maurice was sitting up in his bed, staring out the window. His glasses flashed white as he turned his head, and for an instant, Roy worried the old man didn't recognize him.

Then: "Come in, stranger. Haven't seen you in a while."

"Sorry. I've been busy with all the campaigning."

"And how goes it? You kissing all the babies, hugging all those old women, smiling so hard your face hurts? Welcome to politicking, son."

"Yeah, you made it look easy," Roy said.

The singing grew louder next door, and Maurice suddenly threw his thin arms up.

"Them women down the hall singing bloody murder all the time. A man can't hear himself think."

"You want me to tell them to hold it down?" Roy motioned to get to his feet.

"No. Sit a while. You come in here, looking all serious, like you were about to serve a warrant."

Roy forced a smile but said nothing.

"I heard what happened to poor Junk Jackson, the Harmon girl stabbing him like that," Maurice said. "Too bad she's taking after her late mama."

"Yeah, that was all messed up," Roy agreed.

Roy himself could still wince at the feel of young Walter's clammy flesh when he had him in a half-nelson. He could see how a young girl might have panicked and run that kitchen knife right into that pot belly. Who was right, who was wrong, who deserved mercy and who deserved to be buried under the old jail? Roy used to be dead sure about these things. Nowadays his once clean conscience seemed unsettled.

"Speaking of the Harmons." Roy took a deep breath and blurted out, "Charlie Clyde says you framed him for that church fire."

"Why would you believe that old liar after all this time?" Maurice asked. "He might as well as say you framed him, since you arrested the culprit. You remember?"

Roy had considered it his proudest day as a deputy when Maurice signed the warrant and told him to go get Charlie Clyde for the church fire.

"You ain't coming?" Roy had asked. On a big case, the sheriff usually went with an entourage and someone taking photos for his album, pictures that would always lead the front page of the week's *Coweetsee Chronicle.*

"No, I trust you to handle it," the sheriff had said.

Roy had made sure his badge was pinned straight on his shirt as he drove the cruiser over to the Harmon house and knocked loudly on the broken door. Charlie Clyde looked through the screen, and Roy wondered if he was about to bolt out back.

"Charlie Clyde, I have a warrant for your arrest, charge of arson and murder."

He stepped out on the porch, let Roy read him his rights, how he could remain silent so as not to incriminate himself. "In other words, shut my mouth, right?"

Charlie Clyde even willingly put out his lean wrists for the handcuffs.

"What y'all serving tonight at the jail? I always favored that livermush and hominy y'all fix."

Roy had him by the elbow and escorted him to the car, opened the rear door. Roy had been trained to place his hand atop the detainee's head, bend him into the backseat safely. He felt the warmth coming off the crown, the softness of Harmon's hair beneath his fingers.

Charlie Clyde glanced up at Roy. "Hey, you remember when you pulled that gun on me?"

"Get in the car." Roy slammed the door.

For years afterward Roy would sit in his dead parents' parlor, alone in his house, thinking how his life had taken its twists and turns. He could have saved the lives of maybe two drunks, Drew Adcock and LeRoy Hubbs, if at eight years old, he'd pulled the trigger on his daddy's gun and blew away Charlie Clyde Harmon's smirk. But he would have marked himself as a murderer.

Now, sitting by what was likely Maurice Posey's deathbed, Roy Barker still felt guilty.

"That fire was fucked up. LeRoy Hubbs burned up in the pew."

"We got our man, didn't we? Justice was served," the old man insisted. "Why do you keep harping on this?"

"I've been doing a little digging, talking to folks," Roy said. "Seems more than a little coincidental that Pastor Tomes took out an insurance policy on the sanctuary just a few months before the fire. And that you co-signed."

"Who told you that? Old Tomes is senile. Can't trust a word out of his mouth."

"Birdie was talking to Shawanda Tomes, who called me last night."

"That's your problem right there, son." Maurice lowered his voice. "Listening to women gossiping about things they don't know squat about."

"Shawanda told me that she was curious after that scene the preacher made forgiving Charlie Clyde at my fundraiser. So she went and found the paperwork. That policy for the church was actually for two million dollars, but New Nebuchadnezzar was rebuilt to the tune of one mil."

Maurice's nose wrinkled and he readjusted the oxygen tubes in his nostrils.

Roy pressed on: "Makes you wonder what happened to the missing money."

"I never done nothing but for the good of the people of Coweetsee," the old man wheezed. "You know that. You know me, son, don't you?"

Kezia tapped on the door. "Everything all right, Sheriff?"

"Could you tell those damn women to stop that hollering down there? A man can't hear himself think," Maurice yelled.

Roy hadn't heard any singing from the next room, through Laurel Trace's paper-thin walls. Kezia nodded and left.

Maurice took his thick-stemmed glasses off and pinched the raw red spots on either side of the bridge of his nose. He replaced his spectacles and glared. Roy felt the cold blue steel in Maurice's eyes drilling into him.

"I thought you were loyal," he hissed.

"I'm loyal," Roy protested. "Loyalty goes two ways. You didn't stand up for me at my own fundraiser and give an endorsement, now did you?"

Maurice scowled. "You're too soft for politics. Everyone remembers how you quit wrestling, cost Coweetsee a chance at a state championship."

That old story again, haunting Roy for decades. "I didn't want to hurt nobody. No sport in breaking a boy's arm."

"No killer instinct," the old man said. "You don't have it in you. That's why you don't deserve to be sheriff."

"Maybe we ought to let the people decide who deserves what."

"This ain't no *Andy Griffith Show*. You don't know how the game is played."

"You're the one who broke the rules, the law. You got sent away for vote buying."

"Coweetsee never saw that as a crime back in the day. Remember when you and your daddy were handing out those democracy dollars for old Shad?"

"People looked up to you and you let them down," Roy said somberly.

"Like you, son?"

"Yeah, maybe."

"You're wanting me to confess to all these crimes you're not sure about. Spill my guts, clear my guilty conscience. Or maybe just put your mind at rest. Is that it?"

Roy vaguely shrugged.

"Boy, if you ain't learned life is a thankless thing, you've not been paying attention. How did you think the story would turn out? Look up there atop the courthouse, boy, the blindfold is still tight on Lady Justice and the scales are tipped, the lady don't know the balance is due."

"Don't you ever feel bad about what you've done?" Roy burst out.

"I done some good along the way." The old man rubbed his hands on the thin bedsheets. "I got re-elected seven times. Hell, I'll probably get more write-in votes than you ever get. This is Coweetsee and some things never change."

"Maybe they should." Roy got to his heavy feet. His bad ankle still throbbed when he stood up too fast. He slammed the door on the way out.

❧

Next door, the women looked at each other, wide-eyed and gape-mouthed.

"Did you hear all that?"

They had heard the door slam and Roy's heavy tread down the hall. They had heard some of the fierce back-and-forth. Maurice's voice rising. Roy's slow insistent tone.

"I couldn't hear a word they were saying. All I know is it sounded like a fight," Zip said.

"I didn't hear anybody hitting anybody," Rhonda Jr. said.

"Sounded like Roy giving Maurice a piece of his mind for once," Birdie said proudly.

"What were they were fighting about?" Rhonda Jr. asked.

"What men always fight about in Coweetsee. Politicking and power. That never changes."

The women fell silent. What could they say?

"We ain't done singing yet, are we?" Zip said. "We haven't done 'Barbara Allen.'"

The old woman began to hum deep in her throat, aiming for the right pitch. "Let's go, ladies."

32

On election night, Roy and his campaign advisers gathered in the living room of his parents' old rock house. They watched the vote tallies come in, precinct by precinct, constantly refreshing the state website Dylan had up on his laptop. No counting by hand, but electronic ballots fed into optical scanning machine set up at the courthouse and guarded by a special detail of state troopers and SBI agents at the governor's insistence. No shenanigans, no irregularities as Coweetsee marked its first contested and free democratic election in more than thirty years.

Dylan kept crunching the numbers, matching the early returns to census data and precinct charts he summoned like a wizard on his smudged screen, cursing and crying, unable to make the outcome any different. He hadn't counted on so many newcomers, flat landers who had moved into the Mountain Meadows gated community. The dead stayed buried in their cemeteries. No walking-around money was going to resurrect them. As the percentages of counted votes in the precincts mounted, it became apparent that the Black vote had stayed home. Shawanda's family and others saw no need to support Maurice's successor, not after all the heartbreak the Posey posse had put her folks through.

Write-ins for Maurice Posey didn't help the cause either, adding more salt to the wound for Roy.

By nine o'clock, it was all over.

A chyron scrolled across the bottom of the Asheville TV station, an afterthought to the laugh track of the network sitcom. Coweetsee County Sheriff—Francis Cancro (incumbent) 1770, Roy Barker Jr. 1050.

Jimmy Lee and Cutworm muttered about a stolen vote. How could anyone be certain since Coweetsee no longer had paper ballots that could be thrown into a creek, but invisible electronic votes counted by unseen computer algorithms, perhaps hacked by Cancro's Yankee advisers? Could there be a server somewhere with Roy's missing votes?

"You ought to do a recount. It was rigged, all right," Gene kept insisting.

"Boys, it's all over." Roy stood from his daddy's sagging wingback chair.

He went out on the porch of his childhood home.

He'd programmed the number into his flip phone. His crooked thumb hovered over, then mashed the fatal button.

Cancro picked up on the other end.

"Hey, Frank, didn't turn out the way we thought. Sounds like the county has made its choice. Best man wins. My congratulations."

"I believe you're a good man, Barker. You should know that." The New Jersey accent grated in his ear.

And they hung up on each other, Cancro grinning and flashing a thumbs-up to his room of supporters high on the Mountain Meadows, Roy alone on his porch.

He was afraid he might burst out crying like a little boy, like he'd felt when the Feds hauled off his hero Maurice.

It was indeed over. He had been telling himself the wrong story for so long, the unforeseen ending had poleaxed him. Pinned by a greater weight, he let out a breath, let it all go, every muscle in his wrestler's body gone to flab.

Yet here he was. The pitiless stars blinked over him from the long, cold night that covered Coweetsee.

PART V

The Ballad

33

December dusk, sunlight already fading at five o'clock when W. D. stepped out of Clark's Crossroads Mercantile. He shut the wooden door, then swung the more secure iron grating toward its hasp and padlock. Couldn't keep out the riffraff these days with just a deadbolt in the door. Out of the accordion folds of the grate, a piece of paper fell out and fluttered between his boots.

His knees cracked as he bent to pick it up and squinted his eyes to read it. I GOT SOMETHING FOR YOU. MEET ME DOWN AT YOUR CREEK. DEANA

Not exactly a love letter, but more like an invitation to blackmail. Least, the bitch had signed her name. W. D. wadded the note into his front pants pocket. Them Harmon whores had always spelled trouble. He had his snub-nosed revolver in his hip pocket if things got out of hand.

Down the slope from the store, into the woods, toward the rushing creek, the light was fading. He went slowly, his hips giving him trouble.

She was sitting in the roots of a sycamore on the bank. She scrambled up against the trunk when she heard his footsteps crushing the fallen leaves. She was wearing that loose ratty cardigan with its drooping pockets, likely a hand-me-down from her old man, or maybe that quiet mother. The Harmons had always been a shiftless family who had to make do or do without.

"I thought it was high time we talked, face-to-face, you and me." Deana folded her wiry arms.

"You and me don't have anything to talk about."

"What about the way you stole that election, and you threw that ballot box in the water?" Deana said.

He waved his hand through the chill air, as if batting away

her petty complaints. "All that's ancient history that doesn't have a thing to do with me."

"What about burning down churches, framing innocents?"

"I don't appreciate you spreading lies about me in public, slandering my good name. That was quite the hissy fit you pitched at Barker's fundraiser."

"Not as bad as when that senile preacher got up and started forgiving Charlie Clyde for all his sins, like some Black Jesus."

"Wasn't my idea," W. D. said. "You ask me, forgiveness is overrated, doesn't bring a soul back from the dead. I don't believe Drew Adcock's family ever forgave that brother of yours that ran him over."

"My brother was no saint, but he did his time. I just never did believe my brother would set that church fire y'all sent him away for. Yeah, he'd break in and rob the place, take the wood, anything valuable, then get the hell out. He's crooked, but he ain't stupid."

"That's not what a jury of his peers said."

"He made a convenient scapegoat," Deana said. "Pin all the blame on the bad boy, the black sheep, and no one would be the wiser, nor give a shit."

"You're the one full of shit."

But she kept on: "Now I hear all this talk about how Old Neb Baptist's insurance policy was for two million dollars and not just the one million spent to rebuild that ratty little place. Was it you or Maurice who went in and set that fire, just so that old Black preacher could collect the insurance? Would we find that missing money in another box in one of your barns?"

"You stay off my property. You or your brother comes trespassing on my land, any of my barns or buildings, I'm in my rights to shoot you dead."

"Listen, I left you alone all these years after what you did to me and my sister."

"I don't recollect you complaining at the time."

W. D. was among the men who had enjoyed their young

company when the Harmons were trying to buy off the lawyers likely to hang young Charlie Clyde.

He licked his dry lips. Them girls were a good ride. They'd certainly squealed at all the presents, the silks and jewels, rings and necklaces, the flowers and perfume, fancy dresses and vinyl records and good liquor, even chocolate bonbons. They were getting fat as hogs until the men realized they were knocked up. They'd fixed those problems before they drove those sisters home.

Now years later, Deana Harmon was nothing but a hateful harpy, all tough skin and bitter bones, the soft curves of her youth worn away. Hard to believe he'd once bedded her. He could scarcely remember what pleasure he might have taken.

"You Harmons are all alike. Runs in the blood. Like that loose girl under your charge sticks old Junk Jackson's belly with a knife. That girl's guilty as sin. She ought to be sent away."

"You leave Rhonda Jr. out of this. You leave her be, you hear me?" Deana hissed.

"She ain't my type." W. D. smiled his thin smile that never showed a tooth. "She's just trouble. Any man with a lick of sense would rue the day he got mixed up with her."

"Like you got mixed up with my sister?" She stepped toward him, and the old man could feel the heat of her breath on his face, then a speck of her flying spittle on his cheek.

"You didn't expect that ballot box we found to ever see the light of day again, now did you? What did you say to Rhonda when she brought you that old box?"

W. D. kept silent, just as he said not a word to Rhonda, after that dumb bitch said she'd found the box in the creek. Said it showed hard evidence that the election of '82 had not just been bought with dollars handed out to voters, but outright stolen, the crucial precinct with all the votes for Shad Smathers tossed in the creek. Damn woman trying to blackmail him.

"Why didn't you just give her the money she asked for?" Deana wanted to know.

But he had wanted more. Perhaps they could work out a more pleasurable trade, another ride like the old days. But old Rhonda didn't want to play along. When he grabbed her arm, she pushed back. Maybe he punched her too hard, the way she went down the bank and banged her head on a rock. He left her floating face down, and took the box on home, stashed in the barn for safekeeping, for insurance, for leverage.

"You killed her, didn't you?" Deanna poked her sharp finger in his bony chest.

He took a step back, his heart beating, fumbling now for the firearm in his pocket.

But she was quicker, pulling from her sweater pocket what looked like a black snake whipping at his face. The five smooth river rocks slipped inside that black pantyhose caught his temple. She swung again her homemade blackjack and smashed his eye socket, breaking his glasses. Then again. Blood gushed from his broken nose, and he was falling into the water, his head swimming.

When W. D. went missing, we all wondered where he might have wandered off to. The grate covering the door at Clark's Mercantile remained locked for a couple of days, even as a few folks stopped by and tried to peer into the dark innards of the store through the bars and dirty glass panes. Wasn't like the crotchety storeowner to take a vacation.

Cancro sent a deputy over, who wandered around the premises, stomping down the bank when he spied the body face down in the water. A whiskey bottle was nearby, empty. Later at the morgue when the deceased's pockets were searched, the bankroll was found, the rubber band snapped around more than five hundred dollars, and the keys to his truck and store, even his loaded pistol. Foul play seemed unlikely, just bad luck.

It looked for all the world like that the old man had gotten sloshed, wandering down to the creek behind his store, maybe slipped and banged his noggin on a rock, knocking himself silly, and then drowned, drinking too much of the creek. Sad story. Sad man.

End of an era, we all agreed. The last of the kingdom's election fixers, a man whispered to have stolen the votes for Maurice, the power behind the king.

And none of us bothered to ask Deana Harmon, when she dropped by the dollar store for milk or bread, what she made of that bad news. She might have simply shaken her head, scowled even deeper. "Sounds like an accident all right. Sad, ain't it? But couldn't have happened to a better man if you ask me."

But we wouldn't ask her, thinking better of that conversation, given that her own sister had suffered the same fate as W. D., drunk and drowned, a victim of foolishness.

Deana gathered her plastic bags of foodstuffs and drove home to her trailer. Maybe, out of our sight, she would smile in the dresser mirror. She'd smooth out the note from W. D.'s pocket along with a few Franklins pulled from his fat bankroll before she left him in the water. The wrinkled, wadded note with her careful handwriting in dull pencil, the last message intended for that hateful old man who had hurt her and her family for so long, but no more.

I GOT SOMETHING FOR YOU. MEET ME DOWN AT YOUR CREEK. DEANA

She took the slender chain again, wound its fine gold links around her knuckles. She lay that empty locket on her outstretched tongue and closed her mouth. The cold metal on her tongue made her shudder. At long last, it tasted so good.

34

Deep in the winter, Maurice Posey, the once high sheriff of Coweetsee County and convicted felon, was faring poorly at Laurel Trace. The oxygen fed into his corrupted lungs, but he kept to his bed, no longer sojourning up and down the halls, flirting with the old ladies. He had not been faking his condition after all just to win his freedom.

Kezia had called her mother. "He's not got long now. You might come on over if you need to say something to him."

Shawanda had been praying powerfully with the women of her Bible study about that very moment, what was right and what must be done. Minnie had had the last wise word. "You know what's right. Remember the only unforgivable sin is to deny what the Holy Ghost puts on your heart."

Shawanda turned aside the offer of company from the other women. It was late and those widows needed their rest. She had dressed in her crisp white uniform as a deaconess for the special Sunday services and slipped her tired fingers into her white gloves. She was on a mission now.

It was past visiting hours when Shawanda Tomes drove to Laurel Trace. The sliding doors were unlocked even at midnight. Kezia was working the late shift for a friend, white girl named Patty who had a sick baby to attend to. "Thank you, girl, you're a lifesaver." "You do the same for me one day."

Kezia met her mom at the doors and pointed her down the hall to where the sheriff lay.

The place was quiet, the TVs turned off in each room. Inside came the snoring of old people. The moonlight streaming on their wrinkled white faces. The wheelchairs with their slouched residents wheeled away, stored by the bedside. All the nighttime medications prescribed.

Shawanda came with one of her hand-pieced quilts. She also

had a sheaf of coloring papers with her. She came in quiet as a cat and sat by Maurice's bedside.

◈

He had been half-asleep. Harder now to breathe. His eyelids fluttering, his eyeballs rolling in their orbits. In and out of a dream. Someone, Shad perhaps, had walked him down to the creek by the church and baptized him. Pinching his nose and dunking him into the cold water. He would come up gasping for dream air. "Nope, that don't seem to have done the trick." Shad's thin mustache twitching overhead. And down he'd go again.

He was gasping, his hands pulling at the transparent tube, the lifeline that fed the plastic prong in his nose.

Not the colored girl, but someone else had crept into his room when he wasn't looking. An ebony angel garbed all in a dazzling starched white. The old man was lucid enough to wonder if he was hallucinating.

"Remember me, Sheriff?" the apparition said. "Shawanda Tomes. I remember you at Old Neb Baptist. Our pastor, my great-uncle used to invite you over for dedication services every fall."

He smiled. Otis Tomes was a friend of his, and a real supporter, making sure that all the faithful voters cast their ballots for the right man, which was always Maurice.

"You've had a devil of a time the last few days, my Kezia says. She's been taking care of you."

He tried to say something, but his throat was too dry. He could only grunt and groan and growl. His words weren't working tonight.

"You're shaking awful bad. Good I brought you this." She spread the quilt out over him. "It's not the prettiest pattern. Funny name. Drunkard's Path. You know who was a drunk? My uncle LeRoy, there in that pew. Remember?"

Maurice kept floating away. It was so hot in the room and the sweat was pouring out on his head.

"Charlie Clyde came to the church and scared us bad. Said he had been framed years before, and he pointed the finger at you. Nobody would believe him, that old liar with that smile that won't quit on his face. But he planted a seed of doubt. What if? What if?"

Shawanda leaned forward in her chair, and her voice became a whisper.

"Wasn't until I heard old Pastor Tomes offering the blessing at the fundraiser, how he wanted to forgive Charlie Clyde for all his evil, for burning a drunk man alive in our church. It was our Christian duty to turn the other cheek, to forgive our enemy even if he strikes us seventy times seven, which is an awfully big number and not on the multiplication tables we were taught. How hard it is to live up to what the Bible says.

"Then my old pastor mentioned how you signed the insurance policy. I'd never heard that story before. And I went to look for that old paper and found it buried in files in a closet at Old Neb. Here, you want to see it?"

She opened a yellowed manila folder and a sheaf of official boilerplate and flipped through the pages to the last one with signatures. Put it in his lap on top of the quilt that kept zigzagging in all its possible paths and colors before his eyes.

"See here." She tapped the page with the index finger sheathed in that soft satin glove. "See it's signed by the Reverend Otis T. Tomes, and there underneath as a witness under the seal, why I see your name. Maurice Posey, and lo and behold, you're a beneficiary. And it's all dated just six months before the fire. How convenient. A miracle almost."

გ

If he ever found his voice, maybe he should explain. Tomes needed the cash for his congregation. Maurice didn't mind looking the other way with the law if a greater good was accomplished for his constituents. LeRoy wasn't supposed to be there, sleeping and praying drunk in the back pew on a Thursday night in summer, not anywhere near the Lord's Day.

Lord, how hot it had been, he couldn't help but remember. Maybe the day hits a hundred, but it feels even worse inside the sanctuary. Sweat falls from your fingers like the rain the county had not seen all summer. Damn hot, but nothing like what's to come. Empty that wastebasket down the dusty aisle and across those bone-dry pews, backtracking toward the busted door. Stand in the dark a moment, breathing hard, before you strike the match, that tender flame between your fingers. Takes no thought at all. It's not hard to imagine. All hell falls from your hand.

Easy enough to pin all the blame on Charlie Clyde. Maurice's word against that slick thief's when it came to the 911 call made from the old pay phone at the Gas 'n' Go. Damn shame that LeRoy Hubbs's charred remains turned up. Certainly made Charlie Clyde easier to convict and send away for twenty years. Get him out of town, out of mind, enough troubles.

And the insurance payout went to the church, a chance for that poor congregation to start over and rebuild. And a chance at lining his own nest.

❧

Shawanda leaned over him now, the fragrance of lilac in her braided hair that swept over his face, over his open mouth.

She kissed the old man's hot forehead, not wincing.

"I know what you done. I know who you are. I still forgive you. Jesus told me to."

And she laid out crayoned pictures of angels with wings, and Christ in his white robe and sandals and a yellow sun haloing his head.

"My Sunday school girls colored these. Now I'm giving these to you," Shawanda said. "For the longest time, we blamed the wrong man and thought we needed to forgive him."

"No, no, no!" Maurice was trying to lift his arms against the terrible weight of the bedsheet, the quilt bearing down on him with its crazy patterns, the Drunkard's Path, stumbling one way and staggering the other.

"I know you, what kind of man you are. I know what you done, and I forgive you. But we won't forget."

He was fighting her, trying to kick off the cover, those pieces of coloring, children's work, flying off the bed.

Shawanda gave a faint smile, not so much for him, but grateful that the weight was lifted off her heart, all this time, all this sorrow. She floated out of the room.

But for a man like Maurice Posey, who considered himself not so much above the law, as the law himself, the worst thing you could do to such a man was forgive him. The weight was on him now. The fight was gone, and he had been found out.

Forgiven.

He couldn't stand it. Even with the pure oxygen flowing into his nose, he could scarcely breathe. Like she kinked that little tube feeding his life, filling his rotten lungs. Nary enough air for him, not enough grace, mercy, justice, all them Christian words that hammered at his hardened heart. That mute muscle that drummed irregularly, then seized up as he gasped, finally going under for good, drowning in the darkness.

35

Who knows why Charlie Clyde was rushing down the road that February night, likely all liquored up, or certainly buzzed a bit, unsafe to be behind the wheel, not that that had ever stopped him. Since he was but a boy, not a soul among us could tell what dark schemes shaped themselves behind that sharp smile, that quick wink, the pompadour combed high from his forehead like a jaunty rooster's coxcomb.

Everyone could hear him coming and going, thinking they knew him all right. He was the designated bad seed spat out of the hellmouth of his ravenous kinfolk. He was the man too easy to blame.

What the hell did he have in mind? Did he ever muse or ponder another path? Wonder what if Drew Adcock hadn't picked the wrong place to lay his befuddled head that fatal night in the middle of the very road young Charlie Clyde was headed down? Just having a little fun rolling the car forward like he did, but maybe he got carried away, choosing to back over the body. Surely, he regretted getting caught and the consequences to come.

His truck fishtailed, then the tires found traction around the curve in the light of the moon. Maybe he'd reached the point to finally leave this podunk town behind, head west over the mountains, toward the high plains. Never seen the desert or the big mountains, or the Pacific. High time for a change of scenery, a change of heart.

The blue light suddenly started strobing in the rearview mirror.

Shitfire. Always on his ass when he was minding his own business, never mind the timbers rattling in his truck bed might not be exactly his rightful property. Finders, keepers.

Charlie Clyde stomped his silver-tapped sole to the pedal, and off he flew. Can a man outgun, outrun his past, all those suspicions and false accusations on his tail?

Hell, if he'd let them catch him this time, or ever bow his head willingly, climbing into the back of another patrol car, shackled for easy process back to the penitentiary. Stuffed into a six-by-eight cell with a metal bunk and a metal toilet and no windows, only the white metal walls to climb until you're stir-crazy as a shitbird. Time drifting through your fists as you're supposed to pay some cosmic debt for a church up in flames or the body of your sister floating downriver, when the only crime was being yourself and the only punishable sin is in getting caught.

Never trade sugar for shit, his old man used to say, not that he followed his own advice.

No, thank you—not when the headlights show the black ribbon running west, to the state line and another jurisdiction, the red needle dialing up the speed, and the blue lights sliding in and out of the rearview mirror around each squalling curve. Freedom just ahead.

Too late the orange cones and the sawhorses come up in the headlights, diving now into an abyss opening in the asphalt. Crashing headlong into the windshield as the unseen waters roared in, filling the cab. One silver-tapped shoe floated up through the open window and spun around in the dark cold water in a lonely dance.

Cancro's deputy said later he had only wanted to stop the vehicle for a broken taillight, then the driver had sped off, despite the blue lights and siren. Too late the truck drove past the barricade and into the sinkhole which yawned even wider under the weight and fell fifteen feet below. Took a crane to lift the wreckage and the body inside.

How fitting that the very road that Charlie Clyde had started down as a youth, killing a poor drunk, turned out to be the same road that led surely to his destruction. A sneaky man with his slick smile and the taps on his shoes you never failed to hear coming and going.

It would be a good song, a story we couldn't help but tell ourselves.

Birdie might have to write herself a new ballad one of these days.

36

A century passes, and what do you expect to see? A flu that kills your neighbor down the road and his whole family. The sweats come over your household and two of your baby sisters lying blue faced in the bed you share. A great war and men, even from Coweetsee, marching off to gay Paree. Radio comes into the house, along with electrical wires that snake over the mountain into the kingdom of Coweetsee and the first inkling of that outside world, the music of Tin Pan Alley. The devil's own sound, the preachers say from the pulpits, red-faced and fulminating.

Roads had always been rough, dirt and gravel, with only the U.S. highway angling up the river alongside the railroad grade, which flowed along the old Drovers' Turnpike, which traced the Indian trail, which trailed along a buffalo trace, bison moving like furry bulldozers, grating the river bluffs, herds grazing through the hills.

And one day you wake up and it's been a hundred years fled by. And Coweetsee is not the place you remembered or lived all this time. The trees seem different, certainly the faces. But even the stones in the mountains seemed to have shifted. Nothing in time feels trustworthy.

They call it a celebration when you survive a whole century in a lost kingdom like Coweetsee. And the question keeps coming up. "What's the secret to living so long?"

"Cussing and singing and staying clear of the wrong men," Zip said cantankerously, but secretly pleased at all the attention she was being paid. Simply surviving, and not dying.

Zip could smell that drip of condescension in their voices, like weathering a century of changes and seasons was a miracle. All them old men in the Bible like Methuselah, having to blow out 969 candles on his last cake before he croaked. And Lord knows, his wife probably lived a thousand years but, of course, she wasn't mentioned since the Bible, like all the laws since, was written by boastful if insecure men.

A letter arrived from the president of the USA, though Zipper was unsettled to see it wasn't FDR, that kindly man in the wheelchair, the pince-nez, and the jaunty cigarette. She remembered his Panama hat in the back of the convertible. He had driven through downtown Coweetsee on his way over to commemorate the opening of the Great Smoky Mountains National Park. Or maybe it was the hatless, smiling JFK in another convertible with the First Lady in pink beside him, but she couldn't rightly recollect, had he come to Coweetsee?

Zip found her memories began to jumble and blur, and she shook her head fiercely.

All she could be certain of was surviving. She had outlasted them all. She had seen Depressions and World Wars, sheriffs come and go, buggies and blacksmiths to moonshots and astronauts. Telegraphs to texts, and she was still chipper.

But let it not be said that the staff at Laurel Trace didn't know how to celebrate. It wasn't every day that someone in Coweetsee beat the county's low life expectancy and hit a centenarian mark. Along the pine-scented disinfected hallway that ushered visitors into residents' rooms, they had strung a homemade chain of construction paper. *Happy 100th Birthday, Aunt Zip*. Flowers abounded in the room. They brought her like a princess in her throne, even if it was a wheelchair.

They wheeled in the cake, like it was a frozen body itself. Not a hundred candles, but the top all poked with lighted sparklers, and they were singing that damned song everybody knew. The flames glared in the spectacles of her glasses as she craned her wrinkled face toward the catastrophe.

"Make a wish!"

Make a wish?

Wish I could go back to the beginning, do it all again and again. I wish it would never change.

Zip blew out the candles.

ॐ

Birdie raised her voice over the women in the room. "Now we have a real treat in honor of the occasion. Zip says she's tired of listening to herself, but she'd still like to hear a song."

Roy had slipped in and caught Birdie's eye. He'd come at the last minute at her invitation, back home after a long cross-country haul with his rig. He noticed quickly that he was the only male in the room of women. He knew his place, to melt into the wallpaper and keep his peace.

"Rhonda Jr., you ready?" Birdie asked.

The Harmon girl had cleaned up good, with less makeup, her skin white and paler. She wore plainer clothes, the black Doc Martin boots and the lace bustier all gone, the rings on her fingers and face tucked away in a drawer. She looked younger now, innocent, her face not painted like a queen of the Nile.

Birdie reached over and patted the girl's knee, whispering. "You can do it."

They had been working for weeks for this occasion, knee to knee in Zip's room, memorizing all the lyrics, which Rhonda Jr. was sure she would never remember. "Pshaw, girl. You're bright enough, you just don't like the work. Try again, pitch it higher," Birdie kept repeating what Aunt Zip had taught her.

The girl closed her eyes, searched her mind for the words and began to sing, a trembling lonesome voice:

I first came to this country in eighteen and forty-nine,
I saw many fine lovers, but I never saw mine.
I viewed them all about me. I found I was quite alone,
And me a poor stranger and a long way from home.

It stabbed his heart, the song of a young man who couldn't afford to court a lass he loved, a girl whose pretty head was turned too easily by money and material possessions. A poor potato farmer's son, he ships off for America and wanders lonely in a beautiful wilderness, whose every bird song and glamorous sunset only serve to remind him of the treasure he left behind in his Old World.

Way down in some lonesome valley, way down in some lonesome place,
Where the wild birds they warble and their notes do increase.
My love she is handsome, she's slender and neat,
And I wouldn't find no better pastime than to be with my sweet.

Roy always feared that Birdie would fly away, that she was too good for him, a delicate thing whose love he would crush in his clumsy hands. He was hurt, but not surprised when she had took off with Talmadge, but then that hippie boy had up and died on her, broke her heart clear in two—that, even he could see. Yet she was like Zip and survived and kept going.

Roy listened to Rhonda Jr. singing a song that Birdie had taught her, a song to break any man's heart. He had never been a fan of the murder ballads that Zip had sung to his bride. Roy didn't have the heart for such violence to women, beaten and thrown into the river. When women sang of such things, it brought the hairs of his neck on end, an eeriness, an evil that couldn't be accounted for in this life, no matter how sweet the singer. And the unaccompanied music of their voices, the insistence of their tenor and pitch, the hypnotic rise and fall of their words, wearing on his soul.

He swallowed hard the knot in his throat. He saw his father by the school buses. He saw his mother in the kitchen of the stone house, making a peanut butter and jelly sandwich for her fatherless son. He saw Maurice Posey in his coffin, all his people gone now.

Rhonda Jr. was coming to an end. With all her hurt, her history, her Harmon blood she couldn't live down and hardly live with, but here she was a songbird, resurrected, reassured by Birdie, sitting knee to knee with her, warbling an ancient song from a distant island, a highlands not so different from the cursed kingdom of Coweetsee.

No matter how far the young man wandered in a New World, full of wonders and dangers, seeking his way, he would never be the hero who returns and wins his true love's heart. That was only a dream. Reality was the birds singing of something you've never forgotten. To forgive, you must reach some place of forgetting, no matter how much it hurt.

Roy saw a flash of fur through the window, a pair of chipmunks, scampering in and out of the kudzu that was creeping its tendrils along the red-cut bank at the back of the nursing home. Two chipmunks dodging snakes, looking for their lunch that spring afternoon after a long cold winter. The redbuds were out on the mountains and spring was returning.

Roy couldn't help but rub his eyes, misting up as his former bride, his childhood sweetheart, sat silently, smiling as her protégé sang her heart out.

What the girl was singing struck him as something he couldn't argue with. He'd tried to go on without Birdie after she walked out.

I strolled through the mountains, I strolled through the plains,
I strolled to forget her, but it was all in vain.
On the banks of old Cowley, on the mount of that brow,
Well, I once loved her dearly and I don't hate her now.

37

If you found us, you're likely lost.
Or maybe we've been lost so long, we never could find ourselves, Birdie had decided.

Coweestee was doomed to change, Birdie had come to believe. Looking back now, it's a mystery how she—no, not just her, but all of us—we had denied common sense, fell in love with folk fantasies, nostalgia for a never land. We've been stuck with our old ways, our worn stories that don't explain as much as we think or would like. We have spent years telling ourselves tales that weren't true, spinning yarns we got tangled in, getting everything wrong in a losing argument.

Each one of us scared to death of what we all might think if you step out of line.

But lose that fear, then maybe, just maybe, you have a shot at finding yourself.

Or so Birdie thought as she sat in her porch swing, taking in the mountain air and the long views.

Tal wasn't lost when he found me.

Birdie raised her feet and let herself swing freely forward, and for the first time in years, felt like her old self.

Look back at your days, how time has fled from the skinned knees and skinny legs of your girlhood before your breasts budded and the greased-hair boys took their notice. Lord knows, the day comes when you quit studying the mirror too intently, the crows-feet around your eyes and the gray showing in your head, and you're forty-eight and your life has fled. The girl is gone who used to sing at the top of her lungs, sailing in the tire swing from the tree at Aunt Zip's. But somewhere inside, you're still that girl child at the top of the arc, in that instant before the laws of gravity serve notice, that still moment of floating before you begin to fall forever back into your life.

రిం

With a new state grant from the arts council, and some renovations inside the old jail, Birdie had spruced up the visitor experience at the Coweetsee Historical Society and Museum. She'd sorted through much of what could only be considered flea market and antique shop leftovers. She had cleaned out the front war room with all its sad medals and firearms in favor of a clean and well-lit gallery with overhead track lighting and eggshell-painted walls.

She made sure to hang a fine quilt handmade by her best friend Shawanda Tomes, careful to mount pictures of Nebuchadnezzar Baptist, to tell the story of how quilts had served as signals to escaped slaves on the Underground Railroad that had passed unknown through Coweetsee County before the Civil War.

Tourists were starting to stop by after a write-up in *Southern Living* magazine about the new exhibit "The Barns of Coweetsee County," photos by Talmadge Price of the rural structures many now collapsed or moved. The negatives that Birdie had had specially developed by a printer in Atlanta had proved better than she had hoped. The lighting cast a melancholic, elegiac tone to the weathered timbers and in some shots, you could see the sepia dust of the tobacco and time falling through the enclosed air of the stalls and lofts.

The museum was making its own way, selling postcard reproductions of Talmadge's timeless photos.

Birdie would go in the mornings and run her fingers gingerly over the black frames of each print hung on the wall, the barns standing proud beneath the mountains.

38

What happened to the ballot box that started this story?

Stolen on election night and tossed into the creek. Found by Deana and Rhonda in the fishing hole. Offered to W. D. Clark for fifty dollars to keep quiet, but that deal had cost Rhonda her life. Stashed in the back of W. D.'s barn for decades. Uncovered by Talmadge in rustic explorations, then again by the thieving Charlie Clyde. Brought as a peace offering to his sister, Deana. Deposited with the secret ballots, the evidence on Birdie's doorstep. Put on display at the Coweetsee Historical Society for all to see.

It was history all right and a big lie all along. The missing votes never tallied in the election that started all the troubles, that led to all our woes. That box contained our curse, that nothing would ever change.

Birdie let the historical liquidator lady take the box, along with the bearskin and a few butter churns, for a five-hundred-dollar check and a promise that no one from Coweetsee would ever run across their bartered past in any antique shop this side of Atlanta.

But say, if you're a tired traveler, one of those who take the interstate and blow through Coweetsee County in that steady stream of tourists headed for the Sunshine State, past the scrub pines and the wide cow pastures, you might one day take an exit to one of those country cooking franchises with overpriced, chemically enhanced chicken parts and pinto beans stewed with high-cholesterol fatback, all the things your granny used to fry up to stop your heart one day. You get escorted to your table by the hostess, a young Black girl with her braids tied back, bearing your laminated menus.

You might pass the warm flames in the rock-faced fireplace, even on a summer's day. As you await your order and rub your road-tired eyes and think about how many miles lay ahead, you might even stare at the blue jets and flickering tongues of fire, fueled by a propane tank out back.

On the hearth sits an open box filled with kindling as decoration, the number thirteen etched on its side. Unlucky, like a black cat had crossed your path, or the hostess had led you beneath a ladder against the wall.

You would never know it, but inside the box, hidden from view, uncounted, are ballots from an old election, with the faded names of the high sheriffs, dead kings of a lost kingdom.

ACKNOWLEDGEMENTS

Writing can be a lonely, worrisome business, all that sitting around, staring at a blank page, an empty computer screen or out the window. But in the end, no writer thrives, let alone survives, without a community of like-minded readers.

I'm dedicating this novel to Kevin "Mc" McIlvoy, an amazing writer sorely missed after his sudden death on a tennis court in 2022. Mc proved a gracious friend and fierce reader whose strange brains I tried to pick constantly in our occasional lunches over the years. Mc carefully read through three of my novels, and I always took his suggestions to heart.

I'd also like to thank Nan Cuba, Alison Moore, Diana Lambert, Christine Hale, Emilie White, Rachel Himmelheber, Marjorie Hudson, Kathryn Schwille, Elizabeth Brownrigg, Mimi Herman, all of whom read early drafts and helped me fully imagine this book. I cherish the support and camaraderie of the alumni of the Warren Wilson College MFA Program for Writers.

This is a work of fiction, but any fiction grows out of reality. Going back to my days as a journalist, I drew inspiration for parts of this story from my interviews with Sheila Kay Adams on Appalachian ballads and the late R.L. Clark on vote buying and election shenanigans in Western North Carolina.

Many thanks to Jaynie Royal and Pam Van Dyk at Regal House Publishing for championing this book, and for keeping Southern fiction on the map.

And as always, my gratitude and love to my wife, Cynthia, the reader of my heart.